Chicago *Stories*

Chicago *Stories*

Tales of the City

edited by
John Miller and
Genevieve Anderson

CHRONICLE BOOKS
SAN FRANCISCO

Originally published in 1993 by Chronicle Books LLC.

Page 242 constitutes a continuation of the copyright page.

Library of Congress Cataloging-in-Publication Data:

Chicago stories : tales of the city / edited by John Miller and Genevieve Anderson.

p. cm.
ISBN 0-8118-3974-5 (pbk.)
1. Chicago (Ill.)—Literary Collections. 2. American Literature—Illinois—Chicago. I. Miller, John, 1959– . II. Anderson, Genevieve.
PS572.C5C48 1993
810.8'03277311-dc20 92-20490
CIP

Manufactured in the United States of America
Book design: Big Fish Books
Cover design: Flux

Distributed in Canada by Raincoast Books
9050 Shaughnessy Street
Vancouver, British Columbia V6P 6E5

10 9 8 7 6 5 4 3 2 1

Chronicle Books LLC
85 Second Street
San Francisco, California 94105
www.chroniclebooks.com

Table of Contents

Special Thanks to William Swislow and The Chicago Tribune

Chicago

Chicago, Chicago,
That tawdlin' town.
Chicago, Chicago,
I'll show you around.
I love it.

Bet your bottom dollar
You'll lose the blues in Chicago,
Chicago,
The town that Billy Sunday
Couldn't put down.

On State Street, that great street
I just want to say,
They do things
They don't do on Broadway.

They have the time,
The time of their life,
I saw a man
He danced with his wife
In Chicago

Chicago
Chicago . . . That's my home town.

FRED FISHER,
AS SUNG BY FRANK SINATRA

STUART DYBEK

Introduction

A WRITER'S TOWN and a fighter's town is what Nelson Algren called Chicago. Perhaps, more than any other American city, Chicago draws its identity from its writers, and, in the process, imposes its identity upon them as well. In this powerful relationship between a city and its writers, Chicago seems more akin to the London of Charles Dickens than it does to Cleveland or Detroit, its neighbors across the lake.

What makes Chicago so unique as a writer's town is the lineage between writers as different as Theodore Dreiser, James Farrell, Nelson Algren, Richard Wright, Studs Terkel, Mike Royko, and Saul Bellow to name a few of the most

---

Chicago native and heir to the city's street-smart, gritty writing tradition, Stuart Dybek is author of the collections The Coast of Chicago *and* Childhood and Other Neighborhoods.

prominent. It's a lineage frequently referred to as the Chicago Tradition. Of course, it's true that most every American city has produced its notable writers, yet one doesn't think about a Pittsburgh Tradition, or a St. Louis Tradition, an L.A. Tradition, or even a New York Tradition. In fact, the closest parallel to the Chicago Tradition is found in the sense of place that seems to connect writers from the South.

There are several recognizable qualities that the writers of the Chicago Tradition share. In all of them, the city is their subject, it pervades their work, broods over it, assuming almost the presence of a character in its own right. And, like everything else in Chicago, its writers divide into ethnic neighborhoods: for Farrell, its the South Side Irish; for Algren, the Poles along Milwaukee Avenue; for Bellow, the Jewish community around Hyde Park. With all this attention to ethnic boundaries, it's only natural that the theme of much of this writing is assimilation, or, more accurately, the lack of it.

But it isn't theme that stamps Chicago writing so much as outlook. It's an outlook from the perspective of the country's third coast, a sweet water inland sea surrounded by prairie, a locus at the center of America where there's not much patience with fads or pretension. It's an outlook in which energy is valued over elegance; instinct over fashionable theories; and street-smarts over the academic; an outlook we used to call "having the scan" in my neighborhood, and that Ernest Hemingway, that kid from Oak Park, called the need for a good crap-detector. It's an outlook that's populist, middle-American, but at the same time too radically anti-establishment to ever be middle-of-the-road; a point of view that takes as a given the rigged, crooked nature of power and authority. And because these writers are constantly aware that the individual confronts a corrupt system, there is as much fascination with outsiders, underdogs, heroic and anti-heroic losers, as there is with success.

No wonder it's a town that has not only endured the Cubs, but loved them.

Finally, at the core of the Chicago Tradition there is an insistence on sentiment. Not on sentimentality, but on basic emotion, the complex mix of passion and empathy we term the human heart. How does such sentiment survive not only the world, but the toughness required to live in it; to what limits can the individual be driven and still rise up human? These are the questions posed by Chicago writers over and over, the same questions posed and answered by the blues. It's an allegiance to the heart that seems only natural coming as it does from the heart of the country.

SAUL BELLOW

Looking for Mr. Green

Whatsoever thy hand findeth to do, do it with thy might. . . .

HARD WORK? No, it wasn't really so hard. He wasn't used to walking and stair-climbing, but the physical difficulty of his new job was not what George Grebe felt most. He was delivering relief checks in the Negro district, and although he was a native Chicagoan this was not a part of the city he knew much about—it needed a depression to introduce him to it. No, it wasn't literally hard work, not as reckoned in foot-pounds, but yet he was beginning to feel the strain of it, to grow aware

---

Chicagoan and Pulitzer Prize–winning author Saul Bellow is renowned for his compassionate novels addressing the issues of prejudice and injustice. "Looking for Mr. Green" is a classic example of his use of the quotidian to illustrate the universal.

of its peculiar difficulty. He could find the streets and numbers, but the clients were not where they were supposed to be, and he felt like a hunter inexperienced in the camouflage of his game. It was an unfavorable day, too—fall, and cold, dark weather, windy. But, anyway, instead of shells in his deep trenchcoat pocket he had the cardboard of checks, punctured for the spindles of the file, the holes reminding him of the holes in player-piano paper. And he didn't look much like a hunter, either; his was a city figure entirely, belted up in this Irish conspirator's coat. He was slender without being tall, stiff in the back, his legs looking shabby in a pair of old tweed pants gone through and fringy at the cuffs. With this stiffness, he kept his head forward, so that his face was red from the sharpness of the weather; and it was an indoors sort of face with gray eyes that persisted in some kind of thought and yet seemed to avoid definiteness of conclusion. He wore sideburns that surprised you somewhat by the tough curl of the blond hair and the effect of assertion in their length. He was not so mild as he looked, nor so youthful; and nevertheless there was no effort on his part to seem what he was not. He was an educated man; he was a bachelor; he was in some ways simple; without lushing, he liked a drink; his luck had not been good. Nothing was deliberately hidden.

He felt that his luck was better than usual today. When he had reported for work that morning he had expected to be shut up in the relief office at a clerk's job, for he had been hired downtown as a clerk, and he was glad to have, instead, the freedom of the streets and welcomed, at least at first, the vigor of the cold and even the blowing of the hard wind. But on the other hand he was not getting on with the distribution of the checks. It was true that it was a city job; nobody expected you to push too hard at a city job. His supervisor, that young Mr. Raynor, had practically told him that. Still, he wanted to do well at it. For one thing, when he knew how quickly he could deliver a batch of checks, he would know also how much time he could expect to clip for himself. And then, too, the clients would be waiting for their money. That was not the most important consideration, though it certainly mattered to him. No, but he wanted to do well, simply for doing-well's sake, to acquit himself decently of a job because he so rarely had a job to do that required just this sort of energy. Of this peculiar energy he now had a superabundance; once it had started to flow, it flowed all too heavily. And, for the time being anyway, he was balked. He could not find Mr. Green.

So he stood in his big-skirted trenchcoat with a large envelope in his hand and papers showing from his pocket, wondering why people should be so hard to locate who were too feeble or sick to come to the station to collect their own checks. But Raynor had told him that tracking them down was not easy at first and had offered him some advice on how to proceed. "If you can see the postman, he's your first man to ask, and your best bet. If you can't connect with him, try the stores and tradespeople around. Then the janitor and the neighbors. But you'll find the closer you come to your man the less people will tell you. They don't want to tell you anything."

"Because I'm a stranger."

"Because you're white. We ought to have a Negro doing this, but we don't at the moment, and of course you've got to eat, too, and this is public employment. Jobs have to be made. Oh, that holds for me too. Mind you, I'm not letting myself out. I've got three years of seniority on you, that's all. And a law degree. Otherwise, you might be back of the desk and I might be going out into the field this cold day. The same dough pays us both and for the same, exact, identical reason. What's my law degree got to do with it? But you have to pass out these checks, Mr. Grebe, and it'll help if you're stubborn, so I hope you are."

"Yes, I'm fairly stubborn."

Raynor sketched hard with an eraser in the old dirt of his desk, left-handed, and said, "Sure, what else can you answer to such a question. Anyhow, the trouble you're going to have is that they don't like to give information about anybody. They think you're a plain-clothes dick or an installment collector, or summons-server or something like that. Till you've been seen around the neighborhood for a few months and people know you're only from the relief."

It was dark, ground-freezing, pre-Thanksgiving weather; the wind played hob with the smoke, rushing it down, and Grebe missed his gloves, which he had left in Raynor's office. And no one would admit knowing Green. It was past three o'clock and the postman had made his last delivery. The nearest grocer, himself a Negro, had never heard the name Tulliver Green, or said he hadn't. Grebe was inclined to think that it was true, that he had in the end convinced the man that he wanted only to deliver a check. But he wasn't sure. He needed experience in interpreting looks and signs and, even more, the will not to be put off or denied and even the force to bully if need be. If the grocer did know, he had got rid of him easily. But since most of his trade was with reliefers, why should he prevent the delivery of a check? Maybe Green, or Mrs. Green, if there was a Mrs. Green, patronized another grocer. And was there a Mrs. Green? It was one of Grebe's great handicaps that he hadn't looked at any of the case records. Raynor should have let him read files for a few hours. But he apparently saw no need for that, probably considering the job unimportant. Why prepare systematically to deliver a few checks?

But now it was time to look for the janitor. Grebe took in the building in the wind and gloom of the late November day—trampled, frost-hardened lots on one side; on the other, an automobile junk yard and the infinite work of Elevated frames, weak-looking, gaping with rubbish fires; two sets of leaning brick porches three stories high and a flight of cement stairs to the cellar. Descending, he entered the underground passage, where he tried the doors until one opened and he found himself in the furnace room. There someone rose toward him and approached, scraping on the coal grit and bending under the canvas-jacketed pipes.

"Are you the janitor?"

"What do you want?"

"I'm looking for a man who's supposed to be living here. Green."

"What Green?"

"Oh, you maybe have more than one Green?" said Grebe with new, pleasant hope. "This is Tulliver Green."

"I don't think I c'n help you, mister. I don't know any."

"A crippled man."

The janitor stood bent before him. Could it be that he was crippled? Oh, God! what if he was. Grebe's gray eyes sought with excited difficulty to see. But no, he was only very short and stooped. A head awakened from meditation, a strong-haired beard, low, wide shoulders. A staleness of sweat and coal rose from his black shirt and the burlap sack he wore as an apron.

"Crippled how?"

Grebe thought and then answered with the light voice of unmixed candor, "I don't know. I've never seen him." This was damaging, but his only other choice was to make a lying guess, and he was not up to it. "I'm delivering checks for the relief to shut-in cases. If he weren't crippled he'd come to collect himself. That's why I said crippled. Bedridden, chair-ridden—is there anybody like that?"

This sort of frankness was one of Grebe's oldest talents,

going back to childhood. But it gained him nothing here.

"No suh. I've got four buildin's same as this that I take care of. I don' know all the tenants, leave alone the tenants' tenants. The rooms turn over so fast, people movin' in and out every day. I can't tell you."

The janitor opened his grimy lips but Grebe did not hear him in the piping of the valves and the consuming pull of air to flame in the body of the furnace. He knew, however, what he had said.

"Well, all the same, thanks. Sorry I bothered you. I'll prowl around upstairs again and see if I can turn up someone who knows him."

Once more in the cold air and early darkness he made the short circle from the cellarway to the entrance crowded between the brickwork pillars and began to climb to the third floor. Pieces of plaster ground under his feet; strips of brass tape from which the carpeting had been torn away marked old boundaries at the sides. In the passage, the cold reached him worse than in the street; it touched him to the bone. The hall toilets ran like springs. He thought grimly as he heard the wind burning around the building with a sound like that of the furnace, that this was a great piece of constructed shelter. Then he struck a match in the gloom and searched for names and numbers among the writings and scribbles on the walls. He saw WHOODY-DOODY GO TO JESUS, and zigzags, caricatures, sexual scrawls, and curses. So the sealed rooms of pyramids were also decorated, and the caves of human dawn.

The information on his card was, TULLIVER GREEN—APT 3D. There were no names, however, and no numbers. His shoulders drawn up, tears of cold in his eyes, breathing vapor, he went the length of the corridor and told himself that if he had been lucky enough to have the temperament for it he would bang on one of the doors and bawl out "Tulliver

Green!" until he got results. But it wasn't in him to make an uproar and he continued to burn matches, passing the light over the walls. At the rear, in a corner off the hall, he discovered a door he had not seen before and he thought it best to investigate. It sounded empty when he knocked, but a young Negress answered, hardly more than a girl. She opened only a bit, to guard the warmth of the room.

"Yes suh?"

"I'm from the district relief station on Prairie Avenue. I'm looking for a man named Tulliver Green to give him his check. Do you know him?"

No, she didn't; but he thought she had not understood anything of what he had said. She had a dream-bound, dream-blind face, very soft and black, shut off. She wore a man's jacket and pulled the ends together at her throat. Her hair was parted in three directions, at the sides and transversely, standing up at the front in a dull puff.

"Is there somebody around here who might know?"

"I jus' taken this room las' week."

He observed that she shivered, but even her shiver was somnambulistic and there was no sharp consciousness of cold in the big smooth eyes of her handsome face.

"All right, miss, thank you. Thanks," he said, and went to try another place.

Here he was admitted. He was grateful, for the room was warm. It was full of people, and they were silent as he entered—ten people, or a dozen, perhaps more, sitting on benches like a parliament. There was no light, properly speaking, but a tempered darkness that the window gave, and everyone seemed to him enormous, the men padded out in heavy work clothes and winter coats, and the women huge, too, in their sweaters, hats, and old furs. And, besides, bed and bedding, a black cooking range, a piano piled towering to the ceiling with papers, a dining-room table of the old style of prosperous Chicago. Among these people Grebe, with his cold-heightened fresh color and his smaller stature, entered like a schoolboy. Even though he was met with smiles and good will, he knew, before a single word was spoken, that all the currents ran against him and that he would make no headway. Nevertheless he began. "Does anybody here know how I can deliver a check to Mr. Tulliver Green?"

"Green?" It was the man that had let him in who answered. He was in short sleeves, in a checkered shirt, and had a queer, high head, profusely overgrown and long as a shako; the veins entered it strongly from his forehead. "I never heard mention of him. Is this where he live?"

"This is the address they gave me at the station. He's a sick man, and he'll need his check. Can't anybody tell me where to find him?"

He stood his ground and waited for a reply, his crimson wool scarf wound about his neck and drooping outside his trenchcoat, pockets weighted with the block of checks and official forms. They must have realized that he was not a college boy employed afternoons by a bill collector, trying foxily to pass for a relief clerk, recognized that he was an older man who knew himself what need was, who had had more than an average seasoning in hardship. It was evident enough if you looked at the marks under his eyes and at the sides of his mouth.

"Anybody know this sick man?"

"No suh." On all sides he saw heads shaken and smiles of denial. No one knew. And maybe it was true, he considered, standing silent in the earthen, musky human gloom of the place as the rumble continued. But he could never really be sure.

"What's the matter with this man?" said shako-head.

"I've never seen him. All I can tell you is that he can't

come in person for his money. It's my first day in this district."

"Maybe they given you the wrong number?"

"I don't believe so. But where else can I ask about him?" He felt that this persistence amused them deeply, and in a way he shared their amusement that he should stand up so tenaciously to them. Though smaller, though slight, he was his own man, he retracted nothing about himself, and he looked back at them, gray-eyed, with amusement and also with a sort of courage. On the bench some man spoke in his throat, the words impossible to catch, and a woman answered with a wild, shrieking laugh, which was quickly cut off.

"Well, so nobody will tell me?"

"Ain't nobody who knows."

"At least, if he lives here, he pays rent to someone. Who manages the building?"

"Greatham Company. That's on Thirty-ninth Street."

Grebe wrote it in his pad. But, in the street again, a sheet of wind-driven paper clinging to his leg while he deliberated what direction to take next, it seemed a feeble lead to follow. Probably this Green didn't rent a flat, but a room. Sometimes there were as many as twenty people in an apartment; the real-estate agent would know only the lessee. And not even the agent could tell you who the renters were. In some places the beds were even used in shifts, watchmen or jitney drivers or short-order cooks in night joints turning out after a day's sleep and surrendering their beds to a sister, a nephew, or perhaps a stranger, just off the bus. There were large numbers of newcomers in this terrific, blight-bitten portion of the city between Cottage Grove and Ashland, wandering from house to house and room to room. When you saw them, how could you know them? They didn't carry bundles on their backs or look picturesque. You only saw a man, a Negro, walking in the street or riding in the car, like everyone else, with his thumb closed on a transfer. And therefore how were you supposed to tell? Grebe thought the Greatham agent would only laugh at his question.

But how much it would have simplified the job to be able to say that Green was old, or blind, or consumptive. An hour in the files, taking a few notes, and he needn't have been at such a disadvantage. When Raynor gave him the block of checks he asked, "How much should I know about these people?" Then Raynor had looked as though he were preparing to accuse him of trying to make the job more important than it was. He smiled, because by then they were on fine terms, but nevertheless he had been getting ready to say something like that when the confusion began in the station over Staika and her children.

Grebe had waited a long time for this job. It came to him through the pull of an old schoolmate in the Corporation Counsel's office, never a close friend, but suddenly sympathetic and interested—pleased to show, moreover, how well he had done, how strongly he was coming on even in these miserable times. Well, he was coming through strongly, along with the Democratic administration itself. Grebe had gone to see him in City Hall, and they had had a counter lunch or beers at least once a month for a year, and finally it had been possible to swing the job. He didn't mind being assigned the lowest clerical grade, nor even being a messenger, though Raynor thought he did.

This Raynor was an original sort of guy and Grebe had taken to him immediately. As was proper on the first day, Grebe had come early, but he waited long, for Raynor was late. At last he darted into his cubicle of an office as though he had just jumped from one of those hurtling huge red Indian Avenue cars. His thin, rough face was wind-stung and he was grinning and saying something breathlessly to himself. In his hat, a small fedora, and his coat, the velvet collar a neat fit about his neck, and his silk muffler that set off the nervous twist of his chin, he swayed and turned himself in his swivel chair, feet leaving the ground; so that he pranced a little as he sat. Meanwhile he took Grebe's measure out of his eyes, eyes of an unusual vertical length and slightly sardonic. So the two men sat for a while, saying nothing, while the supervisor raised his hat from his miscombed hair and put it in his lap. His cold-darkened hands were not clean. A steel beam passed through the little makeshift room, from which machine belts once had hung. The building was an old factory.

"I'm younger than you; I hope you won't find it hard taking orders from me," said Raynor. "But I don't make them up, either. You're how old, about?"

"Thirty-five."

"And you thought you'd be inside doing paper work. But it so happens I have to send you out."

"I don't mind."

"And it's mostly a Negro load we have in this district."

"So I thought it would be."

"Fine. You'll get along. *C'est un bon boulot*. Do you know French?"

"Some."

"I thought you'd be a university man."

"Have you been in France?" said Grebe.

"No, that's the French of the Berlitz School. I've been at it for more than a year, just as I'm sure people have been, all over the world, office boys in China and braves in Tanganyika. In fact, I damn well know it. Such is the attractive power of civilization. It's overrated, but what do you want? *Que voulez-vous?* I get *Le Rire* and all the spicy papers, just like in Tanganyika. It must be mystifying, out there. But my reason is that I'm aiming at the diplomatic service. I have a cousin who's a courier, and the way he describes it is awfully attractive. He rides in the *wagon-lits* and reads books. While we— What did you do before?"

"I sold."

"Where?"

"Canned meat at Stop and Shop. In the basement."

"And before that?"

"Window shades, at Goldblatt's."

"Steady work?"

"No, Thursdays and Saturdays. I also sold shoes."

"You've been a shoe-dog too. Well. And prior to that? Here it is in your folder." He opened the record. "Saint Olaf's College, instructor in classical languages. Fellow, University of Chicago, 1926–27. I've had Latin, too. Let's trade quotations—'*Dum spiro spero.*'"

"'*Da dextram misero.*'"

"'*Alea jacta est.*'"

"'*Excelsior.*'"

Raynor shouted with laughter, and other workers came to look at him over the partition. Grebe also laughed, feeling pleased and easy. The luxury of fun on a nervous morning.

When they were done and no one was watching or listening, Raynor said rather seriously, "What made you study Latin in the first place? Was it for the priesthood?"

"No."

"Just for the hell of it? For the culture? Oh, the things people think they can pull!" He made his cry hilarious and tragic. "I ran my pants off so I could study for the bar, and I've passed the bar, so I get twelve dollars a week more than you as a bonus for having seen life straight and whole. I'll tell you, as a man of culture, that even though nothing looks to be real, and everything stands for something else, and that thing for another thing, and that thing for a still further one—there ain't any comparison between twenty-five and thirty-seven dollars a week, regardless of the last reality. Don't you think that was clear to your Greeks? They were a thoughtful people, but they didn't part with their slaves."

This was a great deal more than Grebe had looked for in his first interview with his supervisor. He was too shy to show all the astonishment he felt. He laughed a little, aroused, and brushed at the sunbeam that covered his head with its dust. "Do you think my mistake was so terrible?"

"Damn right it was terrible, and you know it now that you've had the whip of hard times laid on your back. You should have been preparing yourself for trouble. Your people must have been well off to send you to the university. Stop me, if I'm stepping on your toes. Did your mother pamper you? Did your father give in to you? Were you brought up tenderly, with permission to go and find out what were the last things that everything else stands for while everybody else labored in the fallen world of appearances?"

"Well, no, it wasn't exactly like that." Grebe smiled. *The fallen world of appearances!* no less. But now it was his turn to deliver a surprise. "We weren't rich. My father was the last genuine English butler in Chicago—"

"Are you kidding?"

"Why should I be?"

"In a livery?"

"In livery. Up on the Gold Coast."

"And he wanted you to be educated like a gentleman?"

"He did not. He sent me to the Armour Institute to study chemical engineering. But when he died I changed schools."

He stopped himself, and considered how quickly Raynor had reached him. In no time he had your valise on the table and all your stuff unpacked. And afterward, in the streets, he was still reviewing how far he might have gone, and how much he might have been led to tell if they had not been interrupted by Mrs. Staika's great noise.

But just then a young woman, one of Raynor's workers, ran into the cubicle exclaiming, "Haven't you heard all the fuss?"

"We haven't heard anything."

"It's Staika, giving out with all her might. The reporters are coming. She said she phoned the papers, and you know she did."

"But what is she up to?" said Raynor.

"She brought her wash and she's ironing it here, with our current, because the relief won't pay her electric bill. She has her ironing board set up by the admitting desk, and her kids are with her, all six. They never are in school more than once a week. She's always dragging them around with her because of her reputation."

"I don't want to miss any of this," said Raynor, jumping up. Grebe, as he followed with the secretary, said, "Who is this Staika?"

"They call her the 'Blood Mother of Federal Street.' She's a professional donor at the hospitals. I think they pay ten dollars a pint. Of course it's no joke, but she makes a very big thing out of it and she and the kids are in the papers all the time."

A small crowd, staff and clients divided by a plywood barrier, stood in the narrow space of the entrance, and Staika was shouting in a gruff, mannish voice, plunging the iron on the board and slamming it on the metal rest.

"My father and mother came in a steerage, and I was born in our house, Robey by Huron. I'm no dirty immigrant. I'm a U.S. citizen. My husband is a gassed veteran from France with lungs weaker'n paper, that hardly can he go to the toilet by himself. These six children of mine, I have to buy the shoes for their feet with my own blood. Even a lousy little white

Communion necktie, that's a couple of drops of blood; a little piece of mosquito veil for my Vadja so she won't be ashamed in church for the other girls, they take my blood for it by Goldblatt. That's how I keep goin'. A fine thing if I had to depend on the relief. And there's plenty of people on the rolls—fakes! There's nothin' *they* can't get, that can go and wrap bacon at Swift and Armour any time. They're lookin' for them by the Yards. They never have to be out of work. Only they rather lay in their lousy beds and eat the public's money." She was not afraid, in a predominantly Negro station, to shout this way about Negroes.

Grebe and Raynor worked themselves forward to get a closer view of the woman. She was flaming with anger and with pleasure at herself, broad and huge, a golden-headed woman who wore a cotton cap laced with pink ribbon. She was barelegged and had on black gym shoes, her Hoover apron was open and her great breasts, not much restrained by a man's undershirt, hampered her arms as she worked at the kid's dress on the ironing board. And the children, silent and white, with a kind of locked obstinacy, in sheepskins and lumberjackets, stood behind her. She had captured the station, and the pleasure this gave her was enormous. Yet her grievances were true grievances. She was telling the truth. But she behaved like a liar. The look of her small eyes was hidden, and while she raged she also seemed to be spinning and planning.

"They send me out college case workers in silk pants to talk me out of what I got comin'. Are they better'n me? Who told them? Fire them. Let 'em go and get married, and then you won't have to cut electric from people's budget."

The chief supervisor, Mr. Ewing, couldn't silence her and he stood with folded arms at the head of his staff, bald, bald-headed, saying to his subordinates like the ex-school principal he was, "Pretty soon she'll be tired and go."

"No she won't," said Raynor to Grebe. "She'll get what she wants. She knows more about relief even than Ewing. She's been on the rolls for years, and she always gets what she wants because she puts on a noisy show. Ewing knows it. He'll give in soon. He's only saving face. If he gets bad publicity, the Commissioner'll have him on the carpet, downtown. She's got him submerged; she'll submerge everybody in time, and that includes nations and governments."

Grebe replied with his characteristic smile, disagreeing completely. Who would take Staika's orders, and what changes could her yelling ever bring about?

No, what Grebe saw in her, the power that made people listen, was that her cry expressed the war of flesh and blood, perhaps turned a little crazy and certainly ugly, on this place and this condition. And at first, when he went out, the spirit of Staika somehow presided over the whole district for him, and it took color from her; he saw her color, in the spotty curb fires, and the fires under the El, the straight alley of flamy gloom. Later, too, when he went into a tavern for a shot of rye, the sweat of beer, association with West Side Polish streets, made him think of her again.

He wiped the corners of his mouth with his muffler, his handkerchief being inconvenient to reach for, and went out again to get on with the delivery of his checks. The air bit cold and hard and a few flakes of snow formed near him. A train struck by and left a quiver in the frames and a bristling icy hiss over the rails.

Crossing the street, he descended a flight of board steps into a basement grocery, setting off a little bell. It was a dark, long store and it caught you with its stinks of smoked meat, soap, dried peaches, and fish. There was a fire wrinkling and flapping in the little stove, and the proprietor was waiting, an Italian with a long, hollow face and stubborn bristles. He kept his hands warm under his apron.

No, he didn't know Green. You knew people but not names. The same man might not have the same name twice. The police didn't know, either, and mostly didn't care. When somebody was shot or knifed they took the body away and didn't look for the murderer. In the first place, nobody would tell them anything. So they made up a name for the coroner and called it quits. And in the second place, they didn't give a goddamn anyhow. But they couldn't get to the bottom of a thing even if they wanted to. Nobody would get to know even a tenth of what went on among these people. They stabbed and stole, they did every crime and abomination you ever heard of, men and men, women and women, parents and children, worse than the animals. They carried on their own way, and the horrors passed off like a smoke. There was never anything like it in the history of the whole world.

It was a long speech, deepening with every word in its fantasy and passion and becoming increasingly senseless and terrible: a swarm amassed by suggestion and invention, a huge, hugging, despairing knot, a human wheel of heads, legs, bellies, arms, rolling through his shop.

Grebe felt that he must interrupt him. He said sharply, "What are you talking about! All I asked was whether you knew this man."

"That isn't even the half of it. I been here six years. You probably don't want to believe this. But suppose it's true?"

"All the same," said Grebe, "there must be a way to find a person."

The Italian's close-spaced eyes had been queerly concentrated, as were his muscles, while he leaned across the counter trying to convince Grebe. Now he gave up the effort and sat down on his stool. "Oh—I suppose. Once in a while. But I been telling you, even the cops don't get anywhere."

"They're always after somebody. It's not the same thing."

"Well, keep trying if you want. I can't help you."

But he didn't keep trying. He had no more time to spend on Green. He slipped Green's check to the back of the block. The next name on the list was FIELD, WINSTON.

He found the back-yard bungalow without the least trouble; it shared a lot with another house, a few feet of yard between. Grebe knew these two-shack arrangements. They had been built in vast numbers in the days before the swamps were filled and the streets raised, and they were all the same—a boardwalk along the fence, well under street level, three or four ball-headed posts for clotheslines, greening wood, dead shingles, and a long, long flight of stairs to the rear door.

A twelve-year-old boy let him into the kitchen, and there the old man was, sitting by the table in a wheel chair.

"Oh, it's d' Government man," he said to the boy when Grebe drew out his checks. "Go bring me my box of papers." He cleared a space on the table.

"Oh, you don't have to go to all that trouble," said Grebe. But Field laid out his papers: Social Security card, relief certification, letters from the state hospital in Manteno, and a naval discharge dated San Diego, 1920.

"That's plenty," Grebe said. "Just sign."

"You got to know who I am," the old man said. "You're from the Government. It's not your check, it's a Government check and you got no business to hand it over till everything is proved."

He loved the ceremony of it, and Grebe made no more objections. Field emptied his box and finished out the circle of cards and letters.

"There's everything I done and been. Just the death certificate and they can close book on me." He said this with a certain happy pride and magnificence. Still he did not sign; he merely held the little pen upright on the golden-green corduroy of his thigh. Grebe did not hurry him. He felt the old man's hunger for conversation.

"I got to get better coal," he said. "I send my little gran'son to the yard with my order and they fill his wagon with screening. The stove ain't made for it. It fall through the grate. The order says Franklin County egg-size coal."

"I'll report it and see what can be done."

"Nothing can be done, I expect. You know and I know. There ain't no little ways to make things better, and the only big thing is money. That's the only sunbeams, money. Nothing is black where it shines, and the only place you see black is where it ain't shining. What we colored have to have is our own rich. There ain't no other way."

Grebe sat, his reddened forehead bridged levelly by his close-cut hair and his cheeks lowered in the wings of his collar—the caked fire shone hard within the isinglass-and-iron frames but the room was not comfortable—sat and listened while the old man unfolded his scheme. This was to create one Negro millionaire a month by subscription. One clever, good-hearted young fellow elected every month would sign a contract to use the money to start a business employing Negroes. This would be advertised by chain letters and word of mouth, and every Negro wage earner would contribute a dollar a month. Within five years there would be sixty millionaires.

"That'll fetch respect," he said with a throat-stopped sound that came out like a foreign syllable. "You got to take and organize all the money that gets thrown away on the policy wheel and horse race. As long as they can take it away from you, they got no respect for you. Money, that's d' sun of human kind!" Field was a Negro of mixed blood, perhaps Cherokee, or Natchez; his skin was reddish. And he sounded, speaking about a golden sun in this dark room, and looked, shaggy and slab-headed, with the mingled blood of his face and broad lips, the little pen still upright in his hand, like one of the underground kings of mythology, old judge Minos himself.

And now he accepted the check and signed. Not to soil the slip, he held it down with his knuckles. The table budged and creaked, the center of the gloomy, heathen midden of the kitchen covered with bread, meat, and cans, and the scramble of papers.

"Don't you think my scheme'd work?"

"It's worth thinking about. Something ought to be done, I agree."

"It'll work if people will do it. That's all. That's the only thing, any time. When they understand it in the same way, all of them."

"That's true," said Grebe, rising. His glance met the old man's.

"I know you got to go," he said. "Well, God bless you, boy, you ain't been sly with me. I can tell it in a minute."

He went back through the buried yard. Someone nursed a candle in a shed, where a man unloaded kindling wood from a sprawl-wheeled baby buggy and two voices carried on a high conversation. As he came up the sheltered passage he heard the hard boost of the wind in the branches and against the house fronts, and then, reaching the sidewalk, he saw the needle-eye red of cable towers in the open icy height hundreds of feet above the river and the factories—those keen points. From here, his view was obstructed all the way to the South Branch and its timber banks, and the cranes beside the water. Rebuilt after the Great Fire, this part of the city was, not fifty years later, in ruins again, factories boarded up, buildings deserted or fallen, gaps of prairie between. But it wasn't desolation that this made you feel, but rather a faltering of organization that set free a huge energy, an escaped, unattached, unregulated power from the giant raw place. Not only must people feel it but, it seemed to Grebe, they were compelled to match it. In their very bodies. He no less than others, he realized. Say that his parents had been servants in their time, whereas he was not supposed to be one. He thought that they had never done any service like this, which no one visible asked for, and probably flesh and blood could not even perform. Nor could anyone show why it should be performed; or see where the performance would lead. That did not mean that he wanted to be released from it, he realized with a grimly pensive face. On the contrary. He had something to do. To be compelled to feel this energy and yet have no task to do—that was horrible; that was suffering; he knew what that was. It was now quitting time. Six o'clock. He could go home if he liked, to his room, that is, to wash in hot water, to pour a drink, lie down on his quilt, read the paper, eat some liver paste on crackers before going out to dinner. But to think of this actually made him feel a little sick, as though he had swallowed hard air. He had six checks left, and he was determined to deliver at least one of these: Mr. Green's check.

So he started again. He had four or five dark blocks to go, past open lots, condemned houses, old foundations, closed schools, black churches, mounds, and he reflected that there must be many people alive who had once seen the neighborhood rebuilt and new. Now there was a second layer of ruins; centuries of history accomplished through human massing. Numbers had given the place forced growth; enormous numbers had also broken it down. Objects once so new, so concrete that it could have occurred to anyone they stood for other things, had crumbled. Therefore, reflected Grebe, the secret of them was out. It was that they stood for themselves by agreement, and were natural and not unnatural by agreement, and when the things themselves collapsed the agreement became visible. What was it, otherwise, that kept cities from looking peculiar? Rome, that was almost permanent, did not give rise to thoughts like these. And was it abidingly real? But in Chicago, where the cycles were so fast and the familiar died out, and again rose changed, and died again in thirty years, you saw the common agreement or covenant, and you were forced to think about appearances and realities. (He remembered Raynor and he smiled. Raynor was a clever boy.) Once you had grasped this, a great many things became intelligible. For instance, why Mr. Field should conceive such a scheme. Of course, if people were to agree to create a millionaire, a real millionaire would come into existence. And if you wanted to know how Mr. Field was inspired to think of this, why, he had within sight of his kitchen window the chart, the very bones of a successful scheme—the El with its blue and green confetti of signals. People consented to pay dimes and ride the crash-box cars, and so it was a success. Yet how absurd it looked; how little reality there was to start with. And yet Yerkes, the great financier who built it, had known that he could get people to agree to do it. Viewed as itself, what a scheme of a scheme it seemed, how close to an appearance. Then why wonder at Mr. Field's idea? He had grasped a principle. And then Grebe remembered, too, that Mr. Yerkes had established the Yerkes Observatory and endowed it with millions. Now how did the notion come to him in his New York museum of a palace or his Aegean-bound yacht to give money to astronomers? Was he awed by the success of his bizarre enterprise and therefore ready to spend money to find out where in the universe being and seeming were identical? Yes, he wanted to know what abides; and whether flesh is Bible grass; and he offered money to be burned in the fire of suns. Okay, then, Grebe thought further, these things exist because people consent to exist with them—we have got so far—and also there is a reality which doesn't depend on consent but within which consent is a game. But what about need, the need that keeps so many vast thousands in position? You tell me that, you *private* little gentleman and *decent* soul—he used these words against himself scornfully. Why is the consent given to misery? And why so painfully ugly? Because there is *something* that is dismal and permanently ugly? Here he sighed and gave it up, and thought it was enough for the present moment that he had a real check in his pocket for a Mr. Green who must be real beyond question. If only his neighbors didn't think they had to conceal him.

This time he stopped at the second floor. He struck a match and found a door. Presently a man answered his knock and Grebe had the check ready and showed it even before he began. "Does Tulliver Green live here? I'm from the relief."

The man narrowed the opening and spoke to someone at his back.

"Does he live here?"

"Uh-uh. No."

"Or anywhere in this building? He's a sick man and he can't come for his dough." He exhibited the check in the light, which was smoky—the air smelled of charred lard—and the man held off the brim of his cap to study it.

"Uh-uh. Never seen the name."

"There's nobody around here that uses crutches?"

He seemed to think, but it was Grebe's impression that he was simply waiting for a decent interval to pass.

"No, suh. Nobody I ever see."

"I've been looking for this man all afternoon"—Grebe spoke out with sudden force—"and I'm going to have to carry this check back to the station. It seems strange not to be able to find a person to *give* him something when you're looking for him for a good reason. I suppose if I had bad news for him I'd find him quick enough."

There was a responsive motion in the other man's face. "That's right, I reckon."

"It almost doesn't do any good to have a name if you can't be found by it. It doesn't stand for anything. He might as well not have any," he went on, smiling. It was as much of a concession as he could make to his desire to laugh.

"Well, now, there's a little old knot-back man I see once in a while. He might be the one you lookin' for. Downstairs."

"Where? Right side or left? Which door?"

"I don't know which. Thin-face little knot-back with a stick."

But no one answered at any of the doors on the first floor. He went to the end of the corridor, searching by match-light, and found only a stairless exit to the yard, a drop of about six feet. But there was a bungalow near the alley, an old house like Mr. Field's. To jump was unsafe. He ran from the front door, through the underground passage into the yard. The place was occupied. There was a light through the curtains, upstairs. The name on the ticket under the broken, scoop-shaped mailbox was Green! He exultantly rang the bell and pressed against the locked door. Then the lock clicked faintly and a long staircase opened before him. Someone was slowly coming down—a woman. He had the impression in the weak light that she was shaping her hair as she came, making herself presentable, for he saw her arms raised. But it was for support that they were raised; she was feeling her way downward, down the wall, stumbling. Next he wondered about the pressure of her feet on the treads; she did not seem to be wearing shoes. And it was a freezing stairway. His ring had got her out of bed, perhaps, and she had forgotten to put them on. And then he saw that she was not only shoeless but naked; she was entirely naked, climbing down while she talked to herself, a heavy woman, naked and drunk. She blundered into him. The contact of her breasts, though they touched only his coat, made him go back against the door with a blind shock. See what he had tracked down, in his hunting game!

The woman was saying to herself, furious with insult, "So I cain't ———k, huh? I'll show that son-of-a-bitch kin I, cain't I."

What should he do now? Grebe asked himself. Why, he should go. He should turn away and go. He couldn't talk to this woman. He couldn't keep her standing naked in the cold. But when he tried he found himself unable to turn away.

He said, "Is this where Mr. Green lives?"

But she was still talking to herself and did not hear him.

"Is this Mr. Green's house?"

At last she turned her furious drunken glance on him. "What do you want?"

Again her eyes wandered from him; there was a dot of blood in their enraged brilliance. He wondered why she didn't feel the cold.

"I'm from the relief."

"Awright, what?"

"I've got a check for Tulliver Green."

This time she heard him and put out her hand.

"No, no, for *Mr.* Green. He's got to sign," he said. How was he going to get Green's signature tonight!

"I'll take it. He cain't."

He desperately shook his head, thinking of Mr. Field's precautions about identification. "I can't let you have it. It's for him. Are you Mrs. Green?"

"Maybe I is, and maybe I ain't. Who want to know?"

"Is he upstairs?"

"Awright. Take it up yourself, you goddamn fool."

Sure, he was a goddamn fool. Of course he could not go up because Green would probably be drunk and naked, too. And perhaps he would appear on the landing soon. He looked eagerly upward. Under the light was a high narrow brown wall. Empty! It remained empty!

"Hell with you, then!" he heard her cry. To deliver a check for coal and clothes, he was keeping her in the cold. She did not feel it, but his face was burning with frost and self-ridicule. He backed away from her.

"I'll come tomorrow, tell him."

"Ah, hell with you. Don' never come. What you doin' here in the nighttime? Don' come back." She yelled so that he saw the breadth of her tongue. She stood astride in the long cold box of the hall and held on to the banister and the wall. The bungalow itself was shaped something like a box, a clumsy, high box pointing into the freezing air with its sharp, wintry lights.

"If you are Mrs. Green, I'll give you the check," he said, changing his mind.

"Give here, then." She took it, took the pen offered with it in her left hand, and tried to sign the receipt on the wall. He looked around, almost as though to see whether his madness was being observed, and came near believing that someone was standing on a mountain of used tires in the auto-junking shop next door.

"But are you Mrs. Green?" he now thought to ask. But she was already climbing the stairs with the check, and it was too late, if he had made an error, if he was now in trouble, to undo the thing. But he wasn't going to worry about it. Though she might not be Mrs. Green, he was convinced that Mr. Green was upstairs. Whoever she was, the woman stood for Green, whom he was not to see this time. Well, you silly bastard, he said to himself, so you think you found him. So what? Maybe you really did find him—what of it? But it was important that there was a real Mr. Green whom they could not keep him from reaching because he seemed to come as an emissary from hostile appearances. And though the self-ridicule was slow to diminish, and his face still blazed with it, he had, nevertheless, a feeling of elation, too. "For after all," he said, "he *could* be found!"

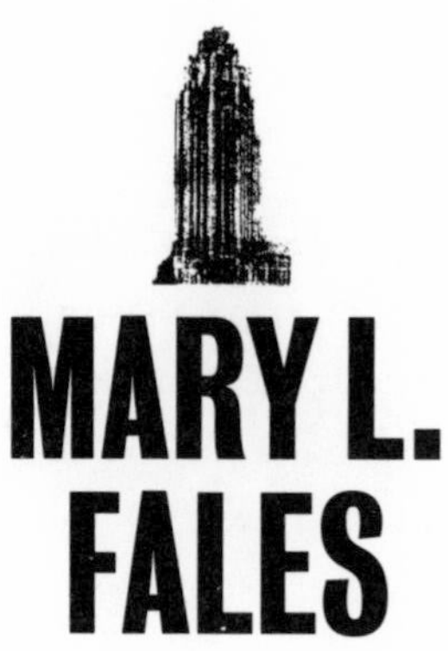

MARY L. FALES

The Great Chicago Fire

[From a letter written by Mrs. David Fales to her mother, October 10, 1871, and now in the possession of the Chicago Historical Society.]

YOU HAVE PROBABLY heard of our fire, and will be glad to know we are safe, after much tribulation. Sunday night a fire broke out on the West Side, about three miles southwest of us. The wind was very high, and David said it was a bad night for a fire. About two o'clock we were awakened by a very bright light, and a great noise of carts and wagons. Upon examination, David found that the fire was not at all on the North Side, but was burning so furiously on the South Side that the whole sky

---

Mary L. Fales, a typical Chicagoan, was caught in the city's devastating 1871 fire, which left 90,000 homeless and some 250 dead. She recorded it in this letter to her mother.

was bright. They thought it would stop when it came to the river, but it proved no obstacle, and the North Side was soon on fire, and Wells and La Salle streets were crowded with carts and people going north.

We saw that with such a wind it would soon reach our neighborhood, and David told me to pack what I most valued. It seemed useless to pack in trunks, as every vehicle demanded an enormous price and was engaged. Several livery stables were already burned, and loose horses were plenty. One of the Wheeler boys had a horse given him for nothing, excepting a promise to lead it to a safe place. He took it home and tied it in their yard. Having no wagon, it was of no use to him, so David took it, and after a while succeeded in finding a no-top buggy; we felt very lucky, as nobody around could get either horse or conveyance. David packed it full, set me and himself on top, and started to the Hutchinson's.

I cannot convey to you how the streets looked. Everybody was out of their houses, without exception, and the sidewalks were covered with furniture and bundles of every description. The middle of the street was a jam of carts, carriages, wheelbarrows, and every sort of vehicle—many horses being led along, all excited and prancing, some running away. I scarcely dared look right or left, as I kept my seat by holding tightly to the trunk. The horse would not be restrained, and I had to use all my powers to keep on. I was glad to go fast, for the fire behind us raged, and the whole earth, or all we saw of it, was a lurid yellowish red.

David left me at Aunt Eng's and went for another load of things. This he soon brought back, and he went off again, and I saw him no more for seven hours. People came crowding to Aunt Eng's, and the house was full of strangers and their luggage. One young lady, who was to have had a fine wedding tomorrow, came dragging along some of her wedding presents.

One lady came with four servants, and one with six blankets of clothing. One lady came with nurse and baby, and, missing her little boy, went off to look for him; this was about daylight, and she did not come back at all. Now and then somebody's husband would come back for a minute; but there was work for everybody, and they only stayed long enough to say how far the fire advanced, and assured us of safety.

At twelve David came and said that he had taken everything out of our house, and buried the piano and books, together with the china, in Mr. Hubbard's grounds. He saw persons taking off all the chairs, tables, and light furniture, without saying a word, for he knew they would burn, even in the street, and my nice preserves, which Maggie had set out on the piazza, he gave freely to anybody who cared to take them.

The Hubbards thought they were safe in a brick house with so much ground around it; but wet their carpets and hung them over the wooden facings for additional safety. It was all to no purpose. David saw ours burn and fall; then theirs shared the same fate. The McCagg's large house and stables burned in a few minutes, also the New England Church and Mr. Collyer's. In the afternoon the wind blew more furiously, the dust was blinding, the sky gray and leaden, and the atmosphere dense with smoke. We watched the swarms of wagons and people pass. All the men, and many of the women, were dragging trunks by cords tied in handles; the children were carrying and pulling big bundles.

Soon they saw Aunt Eng's house must go too. Then such confusion as there was! Everybody trying to get a cart, and not one to be had at any price. After a while, two of the gentlemen who had wagons carried their wives farther north, and those that were left watched for empty wagons, but nobody spoke a word. Mr. Hutchinson, David, and some others, were taking things out and burying them, and many of the ladies fairly lost their wits. Poor Aunt Eng even talked of sending home a shawl that somebody left there long ago. David started for a cart. Again he was successful, and got an old sand cart, with no springs, one board out of the bottom, with a horse that had not been out of harness for twenty-four hours. He put in all our things, and one trunk of Aunt Eng's, to which Miss M. added a bandbox.

The West Side was safe; but to get there was the question. The bridges were blocked and some burned, but the man who owned the cart thought we could get there. We thought of Judge Porter's and Mr. Dupee's, where we believed we would be welcome. Wherever Aunt Eng's family went, they must walk, and our prospects seemed so fair that we took May with us. Our ride was an anxious one. The horse had been overused, and when urged on would kick till the old cart bid fair to break in pieces; then he would go on, and finally kicking no use, gave it up, much to my relief. Many times we were blocked, and it seemed as if the fire must reach the bridge before we did. But we were much too well off to complain.

Some carts had broken down, horses had given out, and many people were walking and pulling big things, and seemed almost exhausted. Furniture and clothing lay all along the road. Mrs. Hamilton hailed us from a mean little hut, two miles from her house and ours, and asked us to take a bag of Mr. Hubbard's silver. It must have been some servant's house. Anyway, it burnt soon after, and we still have the silver. The fences were broken in all the unbuilt fields; and furniture and people covered every yard of space. After a ride of two hours and a half we reached Judge Porter's at dusk, and found a warm welcome.

Every family I know on the North Side is burned out. I can't enumerate them. It would be useless. It is sufficient to say every individual one. We were the only ones who took our things from Aunt Eng's. The lady with the six bundles left five behind her; the lady with the four servants left a bundle of French dresses to burn, but, worst of all, the baby and nurse. They went with the Hutchinsons. At the last minute, a Miss M. insisted on David taking charge of her watch; she said she could trust it to no one else, and it did not occur to her to keep it herself. All of our clothing is saved, and much we have with us.

I never felt so grateful in my life as to hear the rain pour down at three o'clock this morning. That stopped the fire.

The gentlemen have come in, and David says the piano burned under the ground; nothing was left but the iron plates. The North Side is level, as is the burned part of the South Side, so that the streets are not distinguishable. They say people in every class of life are out of doors. The churches are full, and food is sent to them, but hardly anyone has any to spare. My watch was at the jeweler's, and may have been in a safe, but the safes have not yet been uncovered. I shall write soon again; meanwhile, direct to 448 West Washington Street.

ELIOT NESS

The Untouchables

We had been in the brewery-busting business almost six months when the prison gates swung open at Holmesburg, Pennsylvania, and Al Capone walked out a free man on the morning of March 17, 1930.

There was wild excitement in Chicago as the public and the underworld awaited the homecoming of the scarfaced chieftain who ruled the city with an iron fist in a glove of steel.

Speculation was rife as to what he was going to do, how the gangs of Chicago would react to his return and what sort of reception was being planned by the city and federal governments. The newspapers devoted lurid black headlines to the story.

Hard-boiled detective Eliot Ness popularized his pursuit of legendary Chicago mobster Al Capone in The Untouchables. *Thanks to Robert Stack and Kevin Costner, Ness is as popular now as he was in the 1940s.*

Chicago officials had been making eye-catching statements as the time drew near for Capone's release. The law promised he would be given a hot reception.

"We'll clap him in jail as soon as he sets foot in the city," boasted one high police figure.

Captain John Stege, head of the Chicago detective bureau, posted twenty-five men in the vicinity of Capone's home on Prairie Avenue. Their instructions were to take the chubby-faced gang overlord into custody as soon as he arrived, but they waited four days and nights without avail.

"Scarface Al" had apparently disappeared into thin air after being met at the prison by a "royal" entourage that whisked him out of sight. Since there was no indictment against him, however, the police obviously weren't too anxious to locate him.

But we knew immediately where he was, thanks to the wire tap on the Montmartre.

When word came that Capone had disappeared, I laid siege to the headset in our rented basement apartment.

One of the first orders of business among the mob when he returned, I knew, would be the extermination of the Eliot Ness squad which had become a thorn in Al's pasty white side. The orders, I was fairly certain, would filter through brother Ralph's telephone.

On March 18, the day after Capone's release, I was at the headset when the buzzer sounded and an urgent voice demanded:

"Is Ralph there?"

"On the phone," was the reply.

"Listen, Ralph," the voice pleaded frantically. "We're up in Room 718 in the Western and Al is really getting out of hand. He's in terrible shape. Will you come up, please? You're the only one who can handle him when he gets like this. We've sent for a lot of towels."

"Okay," Ralph replied. "I'll be up a little later. Just take care of things the best you can right now."

Without question, Al Capone, celebrating his release from prison not wisely but much too well, was drunk and almost out of control up in Room 718 at the Western Hotel. I didn't know what the towels were for, whether to wet him down or clean him up, but it was obvious that Ralph wasn't worried.

About fifteen minutes after that call, the buzzer sounded again.

"Ralph," said the caller, "this is Jake Lingle. Where's Al? I've been looking all over for him and nobody seems to know where he is."

Ralph pretended ignorance.

"I don't know where he is, either, Jake," he hedged. "I haven't heard a word from him since he got out."

Lingle, a Chicago *Tribune* police reporter, sounded agitated and I marveled at his effrontery.

"Jesus, Ralph, this makes it very bad for me. I'm supposed to have my finger on these things, y'know. It makes it very embarrassing with my paper. Now get this, I want you to call me the minute you hear from him. Tell him I want to see him right away."

"All right," Ralph replied. "I will."

Within an hour, Lingle called Ralph again.

"Ralph?"

"Yes."

"This is Jake again. Have you heard from Al yet?"

"No. Not yet."

Lingle's voice became aggressively indignant.

"Listen, you guys ain't giving me the runaround are you? Just remember, I wouldn't do that if I was you."

Ralph's voice became a bit warmer and friendlier.

"Now, Jake, you know I wouldn't do that. It's just that I haven't heard from Al. What else can I tell you?"

"Okay, okay," Lingle growled. "Just remember to tell him that I want to talk to him right away."

The phone banged down and I wondered what reason Lingle had to play it so high and mighty with the Capones.

Four days after his return from prison, Capone finished up his celebration. Defying the law to pin anything on him, he walked blithely into police headquarters accompanied by his lawyer.

"I hear you want me," Capone challenged.

No one did, as it developed, and "Scarface Al" returned in triumph to his headquarters at the Lexington Hotel, where he occupied the three top floors.

It was an ironic demonstration of the power of this man who had started out as a hardfisted roughneck addicted to red neckties, gaudy shirts and flashy jewelry.

His fortune was estimated at $50,000,000. He rode around in a $30,000 automobile which, with its body armor of steel plate and bulletproof windows, weighed seven tons. He owned an estate in Florida worth $500,000, and on one meaty finger he wore an eleven-carat diamond which had cost $50,000. Capone never carried less than $50,000 cash, scattering $25 tips to hat check girls and $100 gratuities to waiters. He was known around the gambling spots as "a sucker for the ponies."

But those who took him for a "sucker" elsewhere usually wound up dead. Acquiring the poise which comes with power, Capone had become even more dangerous: together with his ruthlessness, he had the quality of a great businessman. Under that patent leather hair he had sound judgment, diplomatic shrewdness and the diamond-hard nerves of a gambler, all balanced by cold common sense.

He had always been a fighter, this man who scorned the law, but even more deadly was the fact that he held with the Sicilian tradition of secret murder. Catching an enemy off guard was the cornerstone of his strategy. Rarely did hate actuate him; when it did, however, those who had incurred his wrath were marked for death.

We weren't going to be caught off guard if I could help it. To prepare for an emergency, I decided to make a survey of the area around his Lexington headquarters.

Taking Lahart with me, I had Basile drive us around the block several times while we charted exits, parking areas and alleyways.

As we swung past the main entrance, a hoodlum named Frank Foster, alias Frankie Frost, who acted as a liaison man between Capone and "Bugs" Moran, swaggered out of the lobby. We were almost face to face through the car window for a fleeting second, and from his startled expression I knew that he had recognized me.

Looking back, I saw him stare after us for a moment, then hurry across the street and leap into a parked car facing in the opposite direction.

"Swing it around fast, Frank," I tapped Basile on the shoulder, "and follow the black sedan just pulling out behind the bread truck."

Foster swung left at the first intersection, and we could see him peering back. Then his car shot forward in an effort to lose us.

"Get him, Frank," I urged. "Swing him into the curb."

The chase covered two miles as we raced block after block through crowded city streets, the speedometer flicking past sixty miles an hour. Careening around corners, weaving between cars, ignoring traffic lights and scattering pedestrians with a blaring horn, we missed disaster several times by a matter of inches.

Basile, hunched over the wheel with cold concentration, finally drew abreast of Foster's sedan. The gangster threw us a wide-eyed stare as we shot ahead of him and then, with a quick wrench of the wheel accompanied by a shrieking of rubber and a squealing of breaks, we slued in front to force the sedan to the curb.

Lahart and I leaped from the car before it had stopped rolling. Sprinting back as Marty raced to the other side of Foster's car, I wrenched open the door. Foster shrank back as I pushed my revolver into his face. Reaching in, I grabbed a handful of coat, dragged him out of the car and slammed him up against the side of the sedan.

"Make one move and you'll wish you hadn't," I said.

But Foster, a swarthy, hard-faced man of about five feet eight inches, wasn't ready to act as tough as he looked. He was shaking as his hands shot meekly into the air. Jamming my pistol into his midriff, I searched him quickly.

From a hand-tooled shoulder holster under the left armpit of his dapper pin-striped suit, I lifted a snub-nosed .38 Colt revolver exactly like the one I had pointed at his diamond-studded belt buckle.

Strangely enough, I noted as the excitement of the chase ebbed and I looked around to take my bearings, we had brought him to heel right in front of the Transportation Building where our offices were located.

"Now we'll go up to my office and talk awhile," I told Foster, putting away my gun and pocketing his. "And don't get any funny ideas about making a break for it."

Foster marched docilely between us, but once assured that he wasn't going to receive rough physical treatment, remained firmly silent when we questioned him about Capone and the rackets.

"I don't have to say nothin'," he repeated over and over, so after a fruitless half hour we turned him in on a gun-carrying charge.

There had been frequent gang murders in the few months preceding "Scarface Al's" return. A serious breach was threatening to disrupt the "peace treaty" Capone had negotiated at Atlantic City. Meanwhile, the Secret Six had established the nation's first large-scale crime detection laboratory at Northwestern University.

I had met Major Calvin Goddard, the ballistics expert in charge of the laboratory, and on a hunch I decided to drive out to Evanston and show him the gun I had taken from Foster.

Goddard's big body was hunched over a microscope as I walked into a laboratory crammed with steel files and numerous glass-fronted cases. His dark hair was rumpled and a shoulder holster was pushed around to the center of his back so it wouldn't interfere with his arms as he worked.

The major was never without a gun, even in the privacy of his laboratory on the quiet Northwestern campus. There was a tremendous amount of damning material stored in those bulging files, and so bold were the gangsters who infested Chicago that even this serene spot wasn't completely safe from an invasion aimed at the destruction of evidence.

Peering at me through thick-rimmed glasses, the major waved his recognition, his deep voice hearty as he said:

"Be with you in a second, Eliot."

He straightened up and shook hands with a hard, firm grip.

"Just ran a test on a bullet fired from a gun we picked up and found out it's the same gun used in a killing on the South Side a couple of months ago," he told me in the manner of a proud parent recounting a child's cute saying.

Reaching into my topcoat pocket, I pulled out the gun I had taken from Foster and handed it to him.

"Major, I'm not quite certain just how this ballistics business works, but I thought maybe you'd like to look at this gun I picked up from a punk named Frank Foster."

Goddard took it, examined it and checked to make certain it was loaded.

"Come here," he directed. "I'll show you exactly how it works."

Moving to a large wastebasket solidly packed with cotton waste, he fired into the wadding. The sound of the shot reverberated through the room like summer thunder. He was digging into the waste for the expended bullet when a uniformed guard poked his head through the doorway and made a quick inspection of the room.

"It's okay, George. Just running a test," Goddard grunted.

The guard flicked his hand in a semisalute and withdrew.

"We take our precautions," the major said, jerking his head toward the door. "Now, look, here's the way this thing works."

He placed the bullet under his microscope and adjusted the lens.

"Take a look through there and you'll see lines along the side of the bullet which were left by the rifling of the pistol barrel." I peered into the microscope and saw these long scratches. "Every pistol's rifling varies somewhat so that by comparing two bullets you can tell whether or not they were shot from the same weapon," he added.

He then went on to explain how a bullet taken from a body could be compared with a test bullet from a gun taken from a suspect to determine whether the pistol carried by the suspect had fired the killing shot.

When I was ready to leave, Goddard picked up the bullet he had fired from the Foster gun and dropped it into an envelope. His voice sounded eager.

"I'll check this against some of the bullets in our unsolved file. But whether I can match it or not, I'll keep this one on file in case this gun ever pops up again."

I dropped the Foster gun into my topcoat pocket, drove back to my office in the Transportation Building and locked the revolver in one of the drawers of the steel filing cabinets where we kept our own records.

I could see already that the return of Capone was having a marked influence on us. We were so few against so many, and the arrogant theatrics of "Scarface Al's" homecoming boasted to the world that he had lost little, if any, of his murderous power. It made you feel like a sitting duck in a shooting gallery.

IMMEDIATELY FOLLOWING the gangster chief's homecoming, I put increased pressure on my men to uncover several more breweries. They didn't need any prodding, but perhaps I was over-eager to show Capone that times and types had changed.

With the unbeatable tactics we had now developed into a science, we cost him another two hundred and fifty thousand dollars in beer, equipment and trucks by wiping out two more breweries. We also took five men into custody, which meant that the bail bond fees were mounting into staggering totals, too. But the next two raids uncovered nothing but dry holes, with obvious indications that the breweries had been hastily moved.

"I can't understand it," I told Lahart as we tried to figure out how the mob could have known in advance about our raids.

Pondering the question, I found myself looking intently at the telephone. Suddenly it occurred to me that if we could tap their phones, wasn't it possible that they could have tapped ours?

Going downstairs to a public booth, I called Harrison at the telephone company and asked him to run a thorough check on my line.

It was exactly as I suspected.

He called back later to say that he had cleared our lines and would run a check each week.

A telephone company investigation showed that several telephone workers had recently left their jobs and "gone over to the syndicate for bigger money," he told me. He had also learned, from a friend of one of those who had left, that the syndicate employed a crew of union electricians to assist their telephone experts.

"But we're on to them now, and we'll make certain that you aren't bothered any more," he promised.

Yet, a few weeks later two more raids proved futile. A check showed that our telephones were clear of taps.

I was puzzling over this newest problem when the "Kid" strutted into my office, and from his manner I knew that he had something out of the ordinary on his mind. As he settled into a chair and went through the usual routine of adjusting his sharply creased trousers, the telephone rang.

"Boss," Basile informed me from the outer office, "I just thought you'd like to know the Kid's got another new car. It's a big splashy job that must of set him back a chunk."

"Fine," I replied. "Thanks."

Turning to the "Kid" I said: "Let's see how much money you have in that getaway fund."

He protested momentarily and then, realizing that I was adamant, pulled out the Postal Savings deposit book. It showed a five-hundred-dollar balance and no recent withdrawals of any large amount.

"They're treating you fairly well, huh?" I asked him.

"Can't kick," he answered expansively.

The young man's blitheness never failed to stagger me. He was sitting astride a powder keg, playing both ends against the middle, and yet he seemed not to be aware that he lived in a dream world which might turn suddenly into a nightmare. My voice was gruff as I held his eyes with mine.

"Today I want some information. And I want straight answers."

He recognized the uncompromising tone and shifted uncomfortably in his chair.

"We've made a couple of raids lately," I snapped. "When we got there the places had been cleaned out, lock, stock and barrel. What I want to know is, how come? Where are they getting their information?"

An injured look came into his eyes; he shook his head vigorously from side to side.

"Search me. Honest to God, Mr. Ness, I don't know where they got the information. But I can tell you one thing."

"What's that?"

"Well, since the boss man got back, the word has gone out that anybody who finds out that you are watching a certain brewery and tips off the mob gets a fast five-hundred-dollar reward," he said. "That means a lot of people must be looking at you whenever your guys leave this office."

It made sense. In the two most recent instances someone had probably recognized one of our men and relayed the information to the mob.

Fidgeting in his chair, the "Kid" coughed nervously. I knew that something important was on his mind.

"Okay, what is it?" I demanded.

He reached into his inside coat pocket and pulled out a plain envelope.

"Mr. Ness," he began uneasily, "I don't want you to get

mad at me. I told them it wouldn't do any good but they told me to try it anyhow. So I gotta try."

Jerking upright, he slid the envelope onto the desk in front of me and then retreated hastily into his chair. I folded back the unsealed flap and came out with two crackling, brand new notes.

Each one was a thousand-dollar bill.

Momentarily hypnotized, I sat there staring down at the first thousand-dollar bills I had ever seen. From a distance I heard the "Kid" saying:

"They said that if you'll take it easy, you'll get the same amount—two thousand dollars—each and every week."

I could feel the anger rising in my chest and reached out to take a viselike grip on my throat. My jaws locked so tightly that my teeth ached; the fingers holding the bills started to shake and I knew, as I jammed the bills back into the envelope and looked up at the "Kid," that my face was a distorted mask. He pushed back in his chair as I rose from my chair and held his arms out in front of him like a man warding off a blow.

"Don't hit me, Mr. Ness," he choked. "I didn't mean to do this but they made me. Honest they did. I told them it wasn't any use trying."

Fighting to get hold of myself, I walked around the desk and stood in front of him. Slowly I reached down, pulled him up and out of the chair and, opening his jacket, stuffed the envelope back into his inner pocket. My voice sounded strange.

"Listen—and listen carefully," I told him. "I want you to take this envelope back to them and tell them that Eliot Ness can't be bought—not for two thousand a week, ten thousand or a hundred thousand. Not for all the money they'll ever lay their scummy hands on."

The "Kid" started backing toward the door.

"Tell them they'll never understand it," I growled,

almost to myself.

White faced, the "Kid" had the door half open when I stopped him. He flinched as I walked toward him.

"Get this straight," I glared. "Make damned sure that that money gets back to the person who gave it to you. I mean *all* of it. Because if I ever find out that you kept it, so help me God I'll break you into tiny pieces with my bare hands."

Gulping audibly, the "Kid" held up his right hand like a man taking an oath.

"I swear it, Mr. Ness. I swear it."

With that, the door banged behind him. The flood of anger was receding now, and I turned back to my desk.

With the "boss man" back, the first step was bribery. What next?

That night my car was stolen again. I wondered, as I called Betty and broke another date and took a taxi home, whether it would be found this time or whether it would disappear as completely as Marty's had.

Next morning the indignant Basile popped in to tell me that it had been found abandoned on the South Side.

"Only one thing, boss," he fumed. "The bastards who took it also took the front wheels off of it. I had to get it towed into the garage."

Nuisance retaliation! They still hadn't given up their hopes of diminishing the efficiency of my outfit through bribery. This was clear later that morning when Lahart and Seager burst into my office. Marty was volubly incredulous.

"Chief," he gasped, "those monkeys tried to buy us off."

I listened with interest as he told me how he and Seager had been tracking a load of barrels from the cleaning plant at 38th and Shields.

"Sam's driving down the street about two blocks behind the load, and as far as we can tell there isn't a convoy with the barrel truck this time," Marty was saying. "All of a sudden—zoom, there's the Ford coupé right beside us and one of the pearl gray hats flips something into our car. It sails right past Sam's nose and lands right in my lap."

Sam bit the end off a cigar and his head disappeared behind a bluish cloud of smoke as he lit up while Marty continued breathlessly.

"Well, I thought for a second maybe we were on the receiving end of a pineapple. But what am I holding but a roll of bills big enough to choke a horse!"

Marty chuckled.

"Sam takes one look, sees what it is and says: 'Watch me catch 'em. Then you can give them a lateral pass.' So off we go, and while he's running down that souped-up Ford I make a quick count and as near as I can estimate—because of the way we're bouncing along—there has to be two thousand bucks in that roll."

Nodding, I asked Marty: "Did you catch them?"

"I'll say," he laughed. "Sam came so close beside them we'll both need a new paint job. Then I pitched a pass that would have made Frank Carideo of Notre Dame look like a substitute. It hit the monkey who was driving right in the eye—and he almost wrecked both of us."

A new surge of confidence swept through me as I heard Marty's story. These two men earned the sum total of twenty-eight hundred dollars a year. They had been tempted with the better part of a year's salary, yet had scorned a bribe which probably would have been impossible to trace. My voice was gruff.

"At the risk of being awfully corny, I want you guys to know that I'm pretty damned proud of you."

"What the hell, Eliot," Sam said. "We want to beat 'em, not join 'em."

"I've got to admit one thing," Marty interrupted kiddingly. "I had to make three or four swings before I got off that pass. Those bills just didn't seem to want to leave Pappa's hand."

"Bunk," Sam grunted. "You hit that guy on the first peg, and you were so mad I thought you were going right through the window after him."

I told them of the offer which had been made to me through the "Kid," the anger rising in me again as I related the details. Marty let loose a reflective whistle.

"Boy, what they tossed us was just carfare, huh?"

"No," I replied. "They know that's big money to people like us. They just can't understand that some people won't be bought. But sooner or later the idea will simmer through their thick skulls and then, in all probability, they'll try some rough stuff. But it sure is nice to know that my guys can't be bought."

"You can tell the world!" Marty cracked.

His words rang in my ears insistently.

Why not? I thought. Why not do just that?—and "tell the world"—and "Scarface Al" Capone—that Eliot Ness and his men couldn't be bought. The idea kept bouncing around inside my head as Marty and Sam filled me in on their progress in trying to locate another brewery.

"That's exactly what we're going to do," I declared.

"What's that?" Sam asked.

"Tell the world, just as Marty suggested. I'm going to make a few calls and then I'm going to take you two to lunch—on the government—to make up in a very minor way for that two thousand dollars you tossed away this morning. Then we're coming back here and 'tell the world.'"

They both looked puzzled. But they got the drift as I leafed through the telephone book and began to call the newspapers and newsreel outfits.

"This is going to ruin my social life in places like the Montmartre," Marty chuckled as I called the *Tribune* and, having attained some notoriety as a "gangbuster," was swiftly put through to the city desk.

"But you'll be a big hero," I joked.

Completing my calls, in which I informed each newspaper and motion-picture company that I was having a "sensational" press conference at two o'clock that afternoon, I took my two men to lunch.

"And," I told them in the elevator, "you can have all you can eat—as long as you take the thirty-five-cent blue-plate special."

There was little conversation as we ate, each busy with his own thoughts. I began to study these two vastly different men—the gusty, irrepressible Lahart, and the stolid, unemotional Seager. Why, I wondered, were they in this? In my case, it was a heterogeneous mixture, a passion for police work, a dislike of seeing people abused and, basically, the thrill of action.

"Sam," I finally asked Seager as he waded through a chunk of apple pie, "what made you come into this thing?"

He chewed reflectively for several seconds, his square jaw working steadily, and then laid aside his fork.

"Police work is about all I've ever known, Eliot. I couldn't take that tour of duty in the death house any more. I had to get outside where I could move around and see people who still had some sort of hope. Then this came along and, well, it's quite an experience."

He prodded a piece of crust with his fork and then looked me right in the eye.

"Maybe it'll surprise you, Eliot, but I've always wanted a chicken farm. Now I've seen just about all the trouble I want. If I get through this one—or I guess I should say 'when'—I think I'll settle for that farm."

I was surprised, because I had never pictured Sam as the country type. Yet I was even more astonished when Lahart chimed in solemnly:

"Damned if I know what my reasons were, except that the job in the post office was driving me crazy and I wanted some kicks. But let me tell you, Sam, that farm idea sounds pretty good. Imagine, nothing to worry about but whether the hens are layin'."

It's getting to all of us, I thought as we left the restaurant. It isn't facing danger that cuts you up inside. It's the waiting and the not knowing what's coming.

When we returned to the office, Basile was shrugging off the questions of more than a dozen reporters and cameramen. Flashbulbs began to pop as we walked in and, raising my hands to quiet them, I told them there would be plenty of time for everything.

"First let's go into my office and I'll give you the story. Then you can take all the pictures you want."

When they were settled, and while the newsreels were setting up their cameras, I told them of the attempted briberies. I related in detail how an emissary of Capone's had tried to buy me off for two thousand dollars a week and how Marty and Sam had thrown back their flying bribe.

Pencils scribbled rapidly, and there was a rush for telephones. Flashlight bulbs popped incessantly and the story had to be repeated for the motion-picture cameras.

It was a long, wearisome process but well worth the effort. Possibly it wasn't too important for the world to know that we couldn't be bought, but I did want Al Capone and every gangster in the city to realize that there were still a few law enforcement agents who couldn't be swerved from their duty.

As the late group was leaving, I heard one of the men say:

"Those guys are dead pigeons."

Pigeons, I thought grimly, who will take a lot of killing. At the very outset I had chosen my men with an eye toward their ability to take care of themselves under almost any conditions. These men were not hoodlums who had all their courage in their trigger finger. They were alert, fearless and extremely fit and capable. They trusted nobody except themselves, and we had long since devised a system of working in pairs. They would be hard to cut down, I knew.

Meanwhile, defiance of the type we had exhibited was unheard of in a racket-infested city where opposition was so consistently bought off or killed off. Our revelation of the bribes was a sensation. The story was splashed across front pages from coast to coast.

One story opened:

Eliot Ness and his young agents have proved to Al Capone that they are untouchable.

A caption writer adopted it for another paper and over our pictures rode the bold, black words:

"THE UNTOUCHABLES"

The wire service picked up the phrase and the words swept across the nation.

So were born "The Untouchables."

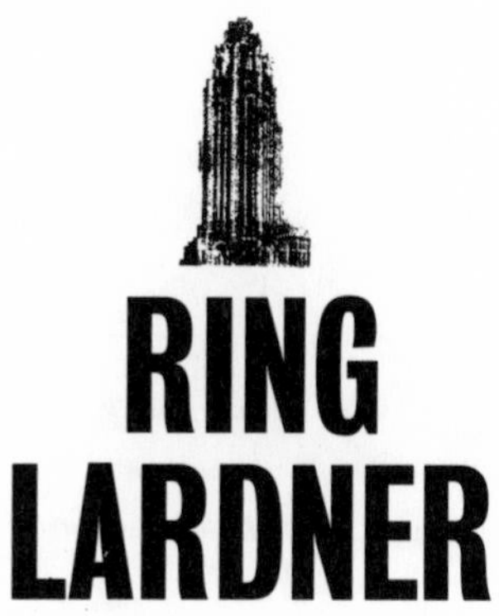

RING LARDNER

You Know Me Al

New York, New York, September 16.

FRIEND AL: I opened the serious here and beat them easy but I know you must of saw about it in the Chi papers. At that they don't give me no fair show in the Chi papers. One of the boys bought one here and I seen in it where I was lucky to win that game in Cleveland. If I knowed which one of them reporters wrote that I would punch his jaw.

Al I told you Boston was some town but this is the real

Ring Lardner's saga of bush-leaguer Jack Keefe began in 1916 with You Know Me Al *and continued on to fill two more volumes:* Treat 'Em Rough *(1918) and* The Real Dope *(1919). Lardner covered sports for* The Chicago Tribune *before becoming a much-loved columnist.* You Know Me Al *was the beginning of Lardner's stellar career, which included coverage of the infamous Black Sox Scandal of 1919.*

one. I never seen nothing like it and I been going some since we got here. I walked down Broadway the Main Street last night and I run into a couple of the ball players and they took me to what they call the Garden but it aint't like the gardens at home because this one is indoors. We sat down to a table and had several drinks. Pretty soon one of the boys asked me if I was broke and I says No, why? He says You better get some lubricateing oil and loosen up. I don't know what he meant but pretty soon when we had had a lot of drinks the waiter brings a check and hands it to me. It was for one dollar. I says Oh I ain't paying for all of them. The waiter says This is just for that last drink.

I thought the other boys would make a holler but they didn't say nothing. So I give him a dollar bill and even then he didn't act satisfied so I asked him what he was waiting for and he said Oh nothing, kind of sassy. I was going to bust him but the boys give me the sign to shut up and not to say nothing. I excused myself pretty soon because I wanted to get some air. I give my check for my hat to a boy and he brought my hat and I started going and he says Haven't you forgot something? I guess he must of thought I was wearing a overcoat.

Then I went down the Main Street again and some man stopped me and asked me did I want to go to the show. He said he had a ticket. I asked him what show and he said the Follies. I never heard of it but I told him I would go if he had a ticket to spare. He says I will spare you this one for three dollars. I says You must take me for some boob. He says No I wouldn't insult no boob. So I walks on but if he had of insulted me I would of busted him.

I went back to the hotel then and run into Kid Gleason. He asked me to take a walk with him so out I go again. We went to the corner and he bought me a beer. He don't drink nothing but pop himself. The two drinks was only ten cents so I says This is the place for me. He says Where have you been? and I told him about paying one dollar for three drinks. He says I see I will have to take charge of you. Don't go round with them ball players no more. When you want to go out and see the sights come to me and I will stear you. So to-night he is going to stear me. I will write to you from Philadelphia.

Your pal, Jack.

Philadelphia, Pa., September 19.

Friend Al: They won't be no game here to-day because it is raining. We all been loafing round the hotel all day and I am glad of it because I got all tired out over in New York City. I and Kid Gleason went round together the last couple of nights over there and he wouldn't let me spend no money. I seen a lot of girls that I would of liked to of got acquainted with but he wouldn't even let me answer them when they spoke to me. We run in to a couple of peaches last night and they had us spotted too. One of them says I'll bet you're a couple of ball players. But Kid says You lose your bet. I am a bell-hop and the big rube with me is nothing but a pitcher.

One of them says What are you trying to do kid somebody? He says Go home and get some soap and remove your disguise from your face. I didn't think he ought to talk like that to them and I called him about it and said maybe they was lonesome and it wouldn't hurt none if we treated them to a soda or something. But he says Lonesome. If I don't get you away from here they will steal everything you got. They won't even leave you your fast ball. So we left them and he took me to a picture show. It was some California pictures and they made me think of Hazel so when I got back to the hotel I sent her three postcards.

Gleason made me go to my room at ten o'clock both nights but I was pretty tired anyway because he had walked me all over town. I guess we must of saw twenty shows. He says I would take you to the grand opera only it would be throwing money away because we can hear Ed Walsh for nothing. Walsh has got some voice Al a loud high tenor.

To-morrow is Sunday and we have a double header

Monday on account of the rain to-day. I thought sure I would get another chance to beat the Athaletics and I asked Callahan if he was going to pitch me here but he said he thought he would save me to work against Johnson in Washington. So you see Al he must figure I am about the best he has got. I'll beat him Al if they get a couple of runs behind me.

Yours truly, Jack.

P.S. They was a letter here from Violet and it pretty near made me feel like crying. I wish they was two of me so both them girls could be happy.

Washington, D. C., September 22.

Dear Old Al: Well Al here I am in the capital of the old United States. We got in last night and I been walking round town all morning. But I didn't tire myself out because I am going to pitch against Johnson this afternoon.

This is the prettiest town I ever seen but I believe they is more colored people here than they is in Evansville or Chi. I seen the White House and the Monumunt. They say that Bill Sullivan and Gabby St. once catched a baseball that was threw off the top of the Monumunt but I bet they couldn't catch it if I throwed it.

I was in to breakfast this morning with Gleason and Bodie and Weaver and Fournier. Gleason says I'm supprised that you ain't sick in bed to-day. I says Why?

He says Most of our pitchers gets sick when Cal tells them they are going to work against Johnson. He says Here's these other fellows all feeling pretty sick this morning and they ain't even pitchers. All they have to do is hit against him but it looks like as if Cal would have to send substitutes in for them. Bodie is complaining of a sore arm which he must of strained drawing to two card flushes. Fournier and Weaver have strained their legs doing the tango dance. Nothing could cure them except to hear that big Walter had got throwed out of his machine and wouldn't be able to pitch against us in this serious.

I says I feel O. K. and I ain't afraid to pitch against Johnson and I ain't afraid to hit against him neither. Then Weaver says Have you ever saw him work? Yes, I says, I seen him in Chi. Then Weaver says Well if you have saw him work and ain't afraid to hit against him I'll bet you would go down to Wall Street and holler Hurrah for Roosevelt. I says No I wouldn't do that but I ain't afraid of no pitcher and what is more if you get me a couple of runs I'll beat him. Then Fournier says Oh we will get you a couple of runs all right. He says That's just as easy as catching whales with a angle-worm.

Well Al I must close and go in and get some lunch. My arm feels great and they will have to go some to beat me Johnson or no Johnson.

Your pal, Jack.

Washington, D. C., September 22

Friend Al: Well I guess you know by this time that they didn't get no two runs for me, only one, but I beat him just the same. I beat him one to nothing and Callahan was so pleased that he give me a ticket to the theater. I just got back from there and it is pretty late and I already have wrote you one letter today but I am going to sit up and tell you about it.

It was cloudy before the game started and when I was warming up I made the remark to Callahan that the dark day ought to make my speed good. He says Yes and of course it will handicap Johnson.

While Washington was takeing their practice their two coachers Schaefer and Altrock got out on the infield and cut up and I pretty near busted laughing at them. They certainly is funny Al. Callahan asked me what I was laughing at and I told him and he says That's the first time I ever seen a pitcher laugh when he was going to work against Johnson. He says Griffith is a pretty good fellow to give us something to laugh at before he shoots that guy at us.

I warmed up good and told Schalk not to ask me for my

spitter much because my fast one looked faster than I ever seen it. He says it won't make much difference what you pitch to-day. I says Oh, yes, it will because Callahan thinks enough of me to work me against Johnson and I want to show him he didn't make no mistake. Then Gleason says No he didn't make no mistake. Wasteing Cicotte or Scotty would of been a mistake in this game.

Well, Johnson whiffs Weaver and Chase and makes Lord pop out in the first inning. I walked their first guy but I didn't give Milan nothing to bunt and finally he flied out. And then I whiffed the next two. On the bench Callahan says That's the way, boy. Keep that up and we got a chance.

Johnson had fanned four of us when I come up with two outs in the third inning and he whiffed me to. I fouled one though that if I had ever got a good hold of I would of knocked out of the park. In the first seven innings we didn't have a hit off of him. They had got five or six lucky ones off of me and I had walked two or three, but I cut loose with all I had when they was men on and they couldn't do nothing with me. The only reason I walked so many was because my fast one was jumping so. Honest Al it was so fast that Evans the umpire couldn't see it half the time and he called a lot of balls that was right over the heart.

Well I come up in the eighth with two out and the score still nothing and nothing. I had whiffed the second time as well as the first but it was account of Evans missing one on me. The eighth started with Shanks muffing a fly ball off of Bodie. It was way out by the fence so he got two bases on it and he went to third while they were throwing Berger out. Then Schalk whiffed.

Callahan says Go up and try to meet one Jack. It might as well be you as anybody else. But your old pal didn't whiff this time Al. He gets two strikes on me with fast ones and then I passed up two bad ones. I took my healthy at the next one and slapped it over first base. I guess I could of made two bases on it but I didn't want to tire myself out. Anyway Bodie scored and I had them beat. And my hit was the only one we got off of him so I guess he is a pretty good pitcher after all Al.

They filled up the bases on me with one out in the ninth but it was pretty dark then and I made McBride and their catcher look like suckers with my speed.

I felt so good after the game that I drunk one of them pink cocktails. I don't know what their name is. And then I sent a postcard to poor little Violet. I don't care nothing about her but it don't hurt me none to try and cheer her up once in a while. We leave here Thursday night for home and they had ought to be two or three letters there for me from Hazel because I haven't heard from her lately. She must of lost my road addresses.

Your pal, Jack.

P.S. I forgot to tell you what Callahan said after the game. He said I was a real pitcher now and he is going to use me in the city serious. If he does Al we will beat them Cubs sure.

Chicago, Illinois, September 27.

Friend Al: They wasn't no letter here at all from Hazel and I guess she must of been sick. Or maybe she didn't think it was worth while writeing as long as she is comeing next week.

I want to ask you to do me a favor Al and that is to see if you can find me a house down there. I will want to move in with Mrs. Keefe, don't that sound funny Al? sometime in the week of October twelfth. Old man Cutting's house or that yellow house across from you would be O. K. I would rather have the yellow one so as to be near you. Find out how much rent they want Al and if it is not no more than twelve dollars a month get it for me. We will buy our furniture here in Chi when Hazel comes.

We have a couple of days off now Al and then we play St. Louis two games here. Then Detroit comes to finish the season the third and fourth of October.

Your pal, Jack.

Chicago, Illinois, October 3.

Dear Old Al: Thanks Al for getting the house. The one-year lease is O. K. You and Bertha and me and Hazel can have all sorts of good times together. I guess the walk needs repairs but I can fix that up when I come. We can stay at the hotel when we first get there.

I wish you could of came up for the city serious Al but anyway I want you and Bertha to be sure and come up for our wedding. I will let you know the date as soon as Hazel gets here.

The serious starts Tuesday and this town is wild over it. The Cubs finished second in their league and we was fifth in ours but that don't scare me none. We would of finished right on top if I had of been here all season.

Callahan pitched one of the bushers against Detroit this afternoon and they beat him bad. Callahan is saveing up Scott and Allen and Russell and Cicotte and I for the big show. Walsh isn't in no shape and neither is Benz. It looks like I would have a good deal to do because most of them others can't work no more than once in four days and Allen ain't no good at all.

We have a day to rest after to-morrow's game with the Tigers and then we go at them Cubs.

Your pal, Jack.

P. S. I have got it figured that Hazel is fixing to surprise me by dropping in on me because I haven't heard nothing yet.

Chicago, Illinois, October 7.

Friend Al: Well Al you know by this time that they beat me to-day and tied up the serious. But I have still got plenty of time Al and I will get them before it is over. My arm wasn't feeling good Al and my fast ball didn't hop like it had ought to. But it was the rotten support I got that beat me. That lucky stiff Zimmerman was the only guy that got a real hit off of me and he must of shut his eyes and throwed his bat because the ball he hit was a foot over his head. And if they hadn't been makeing all them errors behind me they wouldn't of been nobody on bases when Zimmerman got that lucky scratch. The serious now stands one and one Al and it is a cinch we will beat them even if they are a bunch of lucky stiffs. They has been great big crowds at both games and it looks like as if we should ought to get over eight hundred dollars a peace if we win and we will win sure because I will beat them three straight if necessary.

But Al I have got bigger news than that for you and I am the happyest man in the world. I told you I had not heard from Hazel for a long time. To-night when I got back to my room they was a letter waiting for me from her.

Al she is married. Maybe you don't know why that makes me happy but I will tell you. She is married to Kid Levy the middle weight. I guess my thirty dollars is gone because in her letter she called me a cheap skate and she inclosed one one-cent stamp and two twos and said she was paying me for the glass of beer I once bought her. I bought her more than that Al but I won't make no holler. She all so said not for me to never come near her or her husband would bust my jaw. I ain't afraid of him or no one else Al but they ain't no danger of me ever bothering them. She was no good and I was sorry the minute I agreed to marry her.

But I was going to tell you why I am happy or maybe you can guess. Now I can make Violet my wife and she's got Hazel beat forty ways. She ain't nowheres near as big as Hazel but she's classier Al and she will make me a good wife. She ain't never asked me for no money.

I wrote her a letter the minute I got the good news and told her to come on over here at once at my expense. We will be married right after the serious is over and I want you and Bertha to be sure and stand up with us. I will wire you at my own expence the exact date.

It all seems like a dream now about Violet and I haveing our misunderstanding Al and I don't see how I ever could of accused her of sending me that postcard. You and Bertha will be just as crazy about her as I am when you see her Al. Just think Al I will be married inside of a week and to the only girl I ever could of been happy with instead of the woman I never really cared for except as a passing fancy. My happyness would be complete Al if I had not of let that woman steal thirty dollars off of me.

Your happy pal, Jack.

P. S. Hazel probibly would of insisted on us takeing a trip to Niagara falls or somewheres but I know Violet will be perfectly satisfied if I take her right down to Bedford. Oh you little yellow house.

Chicago, Illinois, October 9.

Friend Al: Well Al we have got them beat three games to one now and will wind up the serious to-morrow sure. Callahan sent me in to save poor Allen yesterday and I stopped them dead. But I don't care now Al. I have lost all interest in the game and I don't care if Callahan pitches me to-morrow or not. My heart is just about broke Al and I wouldn't be able to do myself justice feeling the way I do.

I have lost Violet Al and just when I was figureing on being the happyest man in the world. We will get the big money but it won't do me no good. They can keep my share because I won't have no little girl to spend it on.

Her answer to my letter was waiting for me at home to-night. She is engaged to be married to Joe Hill the big lefthander Jennings got from Providence. Honest Al I don't see how he gets by. He ain't got no more curve ball than a rabbit and his fast one floats up there like a big balloon. He beat us the last game of the regular season here but it was because Callahan had a lot of bushers in the game.

I wish I had knew then that he was stealing my girl and I would of made Callahan pitch me against him. And when he come up to bat I would of beaned him. But I don't suppose you could hurt him by hitting him in the head. The big stiff. Their wedding ain't going to come off till next summer and by that time he will be pitching in the Southwestern Texas League for about fifty dollars a month.

Violet wrote that she wished me all the luck and happyness in the world but it is too late for me to be happy Al and I don't care what kind of luck I have now.

Al you will have to get rid of that lease for me. Fix it up the best way you can. Tell the old man I have changed my plans. I don't know just yet what I will do but maybe I will go to Australia with Mike Donlin's team. If I do I won't care if the boat goes down or not. I don't believe I will even come back to Bedford this winter. It would drive me wild to go past that little house every day and think how happy I might of been.

Maybe I will pitch to-morrow Al and if I do the serious will be over to-morrow night. I can beat them Cubs if I get any kind of decent support. But I don't care now Al.

Yours truly, Jack.

Chicago, Illinois, October 12.

Al: Your letter received. If the old man won't call it off I guess I will have to try and rent the house to some one else. Do you know of any couple that wants one Al? It looks like I would have to come down there myself and fix things up someway. He is just mean enough to stick me with the house on my hands when I won't have no use for it.

They beat us the day before yesterday as you probibly know and it rained yesterday and to-day. The papers says it will be all O. K. to-morrow and Callahan tells me I am going to work. The Cub pitchers was all shot to peaces and the bad weather is just nuts for them because it will give Cheney a good rest. But I will beat him Al if they don't kick it away behind me.

I must close because I promised Allen the little left-hander that I would come over to his flat and play cards a while to-night and I must wash up and change my collar. Allen's wife's sister is visiting them again and I would give anything not to have to go over there. I am through with girls and don't want nothing to do with them.

I guess it is maybe a good thing it rained to-day because

I dreamt about Violet last night and went out and got a couple of high balls before breakfast this morning. I hadn't never drank nothing before breakfast before and it made me kind of sick. But I am all O.K. now.

Your pal, Jack.

Chicago, Illinois, October 13.

Dear Old Al: The serious is all over Al. We are the champions and I done it. I may be home the day after to-morrow or I may not come for a couple of days. I want to see Comiskey before I leave and fix up about my contract for next year. I won't sign for no less than five thousand and if he hands me a contract for less than that I will leave the White Sox flat on their back. I have got over fourteen hundred dollars now Al with the city serious money which was $814.30 and I don't have to worry.

Them reporters will have to give me a square deal this time Al. I had everything and the Cubs done well to score a run. I whiffed Zimmerman three times. Some of the boys say he ain't no hitter but he is a hitter and a good one Al only he could not touch the stuff I got. The umps give them their run because in the fourth inning I had Leach flatfooted off of second base and Weaver tagged him O. K. but the umps wouldn't call it. Then Schulte the lucky stiff happened to get a hold of one and pulled it past first base. I guess Chase must of been asleep. Anyway they scored but I don't care because we piled up six runs on Cheney and I drove in one of them myself with one of the prettiest singles you ever see. It was a spitter and I hit it like a shot. If I had hit it square it would of went out of the park.

Comiskey ought to feel pretty good about me winning and I guess he will give me a contract for anything I want. He will have to or I will go to the Federal League.

We are all invited to a show to-night and I am going with Allen and his wife and her sister Florence. She is O. K. Al and I guess she thinks the same about me. She must because she was out to the game to-day and seen me hand it to them. She maybe ain't as pretty as Violet and Hazel but as they say beauty isn't only so deep.

Well Al tell the boys I will be with them soon. I have gave up the idea of going to Australia because I would have to buy a evening full-dress suit and they tell me they cost pretty near fifty dollars.

Yours truly, Jack.

Chicago, Illinois, October 14.

Friend Al: Never mind about that lease. I want the house after all Al and I have got the supprise of your life for you.

When I come home to Bedford I will bring my wife with me. I and Florence fixed things all up after the show last night and we are going to be married to-morrow morning. I am a busy man to-day Al because I have got to get the license and look around for furniture. And I have also got to buy some new cloths but they are having a sale on Cottage Grove Avenue at Clark's store and I know one of the clerks there.

I am the happyest man in the world Al. You and Bertha and I and Florence will have all kinds of good times together this winter because I know Bertha and Florence will like each other. Florence looks something like Bertha at that. I am glad I didn't get tied up with Violet or Hazel even if they was a little bit prettier than Florence.

Florence knows a lot about baseball for a girl and you would be supprised to hear her talk. She says I am the best pitcher in the league and she has saw them all. She all so says I am the best looking ball player she ever seen but you know how girls will kid a guy Al. You will like her O. K. I fell for her the first time I seen her.

Your old pal, Jack.

P. S. I signed up for next year. Comiskey slapped me on the back when I went in to see him and told me I would be a star next year if I took good care of myself. I guess I am a star without waiting for next year Al. My contract calls for twenty-eight hundred a year which is a thousand more than I was getting. And it is pretty near a cinch that I will be in on the World Serious money next season.

P. S. I certainly am relieved about that lease. It would of been fierce to of had that place on my hands all winter and not getting any use out of it. Everything is all O. K. now. Oh you little yellow house.

THE BUSHER'S HONEYMOON

Chicago, Illinois, October, 17

Friend Al: Well Al it looks as if I would not be writeing so much to you now that I am a married man. Yes Al I and Florrie was married the day before yesterday just like I told you we was going to be and Al I am the happyest man in the world though I have spent $30 in the last 3 days incluseive. You was wise Al to get married in Bedford where not nothing is nearly half so dear. My expenses was as follows:

License	$2.00
Preist	3.50
Haircut and shave	.35
Shine	.05
Carfair	.45
New suit	14.50
Show tickets	3.00
Flowers	.50
Candy	.30
Hotel	4.50
Tobacco both kinds	.25

You see Al it costs a hole lot of money to get married here. The sum of what I have wrote down is $29.40 but as I told you I have spent $30 and I do not know what I have did with that other $0.60. My new brother-in-law Allen told me I should ought to give the preist $5 and I thought it should be about $2 the same as the license so I split the difference and gave him $3.50. I never seen him before and probily won't never see him again so why should I give him anything at all when it is his business to marry couples? But I like to do the right thing. You know me Al.

I thought we would be in Bedford by this time but Florrie wants to stay here a few more days because she says she wants to be with her sister. Allen and his wife is thinking about takeing a flat for the winter instead of going down to Waco Texas where they live. I don't see no sense in that when it costs so much to live here but it is none of my business if they want to throw their money away. But I am glad I got a wife with some sense though she kicked because I did not get no room with a bath which would cost me $2 a day instead of $1.50. I says I guess the clubhouse is still open yet and if I want a bath I can go over there and take the shower. She says Yes and I suppose I can go and jump in the lake. But she would not do that Al because the lake here is cold at this time of the year.

When I told you about my expenses I did not include in it the meals because we would be eating them if I was getting married or not getting married only I have to pay for six meals a day now instead of three and I didn't used to eat no lunch in the playing season except once in a while when I knowed I was not going to work that afternoon. I had a meal ticket which had not quite ran out over to a resturunt on Indiana Ave and we eat there for the first day except at night when I took Allen and his wife to the show with us and then he took us to a chop suye resturunt. I guess you have not never had no chop suye Al and I am here to tell you you have not missed nothing but when Allen was going to buy the supper what could I say? I could not say nothing.

Well yesterday and to-day we been eating at a resturunt on Cottage Grove Ave near the hotel and at the resturunt on Indiana that I had the meal ticket at only I do not like to buy no new meal ticket when I am not going to be round here no more than a few days. Well Al I guess the meals has cost me all together about $1.50 and I have eat very little myself. Florrie always wants desert ice cream or something and that runs up money faster than regular stuff like stake and ham and eggs.

Well Al Florrie says it is time for me to keep my promise and take her to the moveing pictures which is $0.20 more because the one she likes round here costs a dime apeace. So I must close for this time and will see you soon.

Your pal, Jack.

Chicago, Illinois, October 22.

Al: Just a note Al to tell you why I have not yet came to Bedford yet where I expected I would be long before this time. Allen and his wife have took a furnished flat for the winter and Allen's wife wants Florrie to stay here untill they get settled. Meentime it is costing me a hole lot of money at the hotel and for meals besides I am paying $10 a month rent for the house you got for me and what good am I getting out of it? But Florrie wants to help her sister and what can I say? Though I did make her promise she would not stay longer than next Saturday at least. So I guess Al we will be home on the evening train Saturday and then may be I can save some money.

I know Al that you and Bertha will like Florrie when you get acquainted with her spesially Bertha though Florrie dreses pretty swell and spends a hole lot of time fusing with her face and her hair.

She says to me to-night Who are you writeing to and I told her Al Blanchard who I have told you about a good many times. She says I bet you are writeing to some girl and acted like as though she was kind of jealous. So I thought I would tease her a little and I says I don't know no girls except you and Violet and Hazel. Who is Violet and Hazel? she says. I kind of laughed and says Oh I guess I better not tell you and then she says I guess you will tell me. That made me kind of mad because no girl can't tell me what to do. She says Are you going to tell me? and I says No.

Then she says If you don't tell me I will go over to Marie's that is her sister Allen's wife and stay all night. I says Go on and she went downstairs but I guess she probily went to get a soda because she has some money of her own that I give her. This was about two hours ago and she is probily down in the hotel lobby now trying to scare me by makeing me believe she has went to her sister's. But she can't fool me Al and I am now going out to mail this letter and get a beer. I won't never tell her about Violet and Hazel if she is going to act like that.

Yours truly Jack.

.....

Chicago, Illinois, Febuery 9.

Old Pal: I want to thank you for asking Florrie to come down there and visit you Al but I find she can't get away. I did not know she had no engagements but she says she may go down to her folks in Texas and she don't want to say that she will come to visit you when it is so indefanate. So thank you just the same Al and thank Bertha too.

Florrie is still at me to take her along to California but honest Al I can't do it. I am right down to my last $50 and I have not payed no rent for this month. I owe the hired girl 2 weeks' salery and both I and Florrie needs some new cloths.

Florrie has just came in since I started writeing this letter and we have been talking some more about California and she says maybe if I would ask Comiskey he would take her along as the club's guest. I had not never thought of that Al and maybe he would because he is a pretty good scout and I guess I will go and see him about it. The league has it skedule meeting here to-morrow and may be I can see him down to the hotel where they meet at. I am so worried Al that I can't write no more but I will tell you how I come out with Comiskey.

Your pal, Jack.

Chicago, Illinois, Febuery 11.

Friend Al: I am up against it right Al and I don't know where I am going to head in at. I went down to the hotel where the league was holding its skedule meeting at and I seen Comiskey and got some money off of the club but I owe all the money I got off of them and I am still wondering what to do about Florrie.

Comiskey was busy in the meeting when I went down there and they was not no chance to see him for a while so I and Allen and some of the boys hung round and had a few drinks and fanned. This here Joe Hill the busher that Detroit has got that Violet is hooked up to was round the hotel. I don't know what for but I felt like busting his jaw only the boys told me I had better not do nothing because I might kill him and any way he probily won't be in the league much longer. Well finally Comiskey got threw the meeting and I seen him and he says Hello Young man what can I do for you? And I says I would like to get $100 advance money. He says Have you been takeing care of yourself down in Bedford? And I told him I had been liveing here all winter and it did not seem to make no hit with him though I don't see what business it is of hisn where I live.

So I says I had been takeing good care of myself. And I have Al. You know that. So he says I should come to the ball park the next day which is to-day and he would have the secretary take care of me but I says I could not wait and so he give me $100 out of his pocket and says he would have it charged against my salery. I was just going to brace him about the California trip when he got away and went back to the meeting.

Well Al I hung round with the bunch waiting for him to get threw again and we had some more drinks and finally Comiskey was threw again and I braced him in the lobby and asked him if it was all right to take my wife along to California. He says Sure they would be glad to have her along. And then I says Would the club pay her fair? He says I guess you must of spent that $100 buying some nerve. He says Have you not got no sisters that would like to go along to? He says Does your wife insist on the drawing room or will she take a lower berth? He says Is my special train good enough for her?

Then he turns away from me and I guess some of the boys must of heard the stuff he pulled because they was laughing when he went away but I did not see nothing to laugh at. But I guess he ment that I would have to pay her fair if she goes along and that is out of the question Al. I am up against it and I don't know where I am going to head in at.

Your pal, Jack.

Chicago, Illinois, Febuery 12.

Dear Old Al: I guess everything will be all O. K. now at least I am hopeing it will. When I told Florrie about how I come out with Comiskey she bawled her head off and I thought for a while I was going to have to call a doctor or something but pretty soon she cut it out and we sat there a while without saying nothing. Then she says If you could get your salery razed a couple of hundred dollars a year would you borrow the money ahead somewheres and take me along to California? I says Yes I would if I could get a couple hundred dollars more salery but how could I do that when I had signed a contract for $2800 last fall allready? She says Don't you think you are worth more than $2800? And I says Yes of coarse I was worth more than $2800. She says Well if you will go and talk the right way to Comiskey I believe he will give you $3000 but you must be sure you go at it the right way and don't go and ball it all up.

Well we argude about it a while because I don't want to hold nobody up Al but finally I says I would. It would not be holding nobody up anyway because I am worth $3000 to the club if I am worth a nichol. The papers is all saying that the club has got a good chance to win the pennant this year and talking about the pitching staff and I guess they would not be no pitching staff much if it was not for I and one or two others—about one other I guess.

So it looks as if everything will be all O. K. now Al. I am going to the office over to the park to see him the first thing in the morning and I am pretty sure that I will get what I am after because if I do not he will see that I am going to quit and then he will see what he is up against and not let me get away.

I will let you know how I come out.

Your pal, Jack.

Chicago, Illinois, Febuery 14.

Friend Al: Al old pal I have got a big supprise for you. I am going to the Federal League. I had a run in with Comiskey yesterday and I guess I told him a thing or 2. I guess he would of been glad to sign me at my own figure before I got threw but I was so mad I would not give him no chance to offer me another contract.

I got out to the park at 9 oclock yesterday morning and it was a hour before he showed up and then he kept me waiting another hour so I was pretty sore when I finally went in to see him. He says Well young man what can I do for you? I says I come to see about my contract. He says Do you want to sign up for next year all ready? I says No I am talking about this year. He says I thought I and you talked business last fall. And I says Yes but now I think I am worth more money and I want to sign a contract for $3000. He says If you behave yourself and work good this year I will see that you are took care of. But I says That won't do because I have got to be sure I am going to get $3000.

Then he says I am not sure you are going to get anything. I says What do you mean? And he says I have gave you a very fare contract and if you don't want to live up to it that is your own business. So I give him a awful call Al and told him I would jump to the Federal League. He says Oh, I would not do that if I was you. They are haveing a hard enough time as it is. So I says something back to him and he did not say nothing to me and I beat it out of the office.

I have not told Florrie about the Federal League business yet as I am going to give her a big supprise. I bet they will take her along with me on the training trip and pay her fair but even if they don't I should not worry because I will make them give me a contract for $4000 a year and then I can afford to take her with me on all the trips.

I will go down and see Tinker to-morrow morning and I will write you to-morrow night Al how much salery they are going to give me. But I won't sign for no less than $4000. You know me Al.

Yours, Jack.

Chicago, Illinois, Febuery 15.

Old Pal: It is pretty near midnight Al but I been to bed a couple of times and I can't get to sleep. I am worried to death Al and I don't know where I am going to head in at. Maybe I will go out and buy a gun Al and end it all and I guess it would be better for everybody. But I cannot do that Al because I have not got the money to buy a gun with.

I went down to see Tinker about signing up with the Federal League and he was busy in the office when I come in. Pretty soon Buck Perry the pitcher that was with Boston last year come out and seen me and as Tinker was still busy we went out and had a drink together. Buck shows me a contract for $5000 a year and Tinker had allso gave him a $500 bonus. So pretty soon I went up to the office and pretty soon Tinker seen me and called me into his private office and asked what did I want. I says I was ready to jump for $4000 and a bonus. He says I thought you was signed up with the White Sox. I says Yes I was but I was not satisfied. He says That does not make no difference to me if you are satisfied or not. You ought to of came to me before you signed a contract. I says I did not know enough but I know better now. He says Well it is to late now. We cannot have nothing to do with you because you have went and signed a contract with the White Sox. I argude with him a while and asked him to come out and have a drink so we could talk it over but he said he was busy so they was nothing for me to do but blow.

So I am not going to the Federal League Al and I will

not go with the White Sox because I have got a raw deal. Comiskey will be sorry for what he done when his team starts the season and is up against it for good pitchers and then he will probily be willing to give me anything I ask for but that don't do no good now Al. I am way in debt and no chance to get no money from nobody. I wish I had of stayed with Terre Haute Al and never saw this league.

Your pal, Jack.

Chicago, Illinois, Febuery 17.

Friend Al: Al don't never let nobody tell you that these here lefthanders is right. This Allen my own brother-in-law who married sisters has been grafting and spongeing on me all winter Al. Look what he done to me now Al. You know how hard I been up against it for money and I know he has got plenty of it because I seen it on him. Well Al I was scared to tell Florrie I was cleaned out and so I went to Allen yesterday and says I had to have $100 right away because I owed the rent and owed the hired girl's salery and could not even pay no grocery bill. And he says No he could not let me have none because he has got to save all his money to take his wife on the trip to California. And here he has been liveing on me all winter and maybe I could of took my wife to California if I had not of spent all my money takeing care of this no good lefthander and his wife. And Al honest he has not got a thing and ought not to be in the league. He gets by with a dinky curve ball and has not got no more smoke than a rabbit or something.

Well Al I felt like busting him in the jaw but then I thought No I might kill him and then I would have Marie and Florrie both to take care of and God knows one of them is enough besides paying his funeral expenses. So I walked away from him without takeing a crack at him and went into the other room where Florrie and Marie was at. I says to Marie I says Marie I wish you would go in the other room a minute because I want to talk to Florrie. So Marie beats it into the other room and then I tells Florrie all about what Comiskey and the Federal

League done to me. She bawled something awful and then she says I was no good and she wished she had not never married me. I says I wisht it too and then she says Do you mean that and starts to cry.

I told her I was sorry I says that because they is not no use fusing with girls Al specially when they is your wife. She says No California trip for me and then she says What are you going to do? And I says I did not know. She says Well if I was a man I would do something. So then I got mad and I says I will do something. So I went down to the corner salloon and started in to get good and drunk but I could not do it Al because I did not have the money.

Well old pal I am going to ask you a big favor and it is this I want you to send me $100 Al for just a few days till I can get on my feet. I do not know when I can pay it back Al but I guess you know the money is good and I know you have got it. Who would not have it when they live in Bedford? And besides I let you take $20 in June 4 years ago Al and give it back but I would not have said nothing to you if you had of kept it. Let me hear from you right away old pal.

Yours truly, Jack.

Chicago, Illinois, Febuery 19.

Al: I am certainly greatful to you Al for the $100 which come just a little while ago. I will pay the rent with it and part of the grocery bill and I guess the hired girl will have to wait a while for hern but she is sure to get it because I don't never forget my debts. I have changed my mind about the White Sox and I am going to go on the trip and take Florrie along because I don't think it would not be right to leave her here alone in Chi when her sister and all of us is going.

I am going over to the ball park and up in the office pretty soon to see about it. I will tell Comiskey I changed my mind and he will be glad to get me back because the club has not got no chance to finish nowheres without me. But I won't go on no trip or give the club my services without them giveing me some more advance money so as I can take Florrie along with me because Al I would not go without her.

Maybe Comiskey will make my salery $3000 like I wanted him to when he sees I am willing to be a good fellow and go along with him and when he knows that the Federal League would of gladly gave me $4000 if I had not of signed no contract with the White Sox.

I think I will ask him for $200 advance money Al and if I get it may be I can send part of your $100 back to you but I know you cannot be in no hurry Al though you says you wanted it back as soon as possible. You could not be very hard up Al because it don't cost near so much to live in Bedford as it does up here.

Anyway I will let you know how I come out with Comiskey and I will write you as soon as I get out to Paso Robles if I don't get no time to write you before I leave.

Your pal, Jack.

P. S. I have took good care of myself all winter Al and I guess I ought to have a great season.

P. S. Florrie is tickled to death about going along and her and I will have some time together out there on the Coast if I can get some money somewheres.

Chicago, Illinois, Febuery 21.

Friend Al: I have not got the heart to write this letter to you Al. I am up here in my $42.50 a month flat and the club has went to California and Florrie has went too. I am flat broke Al and all I am asking you is to send me enough money to pay my fair to Bedford and they and all their leagues can go to hell Al.

I was out to the ball park early yesterday morning and some of the boys was there allready fanning and kidding each other. They tried to kid me to when I come in but I guess I give them as good as they give me. I was not in no mind for kidding Al because I was there on business and I wanted to see Comiskey and get it done with.

Well the secretary come in finally and I went up to him and says I wanted to see Comiskey right away. He says The boss was busy and what did I want to see him about and I says I wanted to get some advance money because I was going to take my wife on the trip. He says This would be a fine time to be telling us about it even if you was going on the trip.

And I says What do you mean? And he says You are not going on no trip with us because we have got wavers on you and you are sold to Milwaukee.

Honest Al I thought he was kidding at first and I was waiting for him to laugh but he did not laugh and finally I says What do you mean? And he says Cannot you understand no English? You are sold to Milwaukee. Then I says I want to see the boss. He says It won't do you no good to see the boss and he is to busy to see you. I says I want to get some money. And he says You cannot get no money from this club and all you get is your fair to Milwaukee. I says I am not going to no Milwaukee anyway and he says I should not worry about that. Suit yourself.

Well Al I told some of the boys about it and they was pretty sore and says I ought to bust the secretary in the jaw and I was going to do it when I thought No I better not because he is a little guy and I might kill him.

I looked all over for Kid Gleason but he was not nowheres round and they told me he would not get into town till late in the afternoon. If I could of saw him Al he would of fixed me all up. I asked 3 or 4 of the boys for some money but they says they was all broke.

But I have not told you the worst of it yet Al. When I come back to the flat Allen and Marie and Florrie was busy packing up and they asked me how I come out. I told them and Allen just stood there stareing like a big rummy but Marie and Florrie both begin to cry and I almost felt like as if I would like to cry to only I am not no baby Al.

Well Al I told Florrie she might just as well quit packing and make up her mind that she was not going nowheres till I got money enough to go to Bedford where I belong. She kept right on crying and it got so I could not stand it no more so I went out to get a drink because I still had just about a dollar left yet.

It was about 2 oclock when I left the flat and pretty near 5 when I come back because I had ran in to some fans that knowed who I was and would not let me get away and besides I did not want to see no more of Allen and Marie till they was out of the house and on their way.

But when I come in Al they was nobody there. They was not nothing except the furniture and a few of my things scattered round. I sit down for a few minutes because I guess I must of had to much to drink but finally I seen a note on the table addressed to me and I seen it was Florrie's writeing.

I do not remember just what was there in the note Al because I tore it up the minute I read it but it was something about I could not support no wife and Allen had gave her enough money to go back to Texas and she was going on the 6 oclock train and it would not do me no good to try and stop her.

Well Al they was not no danger of my trying to stop her. She was not no good Al and I wisht I had not of never saw either she or her sister or my brother-in-law.

For a minute I thought I would follow Allen and his wife down to the deepo where the special train was to pull out of and wait till I see him and punch his jaw but I seen that would not get me nothing.

So here I am all alone Al and I will have to stay here till you send me the money to come home. You better send me $25 because I have got a few little debts I should ought to pay before I leave town. I am not going to Milwaukee Al because I did not get no decent deal and nobody cannot make no sucker out of me.

Please hurry up with the $25 Al old friend because I am sick and tired of Chi and want to get back there with my old pal.

Yours, Jack.

P. S. Al I wish I had of took poor little Violet when she was so stuck on me.

EDNA FERBER

The Gay Old Dog

THOSE OF YOU who have dwelt—or even lingered—in Chicago, Illinois, are familiar with the region known as the Loop. For those others of you to whom Chicago is a transfer point between New York and California there is presented this brief explanation:

The Loop is a clamorous, smoke-infested district embraced by the iron arms of the elevated tracks. In a city boasting fewer millions, it would be known familiarly as downtown.

The popular and prolific Edna Ferber traveled around America for forty years, romanticizing the unsung heroes of the Midwest. Writing an average of 1,000 words a day, 350 days a year, the author of such film classics as Giant *and* Showboat *originally conceived "The Gay Old Dog" as a filmscript.*

From Congress to Lake Street, from Wabash almost to the river, those thunderous tracks make a complete circle, or loop. Within it lie the retail shops, the commercial hotels, the theaters, the restaurants. It is the Fifth Avenue and the Broadway of Chicago. And he who frequents it by night in search of amusement and cheer is known, vulgarly, as a Loop-hound.

Jo Hertz was a Loop-hound. On the occasion of those sparse first nights granted the metropolis of the Middle West he was always present, third row, aisle, left. When a new Loop café was opened, Jo's table always commanded an unobstructed view of anything worth viewing. On entering he was wont to say, "Hello, Gus," with careless cordiality to the headwaiter, the while his eye roved expertly from table to table as he removed his gloves. He ordered things under glass, so that his table, at midnight or thereabouts, resembled a hotbed that favors the bell system. The waiters fought for him. He was the kind of man who mixes his own salad dressing. He liked to call for a bowl, some cracked ice, lemon, garlic, paprika, salt, pepper, vinegar, and oil and make a rite of it. People at near-by tables would lay down their knives and forks to watch, fascinated. The secret of it seemed to lie in using all the oil in sight and calling for more.

That was Jo—a plump and lonely bachelor of fifty. A plethoric, roving-eyed, and kindly man, clutching vainly at the garments of a youth that had long slipped past him. Jo Hertz, in one of those pinch-waist suits and a belted coat and a little green hat, walking up Michigan Avenue of a bright winter's afternoon, trying to take the curb with a jaunty youthfulness against which every one of his fat-encased muscles rebelled, was a sight for mirth or pity, depending on one's vision.

The gay-dog business was a late phase in the life of Jo Hertz. He had been a quite different sort of canine. The staid and harassed brother of three unwed and selfish sisters is an underdog.

At twenty-seven Jo had been the dutiful, hard-working son (in the wholesale harness business) of a widowed and gum-midging mother, who called him Joey. Now and then a double wrinkle would appear between Jo's eyes—a wrinkle that had no business there at twenty-seven. Then Jo's mother died, leaving him handicapped by a deathbed promise, the three sisters, and a three-story-and-basement house on Calumet Avenue. Jo's wrinkle became a fixture.

"Joey," his mother had said, in her high, thin voice, "take care of the girls."

"I will, Ma," Jo had choked.

"Joey," and the voice was weaker, "promise me you won't marry till the girls are all provided for." Then as Jo had hesitated, appalled: "Joey, it's my dying wish. Promise!"

"I promise, Ma," he had said.

Whereupon his mother had died, comfortably, leaving him with a completely ruined life.

They were not bad-looking girls, and they had a certain style, too. That is, Stell and Eva had. Carrie, the middle one, taught school over on the West Side. In those days it took her almost two hours each way. She said the kind of costume she required should have been corrugated steel. But all three knew what was being worn, and they wore it—or fairly faithful copies of it. Eva, the housekeeping sister, had a needle knack. She could skim the State Street windows and come away with a mental photograph of every separate tuck, hem, yoke, and ribbon. Heads of departments showed her the things they kept in drawers, and she went home and reproduced them with the aid of a seamstress by the day. Stell, the youngest, was the beauty. They called her Babe.

Twenty-three years ago one's sisters did not strain at the household leash, nor crave a career. Carrie taught school, and hated it. Eva kept house expertly and complainingly. Babe's profession was being the family beauty, and it took all her spare time. Eva always let her sleep until ten.

This was Jo's household, and he was the nominal head of it. But it was an empty title. The three women dominated his life. They weren't consciously selfish. If you had called them cruel they would have put you down as mad. When you are the lone brother of three sisters, it means that you must constantly be calling for, escorting, or dropping one of them somewhere. Most men of Jo's age were standing before their mirror of a Saturday night, whistling blithely and abstractedly while they discarded a blue polka-dot for a maroon tie, whipped off the maroon for a shot-silk, and at the last moment decided against the shot-silk in favor of a plain black-and-white because she had once said she preferred quiet ties. Jo, when he should have been preening his feathers for conquest, was saying:

"Well, my God, I *am* hurrying! Give a man time can't you? I just got home. You girls been laying around the house all day. No wonder you're ready."

He took a certain pride in seeing his sisters well dressed, at a time when he should have been reveling in fancy waistcoats and brilliant-hued socks, according to the style of that day and the inalienable right of any unwed male under thirty, in any day. On those rare occasions when his business necessitated an out-of-town trip, he would spend half a day floundering about the shops selecting handkerchiefs, or stockings, or feathers, or gloves for the girls, They always turned out to be the wrong kind, judging by their reception.

From Carrie, "What in the world do I want of long white gloves!"

"I thought you didn't have any," Jo would say.

"I haven't. I never wear evening clothes."

Jo would pass a futile hand over the top of his head, as was his way when disturbed. "I just thought you'd like them. I thought every girl liked long white gloves. Just," feebly, "just to—to have."

"Oh, for pity's sake!"

And from Eva or Babe, "I've *got* silk stockings, Jo." Or, "You brought me handkerchiefs the last time."

There was something selfish in his giving, as there always is in any gift freely and joyfully made. They never suspected the exquisite pleasure it gave him to select these things, these fine, soft, silken things. There were many things about this slow-going, amiable brother of theirs that they never suspected. If you had told them he was a dreamer of dreams, for example, they would have been amused. Sometimes, dead-tired by nine o'clock after a hard day downtown, he would doze over the evening paper. At intervals he would wake, red-eyed, to a snatch of conversation such as, "Yes, but if you get a blue you can wear it anywhere. It's dressy, and at the same time it's quiet, too." Eva, the expert, wrestling with Carrie over the problem of the new spring dress. They never guessed that the commonplace man in the frayed old smoking jacket had banished them all from the room long ago; had banished himself, for that matter. In his place was a tall, debonair, and rather dangerously handsome man to whom six o'clock spelled evening clothes. The kind of man who can lean up against a mantel, or propose a toast, or give an order to a manservant, or whisper a gallant speech in a lady's ear with equal ease. The shabby old house on Calumet Avenue was transformed into a brocaded and chandeliered rendezvous for the brilliance of the city. Beauty was here, and wit. But none so beautiful and witty as She. Mrs.—er—Jo Hertz. There was wine, of course, but no vulgar display. There was music; the soft sheen of satin; laughter. And he, the gracious, tactful host, king of his own domain—

"Jo, for heaven's sake, if you're going to snore, go to bed!"

"Why—did I fall asleep?"

"You haven't been doing anything else all evening. A person would think you were fifty instead of thirty."

And Jo Hertz was again just the dull, gray, commonplace brother of three well-meaning sisters.

Babe used to say petulantly, "Jo, why don't you ever bring home any of your men friends? A girl might as well not have any brother, all the good you do."

Jo, conscience-stricken did his best to make amends. But a man who has been petticoat-ridden for years loses the knack, somehow, of comradeship with men.

One Sunday in May Jo came home from a late-Sunday-afternoon walk to find company for supper. Carrie often had in one of her schoolteacher friends, or Babe one of her frivolous intimates, or even Eva a staid guest of the old-girl type. There was always a Sunday-night supper of potato salad, and cold meat, and coffee, and perhaps a fresh cake. Jo rather enjoyed it, being a hospitable soul. But he regarded the guests with the undazzled eyes of a man to whom they were just so many petticoats, timid of the night streets and requiring escort home. If you had suggested to him that some of his sisters' popularity was due to his own presence, or if you had hinted that the more kittenish of these visitors were probably making eyes at him, he would have stared in amazement and unbelief.

This Sunday night it turned out to be one of Carrie's friends.

"Emily," said Carrie, "this is my brother, Jo."

Jo had learned what to expect in Carrie's friends. Drab-looking women in the late thirties, whose facial lines all slanted downward.

"Happy to meet you," said Jo, and looked down at a different sort altogether. A most surprisingly different sort, for one of Carrie's friends. This Emily person was very small, and fluffy, and blue-eyed, and crinkly looking. The corners of her mouth when she smiled, and her eyes when she looked up at you, and her hair, which was brown, but had the miraculous effect, somehow, of looking golden.

Jo shook hands with her. Her hand was incredibly small, and soft, so that you were afraid of crushing it, until you discovered she had a firm little grip all her own. It surprised and amused you, that grip, as does a baby's unexpected clutch on your patronizing forefinger. As Jo felt it in his own big clasp, the strangest thing happened to him. Something inside Jo Hertz stopped working for a moment, then lurched sickeningly, then thumped like mad. It was his heart. He stood staring down at her, and she up at him, until the others laughed. Then their hands fell apart, lingeringly.

"Are you a schoolteacher, Emily?" he said.

"Kindergarten. It's my first year. And don't call me Emily, please."

"Why not? It's your name. I think it's the prettiest name in the world." Which he hadn't meant to say at all. In fact, he was perfectly aghast to find himself saying it. But he meant it.

At supper he passed her things, and stared, until everybody laughed again, and Eva said acidly, "Why don't you feed her?"

It wasn't that Emily had an air of helplessness. She just made him feel he wanted her to be helpless, so that he could help her.

Jo took her home, and from that Sunday night he began to strain at the leash. He took his sisters out, dutifully, but he would suggest, with a carelessness that deceived no one, "Don't you want one of your girl friends to come along? That little What's-her-name—Emily, or something. So long's I've got three of you, I might as well have a full squad."

For a long time he didn't know what was the matter

with him. He only knew he was miserable, and yet happy. Sometimes his heart seemed to ache with an actual physical ache. He realized that he wanted to do things for Emily. He wanted to buy things for Emily—useless, pretty, expensive things that he couldn't afford. He wanted to buy everything that Emily needed, and everything that Emily desired. He wanted to marry Emily. That was it. He discovered that one day, with a shock, in the midst of a transaction in the harness business. He stared at the man with whom he was dealing until that startled person grew uncomfortable.

"What's the matter, Hertz?"

"Matter?"

"You look as if you'd seen a ghost or found a gold mine. I don't know which."

"Gold mine," said Jo. And then, "No. Ghost."

For he remembered that high, thin voice, and his promise. And the harness business was slithering downhill with dreadful rapidity, as the automobile business began its amazing climb. Jo tried to stop it. But he was not that kind of businessman. It never occurred to him to jump out of the down-going vehicle and catch the up-going one. He stayed on, vainly applying brakes that refused to work.

"You know, Emily, I couldn't support two households now. Not the way things are. But if you'll wait. If you'll only wait. The girls might—that is, Babe and Carrie—"

She was a sensible little thing, Emily. "Of course I'll wait. But we mustn't just sit back and let the years go by. We've got to help."

She went about it as if she were already a little matchmaking matron. She corralled all the men she had ever known and introduced them to Babe, Carrie, and Eva separately, in pairs, and en masse. She got up picnics. She stayed home while Jo took the three about. When she was present she tried to look as plain and obscure as possible, so that the sisters should show up to advantage. She schemed, and planned, and contrived, and hoped; and smiled into Jo's despairing eyes.

And three years went by. Three precious years. Carrie still taught school, and hated it. Eva kept house more and more complainingly as prices advanced and allowance retreated. Stell was still Babe, the family beauty. Emily's hair, somehow, lost its glint and began to look just plain brown. Her crinkliness began to iron out.

"Now, look here!" Jo argued, desperately, one night. "We could be happy, anyway. There's plenty of room at the house. Lots of people begin that way. Of course, I couldn't give you all I'd like to, at first. But maybe, after a while—"

No dreams of salons, and brocade, and velvet-footed servitors, and satin damask now. Just two rooms, all their own, all alone, and Emily to work for. That was his dream. But it seemed less possible than that other absurd one had been.

Emily was as practical a little thing as she looked fluffy. She knew women. Especially did she know Eva, and Carrie, and Babe. She tried to imagine herself taking the household affairs and the housekeeping pocketbook out of Eva's expert hands. So then she tried to picture herself allowing the reins of Jo's house to remain in Eva's hands. And everything feminine and normal in her rebelled. Emily knew she'd want to put away her own freshly laundered linen, and smooth it, and pat it. She was that kind of woman. She knew she'd want to do her own delightful haggling with butcher and grocer. She knew she'd want to muss Jo's hair, and sit on his knee, and even quarrel with him, if necessary, without the awareness of three ever-present pairs of maiden eyes and ears.

"No! No! We'd only be miserable. I know. Even if they didn't object. And they would, Jo. Wouldn't they?"

His silence was miserable assent. Then, "But you do

love me, don't you, Emily?"

"I do, Jo. I love you—and love you—and love you. But, Jo, I can't."

"I know it, dear. I knew it all the time, really. I just thought, maybe, somehow—"

The two sat staring for a moment into space, their hands clasped. Then they both shut their eyes with a little shudder, as though what they saw was terrible to look upon. Emily's hand, the tiny hand that was so unexpectedly firm, tightened its hold on his, and his crushed the absurd fingers until she winced with pain.

That was the beginning of the end, and they knew it.

Emily wasn't the kind of girl who would be left to pine. There are too many Jos in the world whose hearts are prone to lurch and then thump at the feel of a soft, fluttering, incredibly small hand in their grip. One year later Emily was married to a young man whose father owned a large, pie-shaped slice of the prosperous state of Michigan.

That being safely accomplished, there was something grimly humorous in the trend taken by affairs in the old house on Calumet. For Eva married. Married well, too, though he was a great deal older than she. She went off in a hat she had copied from a French model at Field's, and a suit she had contrived with a home dressmaker, aided by pressing on the part of the little tailor in the basement over on Thirty-first Street. It was the last of that, though. The next time they saw her, she had on a hat that even she would have despaired of copying, and a suit that sort of melted into your gaze. She moved to the North Side (trust Eva for that), and Babe assumed the management of the household on Calumet Avenue. It was rather a pinched little household now, for the harness business shrank and shrank.

"I don't see how you can expect me to keep house decently on this!" Babe would say contemptuously. Babe's nose, always a little inclined to sharpness, had whittled down to a point of late. "If you knew what Ben gives Eva."

"It's the best I can do, Sis. Business is something rotten."

"Ben says if you had the least bit of—" Ben was Eva's husband, and quotable, as are all successful men.

"I don't care what Ben says," shouted Jo, goaded into rage. "I'm sick of your everlasting Ben. Go and get a Ben of your own, why don't you, if you're so stuck on the way he does things."

And Babe did. She made a last desperate drive, aided by Eva, and she captured a rather surprised young man in the brokerage way, who had made up his mind not to marry for years and years. Eva wanted to give her her wedding things, but at that Jo broke into sudden rebellion.

"No, sir! No Ben is going to buy my sister's wedding clothes, understand? I guess I'm not broke—yet. I'll furnish the money for her things, and there'll be enough of them, too."

Babe had as useless a trousseau, and as filled with extravagant pink-and-blue and lacy and frilly things, as any daughter of doting parents. Jo seemed to find a grim pleasure in providing them. But it left him pretty well pinched. After Babe's marriage (she insisted that they call her Estelle now) Jo sold the house on Calumet. He and Carrie took one of those little flats that were springing up, seemingly overnight, all through Chicago's South Side.

There was nothing domestic about Carrie. She had given up teaching two years before, and had gone into social-service work on the West Side. She had what is known as a legal mind—hard, clear, orderly—and she made a great success of it. Her dream was to live at the Settlement House and give all her time to the work. Upon the little household she bestowed a certain amount of grim, capable attention. It was the same kind of attention she would have given a piece of machinery whose oiling and running had been entrusted to her care. She hated it, and didn't hesitate to say so.

Jo took to prowling about department-store basements and household-goods sections. He was always sending home a bargain in a ham, or a sack of potatoes, or fifty pounds of sugar, or a window clamp, or a new kind of paring knife. He was forever doing odd jobs that the janitor should have done. It was the domestic in him claiming its own.

Then, one night Carrie came home with a dull glow in her leathery cheeks, and her eyes alight with resolve. They had what she called a plain talk.

"Listen, Jo. They've offered me the job of first assistant resident worker. And I'm going to take it. Take it! I know fifty other girls who'd give their ears for it. I go in next month."

They were at dinner. Jo looked up from his plate, dully. Then he glanced around the little dining room, with its ugly tan walls and its heavy, dark furniture (the Calumet Avenue pieces fitted cumbersomely into the five-room flat).

"Away? Away from here, you mean—to live?"

Carrie laid down her fork. "Well, really, Jo! After all that explanation."

"But to go over there to live! Why, that neighborhood's full of dirt, and disease, and crime, and the Lord knows what all. I can't let you do that, Carrie."

Carrie's chin came up. She laughed a short little laugh. "Let me! That's eighteenth-century talk, Jo. My life's my own to live. I'm going."

And she went.

Jo stayed on in the apartment until the lease was up. Then he sold what furniture he could, stored or gave away the rest, and took a room on Michigan Avenue in one of the old stone mansions whose decayed splendor was being put to such purpose.

Jo Hertz was his own master. Free to marry. Free to

come and go. And he found he didn't even think of marrying. He didn't even want to come and go, particularly. A rather frumpy old bachelor, with thinning hair and a thickening neck.

Every Thursday evening he took dinner at Eva's, and on Sunday noon at Stell's. He tucked his napkin under his chin and openly enjoyed the homemade soup and the well-cooked meats. After dinner he tried to talk business with Eva's husband, or Stell's. His business talks were the old-fashioned kind, beginning:

"Well, now, look, here. Take, f'rinstance, your raw hides and leathers."

But Ben and George didn't want to take, f'rinstance, your raw hides and leathers. They wanted, when they took anything at all, to take golf, or politics, or stocks. They were the modern type of businessman who prefers to leave his work out of his play. Business, with them, was a profession—a finely graded and balanced thing, differing from Jo's clumsy, downhill style as completely as does the method of a great criminal detective differ from that of a village constable. They would listen, restively, and say, "Uh-uh," at intervals, and at the first chance they would sort of fade out of the room, with a meaning glance at their wives. Eva had two children now. Girls. They treated Uncle Jo with good-natured tolerance. Stell had no children. Uncle Jo degenerated, by almost imperceptible degrees, from the position of honored guest, who is served with white meat, to that of one who is content with a leg and one of those obscure and bony sections which, after much turning with a bewildered and investigating knife and fork, leave one baffled and unsatisfied.

Eva and Stell got together and decided that Jo ought to marry.

"It isn't natural," Eva told him. "I never saw a man who took so little interest in women."

"Me!" protested Jo, almost shyly. "Women!"

"Yes. Of course. You act like a frightened schoolboy."

So they had in for dinner certain friends and acquaintances of fitting age. They spoke of them as "splendid girls." Between thirty-six and forty. They talked awfully well, in a firm, clear way, about civics, and classes, and politics, and economics, and boards. They rather terrified Jo. He didn't understand much that they talked about, and he felt humbly inferior, and yet a little resentful, as if something had passed him by. He escorted them home, dutifully, though they told him not to bother, and they evidently meant it. They seemed capable not only of going home quite unattended but of delivering a pointed lecture to any highwayman or brawler who might molest them.

The following Thursday Eva would say, "How did you like her, Jo?"

"Like who?" Jo would spar feebly.

"Miss Matthews."

"Who's she?"

"Now, don't be funny, Jo. You know very well I mean the girl who was here for dinner. The one who talked so well on the emigration question."

"Oh, her! Why, I like her all right. Seems to be a smart woman."

"Smart! She's a perfectly splendid girl."

"Sure," Jo would agree cheerfully.

"But didn't you like her?"

"I can't say I did, Eve. And I can't say I didn't. She made me think a lot of a teacher I had in the fifth reader. Name of Himes. As I recall her, she must have been a fine woman. But I never thought of Himes as a woman at all. She was just Teacher."

"You make me tired," snapped Eva impatiently. "A man of your age. You don't expect to marry a girl, do you? A child!"

"I don't expect to marry anybody," Jo had answered.

And that was the truth, lonely though he often was.

The following spring Eva moved to Winnetka. Anyone who got the meaning of the Loop knows the significance of a move to a North Shore suburb, and a house. Eva's daughter, Ethel, was growing up, and her mother had an eye on society.

That did away with Jo's Thursday dinners. Then Stell's husband bought a car. They went out into the country every Sunday. Stell said it was getting so that maids objected to Sunday dinners, anyway. Besides, they were unhealthful, old-fashioned things. They always meant to ask Jo to come along, but by the time their friends were placed, and the lunch, and the boxes, and sweaters, and George's camera, and everything, there seemed to be no room for a man of Jo's bulk. So that eliminatedthe Sunday dinners.

"Just drop in any time during the week," Stell said, "for dinner. Except Wednesday—that's our bridge night—and Saturday. And, of course, Thursday. Cook is out that night. Don't wait for me to phone."

And so Jo drifted into that sad-eyed, dyspeptic family made up of those you see dining in second-rate restaurants, their paper propped up against the bowl of oyster crackers, munching solemnly and with indifference to the stare of the passer-by surveying them through the brazen plate-glass window.

And then came the war. The war that spelled death and destruction to millions. The war that brought a fortune to Jo Hertz, and transformed him, overnight, from a baggy-kneed old bachelor whose business was a failure to a prosperous manufacturer whose only trouble was the shortage of hides for the making of his product. Leather! The armies of Europe called for it. Harnesses! More harnesses! Straps! Millions of straps. More! More!

The musty old harness business over on Lake Street was

magically changed from a dust-covered, dead-alive concern to an orderly hive that hummed and glittered with success. Orders poured in. Jo Hertz had inside information on the war. He knew about troops and horses. He talked with French and English and Italian buyers commissioned by their countries to get American-made supplies. And now, when he said to Ben or George, "Take, f'rinstance, your raw hides and leathers," they listened with respectful attention.

And then began the gay-dog business in the life of Jo Hertz. He developed into a Loop-hound, ever keen on the scent of fresh pleasure. That side of Jo Hertz which had been repressed and crushed and ignored began to bloom, unhealthily. At first he spent money on his rather contemptuous nieces. He sent them gorgeous furs, and watch bracelets, and bags. He took two expensive rooms at a downtown hotel, and there was something more tear-compelling than grotesque about the way he gloated over the luxury of a separate ice-water tap in the bathroom. He explained it.

"Just turn it on. Any hour of the day or night. Ice water!"

He bought a car. Naturally. A glittering affair; in color a bright blue, with pale-blue leather straps and a great deal of gold fittings, and special tires. Eva said it was the kind of thing a chorus girl would use, rather than an elderly businessman. You saw him driving about in it, red-faced and rather awkward at the wheel. You saw him, too, in the Pompeian Room at the Congress Hotel of a Saturday afternoon when roving-eyed matrons in mink coats are wont to congregate to sip pale-amber drinks. Actors grew to recognize the semibald head and the shining, round, good-natured face looming out at them from the dim well of the theater, and sometimes, in a musical show, they directed a quip at him, and he liked it. He could pick out the critics as they came down the aisle, and even had a nodding acquaintance with two of them.

"Kelly, of the *Herald*," he would say carelessly. "Bean, of the *Trib*. They're all afraid of him."

So he frolicked, ponderously. In New York he might have been called a Man About Town.

And he was lonesome. He was very lonesome. So he searched about in his mind and brought from the dim past the memory of the luxuriously furnished establishment of which he used to dream in the evenings when he dozed over his paper in the old house on Calumet. So he rented an apartment, many-roomed and expensive, with a manservant in charge, and furnished it in styles and periods ranging through all the Louis. The living room was mostly rose color. It was like an unhealthy and bloated boudoir. And yet there was nothing sybaritic or uncleanly in the sight of this paunchy, middle-aged man sinking into the rosy-cushioned luxury of his ridiculous home. It was a frank and naïve indulgence of long-starved senses, and there was in it a great resemblance to the rolling-eyed ecstasy of a schoolboy smacking his lips over an all-day sucker.

The war went on, and on, and on. And the money continued to roll in—a flood of it. Then, one afternoon, Eva, in town on a shopping bent, entered a small, exclusive, and expensive shop on Michigan Avenue. Eva's weakness was hats. She was seeking a hat now. She described what she sought with a languid conciseness, and stood looking about her after the saleswoman had vanished in quest of it. The room was becomingly rose-illumined and somewhat dim, so that some minutes had passed before she realized that a man seated on a raspberry brocade settee not five feet away—a man with a walking stick, and yellow gloves, and tan spats, and a check suit—was her brother Jo. From him Eva's wild-eyed glance leaped to the woman who was trying on hats before one of the many long mirrors. She was seated, and a saleswoman was exclaiming discreetly at her elbow.

Eva turned sharply and encountered her own saleswoman returning, hat-laden. "Not today," she gasped. "I'm feeling ill. Suddenly." And almost ran from the room.

That evening she told Stell, relating her news in that telephone pidgin English devised by every family of married sisters as protection against the neighbors. Translated, it ran thus:

"He looked straight at me. My dear, I though I'd die! But at least he had sense enough not to speak. She was one of those limp, willowy creatures with the greediest eyes that she tried to keep softened to a baby stare, and couldn't, she was so crazy to get her hands on those hats. I saw it all in one awful minute. You know the way I do. I suppose some people would call her pretty. I don't. And her color. Well! And the most expensive-looking hats. Not one of them under seventy-five. Isn't it disgusting! At his age! Suppose Ethel had been with me!"

The next time it was Stell who saw them. In a restaurant. She said it spoiled her evening. And the third time it was Ethel. She was one of the guests at a theater party given by Nicky Overton II. The North Shore Overtons. Lake Forest. They came in late, and occupied the entire third row at the opening performance of *Believe Me!* And Ethel was Nicky's partner. She was glowing like a rose. When the lights went up after the first act Ethel saw that her uncle Jo was seated just ahead of her with what she afterward described as a blonde. Then her uncle had turned around, and seeing her, had been surprised into a smile that spread genially all over his plump rubicund face. Then he had turned to face forward again, quickly.

"Who's the old bird?" Nicky had asked. Ethel had pretended not to hear, so he had asked again.

"My uncle," Ethel answered, and flushed all over her delicate face, and down to her throat. Nicky had looked at the blonde, and his eyebrows had gone up ever so slightly.

It spoiled Ethel's evening. More than that, as she told her mother of it later, weeping, she declared it had spoiled her life.

Eva talked it over with her husband in that intimate hour that precedes bedtime. She gesticulated heatedly with her hairbrush.

"It's disgusting, that's what it is. Perfectly disgusting. There's no fool like an old fool. Imagine! A creature like that. At his time of life."

"Well, I don't know," Ben said, and even grinned a little. "I suppose a boy's got to sow his wild oats sometime."

"Don't be any more vulgar than you can help," Eva retorted. "And I think you know, as well as I, what it means to have that Overton boy interested in Ethel."

"If he's interested in her," Ben blundered, "I guess the fact that Ethel's uncle went to the theater with someone who isn't Ethel's aunt won't cause a shudder to run up and down his frail young frame, will it?"

"All right," Eva had retorted. "If you're not man enough to stop it, I'll have to, that's all. I'm going up there with Stell this week."

They did not notify Jo of their coming. Eva telephoned his apartment when she knew he would be out, and asked his man if he expected his master home to dinner that evening. The man had said yes. Eva arranged to meet Stell in town. They would drive to Jo's apartment together, and wait for him there.

When she reached the city Eva found turmoil there. The first of the American troops to be sent to France were leaving. Michigan Boulevard was a billowing, surging mass: flags, pennants, banners, crowds. All the elements that make for demonstration. And over the whole—quiet. No holiday crowd, this. A solid, determined mass of people waiting patient hours to see the khaki-clads go by. Three years had brought them to a clear knowledge of what these boys were going to.

"Isn't it dreadful!" Stell gasped.

"Nicky Overton's too young, thank goodness."

Their car was caught in the jam. When they moved at all, it was by inches. When at last they reached Jo's apartment they were flushed, nervous, apprehensive. But he had not yet come in. So they waited.

No, they were not staying to dinner with their brother, they told the relieved houseman.

Stell and Eva, sunk in rose-colored cushions, viewed the place with disgust and some mirth. They rather avoided each other's eyes.

"Carrie ought to be here," Eva said. They both smiled at the thought of the austere Carrie in the midst of those rosy cushions, and hangings, and lamps. Stell rose and began to walk about restlessly. She picked up a vase and laid it down; straightened a picture. Eva got up, too, and wandered into the hall. She stood there a moment, listening. Then she turned and passed into Jo's bedroom, Stell following. And there you knew Jo for what he was.

This room was as bare as the other had been ornate. It was Jo, the clean-minded and simplehearted, in revolt against the cloying luxury with which he had surrounded himself. The bedroom, of all rooms in any house, reflects the personality of its occupant. True, the actual furniture was paneled, cupid-surmounted, and ridiculous. It had been the fruit of Jo's first orgy of the senses. But now it stood out in that stark little room with an air as incongruous and ashamed as that of a pink tarlatan danseuse who finds herself in a monk's cell. None of those wall pictures with which bachelor bedrooms are reputed to be hung. No satin slippers. No scented notes. Two plain-backed military brushes on the chiffonier (and he so nearly hairless!). A little orderly stack of books on the table near the bed. Eva fingered their titles and gave a little gasp. One of them was on gardening.

"Well, of all things!" exclaimed Stell. A book on the war, by an Englishman. A detective story of the lurid type that lulls us to sleep. His shoes ranged in a careful row in the closet, with a shoe tree in every one of them. There was something speaking about them. They looked so human. Eva shut the door on them quickly. Some bottles on the dresser. A jar of pomade. An ointment such as a man uses who is growing bald and is panic-stricken too late. An insurance calendar on the wall. Some rhubarb-and-soda mixture on the shelf in the bathroom, and a little box of pepsin tablets.

"Eats all kinds of things at all hours of the night," Eva said, and wandered out into the rose-colored front room again with the air of one who is chagrined at her failure to find what she has sought. Stell followed her furtively.

"Where do you suppose he can be?" she demanded. "It's"—she glanced at her wrist—"why, it's after six!"

And then there was a little click. The two women sat up, tense. The door opened. Jo came in. He blinked a little. The two women in the rosy room stood up.

"Why—Eve! Why, Babe! Well! Why didn't you let me know?"

"We were just about to leave. We thought you weren't coming home."

Jo came in slowly.

"I was in the jam on Michigan, watching the boys go by." He sat down, heavily. The light from the window fell on him. And you saw that his eyes were red.

He had found himself one of the thousands in the jam on Michigan Avenue, as he said. He had a place near the curb, where his big frame shut off the view of the unfortunates behind him. He waited with the placid interest of one who has subscribed to all the funds and societies to which a prosperous, middle-aged businessman is called upon to subscribe in wartime. Then, just as he was about to leave, impatient at the delay, the crowd had cried, with a queer, dramatic, exultant note in its voice, "Here they come! Here come the boys!"

Just at that moment two little, futile, frenzied fists began to beat a mad tattoo on Jo Hertz's broad back. Jo tried to turn in the crowd, all indignant resentment. "Say, looka here!"

The little fists kept up their frantic beating and pushing. And a voice—a choked, high little voice—cried, "Let me by! I can't see! You *man*, you! You big fat man! My boy's going by—to war—and I can't see! Let me by!"

Jo scrooged around, still keeping his place. He looked down. And upturned to him in agonized appeal was the face of Emily. They stared at each other for what seemed a long, long time. It was really only the fraction of a second. Then Jo put one great arm firmly around Emily's waist and swung her around in front of him. His great bulk protected her. Emily was clinging to his hand. She was breathing rapidly, as if she had been running. Her eyes were straining up the street.

"Why, Emily, how in the world—!"

"I ran away. Fred didn't want me to come. He said it would excite me too much."

"Fred?"

"My husband. He made me promise to say good-bye to Jo at home."

"Jo?"

"Jo's my boy. And he's going to war. So I ran away. I had to see him. I had to see him go."

She was dry-eyed. Her gaze was straining up the street.

"Why, sure," said Jo. "Of course you want to see him." And then the crowd gave a great roar. There came over Jo a feeling of weakness. He was trembling. The boys went marching by.

"There he is," Emily shrilled, above the din. "There he

is! There he is! There he—" And waved a futile little hand. It wasn't so much a wave as a clutching. A clutching after something beyond her reach.

"Which one? Which on, Emily?"

"The handsome one. The handsome one." Her voice quavered and died.

Jo put a steady hand on her shoulder. "Point him out," he commanded. "Show me." And the next instant, "Never mind. I see him."

Somehow, miraculously, he had picked him from among the hundreds. Had picked him as surely as his own father might have. It was Emily's boy. He was marching by, rather stiffly. He was nineteen, and fun-loving, and he had a girl, and he didn't particularly want to go to France and—to go to France. But more than he had hated going, he had hated not to go. So he marched by, looking straight ahead, his jaw set so that his chin stuck out just a little. Emily's boy.

Jo looked at him, and his face flushed purple. His eyes, the hard-boiled eyes of a Loop-hound, took on the look of a sad old man. And suddenly he was no longer Jo, the sport; old J. Hertz, the gay dog. He was Jo Hertz, thirty, in love with life, in love with Emily, and with the stinging blood of young manhood coursing through his veins.

Another minute and the boy had passed on up the broad street—the fine, flag-bedecked street—just one of a hundred service hats bobbing in rhythmic motion like sandy waves lapping a shore and flowing on.

Then he disappeared altogether.

Emily was clinging to Jo. She was mumbling something, over and over. "I can't. I can't Don't ask me to. I can't let him go. Like that. I can't."

Jo said a queer thing.

"Why, Emily! We wouldn't have him stay home would

we? We wouldn't want him to do anything different, would we? Not our boy. I'm glad he enlisted. I'm proud of him. So are you glad."

Little by little he quieted her. He took her to the car that was waiting, a worried chauffeur in charge. They said good-bye, awkwardly. Emily's face was a red, swollen mass.

So it was that when Jo entered his own hallway half an hour later he blinked, dazedly, and when the light from the window fell on him you saw that his eyes were red.

Eva was not one to beat about the bush. She sat forward in her chair, clutching her bag rather nervously.

"Now, look here, Jo. Stell and I are here for a reason. We're here to tell you that this thing's going to stop."

"Thing? Stop?"

"You know very well what I mean. You saw me at the milliner's that day. And night before last, Ethel. We're all disgusted. If you must go about with people like that, please have some sense of decency."

Something gathering in Jo's face should have warned her. But he was slumped down in his chair in such a huddle, and he looked so old and fat that she did not heed it. She went on "You've got us to consider. Your sisters. And your nieces. Not to speak of your own—"

But he got to his feet then, shaking, and at what she saw in his face even Eva faltered and stopped. It wasn't at all the face of a fat, middle-aged sport. It was a face Jovian, terrible.

"You!" he began, low-voiced, ominous. "You!" He raised a great fist high. "You two murderers! You didn't consider me, twenty years ago. You come to me with talk like that. Where's my boy! You killed him, you two, twenty years ago. And now he belongs to somebody else. Where's my son that should have gone marching by today?" He flung his arms out in a great gesture of longing. The red veins stood out on his forehead. "Where's my son! Answer me that, you two selfish, miserable women. Where's my son!" Then, as they huddled together, frightened, wild-eyed. "Out of my house! Out of my house! Before I hurt you!"

They fled, terrified. The door banged behind them.

Jo stood, shaking, in the center of the room. Then he reached for a chair, gropingly, and sat down. He passed one moist, flabby hand over his forehead and it came away wet. The telephone rang. He sat still. It sounded far away and unimportant, like something forgotten. But it rang and rang insistently. Jo liked to answer his telephone when he was at home.

"Hello!" He knew instantly the voice at the other end.

"That you, Jo?" it said.

"Yes."

"How's my boy?"

"I'm—all right."

"Listen, Jo. The crowd's coming over tonight. I've fixed up a little poker game for you. Just eight of us."

"I can't come tonight, Gert."

"Can't! Why not?"

"I'm not feeling so good."

"You just said you were all right."

"I *am* all right. Just kind of tired."

The voice took on a cooing note. "Is my Joey tired? Then he shall be all comfy on the sofa, and he doesn't need to play if he don't want to. No, sir."

Jo stood staring at the black mouthpiece of the telephone. He was seeing a procession go marching by. Boys, hundreds of boys, in khaki.

"Hello! Hello!" The voice took on an anxious note. "Are you there?"

"Yes," wearily.

"Jo, there's something the matter. You're sick. I'm

coming right over."

"No!"

"Why not? You sound as if you'd been sleeping. Look here—"

"Leave me alone!" cried Jo, suddenly, and the receiver clacked onto the hook. "Leave me alone. Leave me alone." Long after the connection had been broken.

He stood staring at the instrument with unseeing eyes. Then he turned and walked into the front room. All the light had gone out of it. Dusk had come on. All the light had gone out of everything. The zest had gone out of life. The game was over—the game he had been playing against loneliness and disappointment. And he was just a tired old man. A lonely, tired old man in a ridiculous rose-colored room that had grown, all of a sudden, drab.

JEAN GENET

The Members of the Assembly

CHICAGO REMINDS ME of an animal which curiously is trying to climb on top of itself. Part of the city is transformed by the life—or the parade, in both senses of the term—of the hippies.

Saturday night, about ten o'clock, the young people in Lincoln Park have lighted a kind of bonfire. Close by, scarcely visible in the darkness, a good-sized crowd has formed beneath the trees to listen to a black band—flutes and bongo drums. An American Indian, carrying a furled green flag, explains to us

---

The always-controversial novelist and poet Jean Genet was thrown out of five different countries before being dispatched by Esquire *to cover the 1968 Democratic Convention. Genet was considered to be the ultimate critic of bureaucracy; his work gained stature through the admiration of compatriots and existentialists Jean Cocteau and Jean-Paul Sartre.*

that it will be taken tomorrow to the airport when Senator McCarthy is scheduled to arrive and speak. Unfurled, the flag bears upon its green background the painted image of a seventeen-year-old boy—some say he was Indian, others black—killed two days before by the Chicago police.

The cops arrive, in brief but still unangry waves, to put out the fire and disperse the demonstrators. One word about them: the demonstrators are young people of a gentleness almost too gentle, at least this evening. If couples are stretched out on the grass in the park, it seems to me it is for the purpose of angelic exchanges. Everything strikes me as being very chaste. The darkness of the park is not solely responsible for the fact that all I can see are shadows folded in each other's arms.

A group of demonstrators, which had at first dispersed, has re-formed and is singing a kind of two-syllable chant, not unlike a Gregorian chant, a funeral dirge to the memory of the dead boy. I can scarcely speak of the beauty of this plaintive wail, of the anger and the singing.

Around the park, which is almost totally dark, what I first see is a proliferation of American cars, heavy with chrome, and beyond them the gigantic buildings of the city, each of whose floors is lighted, why I don't know.

Are these four democratic days going to begin with a funeral vigil in memory of a young Indian—or black—murdered by the Chicago police?

If man is, or is searching to be, omnipotent, I am willing to accept Chicago's gigantism; but I should like the opposite to be accepted as well: a city which would fit in the hollow of one's hand.

SUNDAY, MIDWAY AIRPORT, Chicago. McCarthy's arrival. Almost no police, and the few who do check our press credentials are extremely casual. Across from the press platform itself, actually the empty back of a parked trailer truck, are three similar platforms, one is occupied by a brass-dominated orchestra whose members are men in their thirties and forties, another by a rock group in its twenties. Between them is the platform reserved for McCarthy and his staff. McCarthy's plane is a few minutes late; the crowd massed behind the press platform consists of men and women whose faces reflect that peculiar image which only profound honesty and hope can give.

McCarthy finally arrives; and the crowd comes dramatically to life: every man, woman, and child shouting "We Want Gene," brandishes signs devoid of the customary slogans but generously bedecked with flowers drawn or painted each according to the bearer's whim, and it is this flower-crowd that McCarthy is going to address. He is extremely relaxed; he smiles; he is about to speak, but the battery of microphones is dead. Sabotage? Smiling, he walks over and tries the mikes of the musical group in its thirties and forties: dead. Still smiling, he tries the mikes of the rock group in its twenties: dead! Finally, he makes his way back to his platform and tries his own microphones, which in the interim have been repaired, at least to some degree. He smiles. He is also serious, and he declares that he will speak only if the men and women the farthest away from the speaker's platform can hear him. Finally, he does speak, and you have all heard what he said on television.

As he leaves the speaker's platform, it seems that no one is protecting him, save for the sea of flowers painted by the hope-filled men and women.

A FEW HOURS later, at McCarthy's headquarters in the Hilton Hotel, there again appears to be almost no police security, or if there is any it is subtle, invisible. We are received with great courtesy.

This leads me to what, in my opinion, is one of the basic questions I ask myself: after eight months of campaigning, in order for this little-known Senator—or known all too well through a name steeped in shame—in order for McCarthy to arouse such enthusiasm, what concessions has he made? In what ways has his moral rectitude been weakened?

And yet the fact remains that all his speeches, all his statements, reveal intelligence and generosity. Is it a trick?

For a city with as large a black population as Chicago has, I note that there were very few blacks out to greet and acclaim him.

The First Day: The Day of the Thighs

THE THIGHS ARE very beautiful beneath the blue cloth, thick and muscular. It all must be hard. This policeman is also a boxer, a wrestler. His legs are long, and perhaps, as you approach his member, you would find a furry nest of long, tight, curly hair. That is all I can see—and I must say it fascinates me—that and his boots, but I can guess that these superb thighs extend on up into an imposing member and a muscled torso, made even firmer every day by his police training in the cops' gymnasium. Higher up, into his arms and hands which must know how to put a black man or a thief out of action.

In the compass of his well-built thighs, I can see . . . but the thighs have moved, and I can see that they are splendid: America has a magnificent, divine, athletic police force, often photographed and seen in dirty books . . . but the thighs have parted slightly, ever so slightly, and through the crack which extends from the knees to the too-heavy member, I can see . . . why, it's the whole panorama of the Democratic Convention with its star-spangled banners, its star-spangled prattle, its star-spangled dresses, its star-spangled undress, its star-spangled songs, its star-spangled fields, its star-spangled candidates, in short the whole ostentatious parade, but the color has too many facets, as you have seen on your television sets.

What your television fails to bring you is the odor. No: the Odor, which may have a certain connection with order? The reason is that the Democratic Convention is being held right next to the stockyards, and I keep asking myself whether the air is being befouled by the decomposition of Eisenhower or by the decomposition of all America.

A few hours later, about midnight, I join Allen Ginsberg to take part in a demonstration of hippies and students in Lincoln Park: their determination to sleep in the park is their very gentle, as yet too gentle, but certainly poetic, response to the nauseating spectacle of the Convention. Suddenly the police begin their charge, with their grimacing masks intended to terrify: and, in fact, everyone turns and runs. But I am well aware that these brutes have other methods, and far more terrifying masks, when they go hunting for blacks in the ghettos, as they have done for the past hundred and fifty years. It is a good, healthy, and ultimately moral thing for these fair-haired, gentle hippies to be charged at by these louts decked out in this amazing snout that protects them from the effects of the gas they have emitted.

AND I SHOULD like to end the first day with this: the person who opens her door to receive us as we try to escape from these brutes in blue is a young and very beautiful black woman. Later, when the streets have finally grown calm again, she offers to let us slip out through a back door, which opens onto another street: without the police suspecting it, we have been conjured away and concealed by a trick house. Nonetheless, these enormous thighs of policemen stuffed with LSD, rage, and patriotism were fascinating to see.

Tomorrow: another sleep-in in Lincoln Park, for this Law which is no law must be resisted.

The Second Day: The Day of the Visor

THE TRUTH OF the matter is that we are bathed in a Mallarméan blue. This second day imposes the azure helmets of the Chicago police. A policeman's black leather visor intrudes between me and the world: a gleaming visor in whose tidy reflections I may be able to read the world, wittingly kept in top condition by numerous, and doubtless daily, polishings. Supporting this visor is the blue cap—Chicago wants us to think that the whole police force, and this policeman standing in front of me, have descended from heaven—made of a top-grade sky-blue cloth. But who is this blue cop in front of me? I look into his eyes, and I can see nothing else there except the blue of the cap. What does this gaze say? Nothing. The Chicago police are, and are not. I shall not pass. The visor and the gaze are there. The visor so gleaming that I can see myself and lose myself in it. I've got to see the continuation of the allegedly Democratic Convention, but the cop in the black visor with the blue eyes is there. Beyond him, I can nonetheless catch a glimpse of a lighted sign above the convention floor: there is an eye and "CBS News," the structure of which, in French as in English, reminds me of "obscene." But who is this policeman in the blue cap and black visor? He is so handsome I could fall into his arms. I look again at his look: at long last I recognize it; it is the look of a beautiful young girl, voluptuous and tender, which is hiding beneath a black visor and blue cap. She loves this celestial color: the Chicago police are feminine and brutal. It does not want its ladies to meekly obey their husbands whose hair is sky blue, dressed in robes of many colors. . . .

And what of the convention? It is democratic, it babbles on, and you have seen it on your screens: it is there for the purpose of concealing from you a game both simple and complex, which you prefer to ignore.

ABOUT TEN O'CLOCK this evening, part of America has detached itself from the American fatherland and remains suspended between earth and sky. The hippies have gathered in an enormous hall, as starkly bare as the Convention Hall is gaudy. Here all is joy, and in the enthusiasm several hippies burn their draft cards, holding them high for everyone to see: they will not be soldiers, but they may well be prisoners for five years. The hippies ask me to come up onto the stage and say a few words: this youth is beautiful and very gentle. It is celebrating the Un-Birthday of a certain Johnson who, it seems to me, hasn't yet been born. Allen Ginsberg is voiceless: he has chanted too loud and too long in Lincoln Park the night before.

Order, real order, is here: I recognize it. It is the freedom offered to everyone to discover and create himself.

About midnight, again in Lincoln Park, the clergy—also between earth and sky in order to escape from America—is conducting a religious service. I am subjected to another, but also very beautiful, kind of poetry. And what of the trees in the park? At night they bear strange fruit, clusters of young people suspended in their branches. I am as yet unfamiliar with this nocturnal variety: but that's the way it is in Chicago. The clergymen invite us to be seated: they are singing hymns in front of an enormous wooden cross. They joke too, and use slang. "Sit or split," says one of the bantering and slangy priests. "Sit or split." The cross, borne by several clergymen, moves away into the night, and this imitation of the Passion is very mov— I don't have time to finish the word: enormous projectors are turned on directly in front of us, and the police, throwing canisters of tear gas, rush at us. We have to run. Once again it is this police, azure but inexorable, who are pursuing us and pursuing the cross. Spellman-the-cop would have had a good laugh.

We take refuge in Ginsberg's hotel, across the street from the Park: my eyes are burning from the gas: a medic pours water into them, and the water spills over me down to my feet. In short, in their blundering clumsiness, the Americans have tried to burn me and a few minutes later to drown me.

We pause to collect ourselves in Allen Ginsberg's hotel room. And what of the convention? And democracy? The newspapers have kept you posted about them.

We leave the hotel: another azure policeman—or the beautiful girl in drag—holding his billy club in his hand the way, exactly the way, I hold a black American's member—escorts us to our car and opens the door for us: there can be no mistake about it: we are White.

The Third Day: The Day of the Belly

CHICAGO HAS FED these policemen's bellies, which are so fat that one must presume that they live on the slaughterhouses required by a city which resembles three hundred Hamburgs piled one on top of the other, and daily consumes three million hamburgers. A policeman's beautiful belly has to be seen in profile: the one barring my route is a medium-sized belly (de Gaulle could qualify as a cop in Chicago). It is medium-sized, but it is well on its way to perfection. Its owner wheedles it, fondles it with both his beautiful but heavy hands. Where did they all come from? Suddenly we are surrounded by a sea of policemen's bellies barring our entrance into the Democratic Convention. When I am finally allowed in, I will understand more clearly the harmony which exists between these bellies and the bosoms of the lady-patriots at the Convention—there is harmony but also rivalry: the arms of the ladies of the gentlemen who rule America have the girth of the policemen's thighs. Walls of bellies. And walls of policemen who encircle us, astonished by our appearance at the Democratic Convention, furious at the unconventional way we're dressed: they are thinking that we are thinking what they know, that is that the Democratic Convention is the Holy of Holies. The mouths of these bellies huddle in hasty conference. Walkie-talkies are barking. All of us in possession of the electronic passes required to enter the Amphitheater. The Chief of Police—wearing civilian clothes and his belly—arrives. He checks our passes, our identification, but, obviously a man of taste and discretion, does not ask to see mine. He offers me his hand. I shake it. The bastard. We enter the corridors of the Convention Hall, but only to be allowed into the press section. New police bellies are there, blocking our route again. Can we go in and sit down? Bellies even heavier and more robust tell us there is no room for us inside: within the hallowed halls of the convention segregation is being practiced against four or five white males, who have had the effrontery to come without ties, a mixed band of long-haired and hairless, with a few beards thrown in. After long discussions, we are allowed to go in and sit down. I gather, from the fatigue which has just overwhelmed me, that what I am witnessing is a resounding lie, voluptuous for those who make their living from it. I hear the numbers being announced: they are counting the votes cast by New Jersey and adding them to those cast by Minnesota: never very good at arithmetic, I am amazed that this science is used to choose a President. Finally triumph and pandemonium—their triumph—Humphrey is nominated. The bellies have chosen a representative. This unmad madness, screaming mauve songs, gaudy but grey, this inordinate lie of talking bellies, you have seen and heard its pale reflections on your television screens.

I have an urge to go outside and touch a tree, graze in the grass, screw a goat, in short do what I'm used to doing.

A few hours before going to the convention, where our free and easy manner has petrified the police and made them suspicious, we have taken part in the Peace March organized by David Dellinger in Grant Park. Thousands of young people were there, peacefully listening to Phil Ochs sing and to others talk; we were covered with flowers. A symbolic march set off in the direction of the slaughterhouse. A first row of blacks, then behind them, in rows of eight abreast, anyone who cared to join the demonstration. No one got very far: more bellies charged, firing tear gas at the young people. Trucks filled with armed soldiers drove endlessly back and forth through the streets of Chicago.

To the Hippies

HIPPIES, YOUNG PEOPLE of the demonstration, you no longer belong to America, which has moreover repudiated you. Hippies with long hair, you are making America's hair curl. But you, between earth and sky, are the beginning of a new continent, an Earth of Fire rising strangely above, or hollowed out below, what once was this sick country—an earth of fire first and if you like, an earth of flowers. But you must begin here and now, another continent.

Fourth Day: The Day of the Revolver

IS IT NECESSARY to write that everything is over? With Humphrey nominated, will Nixon be master of the world?

The Democratic Convention is closing its doors. The police, here as elsewhere, will be less brutal, if it can. And is the revolver, in turn, going to speak?

The Democratic Convention has made its choice, but

where, in what drunken bar, did a handful of democrats make their decision?

ACROSS FROM THE Hotel Hilton, again in Grant Park, a sumptuous happening. The youth have scaled a bronze horse on which is seated a bronze rider. On the horse's mane—whose head is bowed as if in sleep—young blacks and whites are brandishing black flags and red flags. A burning youth, which I hope will burn all its bridges: it is listening, attentive and serious, to a Presidential candidate who was not invited to the convention: Dick Gregory. Gregory is inviting his friends—there are four or five thousand of them in the park—to come home with him. They won't let us march to the Amphitheater, he declares, but there's no law that says you can't come on down to my house for a party. But first, he says, the four or five policemen who have stupidly allowed themselves to be hemmed in by the crowd of demonstrators must be freed. With great wit and humor, Gregory explains how the demonstrators are to walk, no more than two or three abreast, keeping on the sidewalk and obeying all traffic lights. He says that the march may be long and difficult, for he lives in a house in the black ghetto of South Chicago. He invites the two or three beaten delegates (that is, McCarthy delegates) to head the march, for the police whose job it will be to stop the march may be less brutal with them.

We walk along a hedge of armed soldiers.

At long last America is moving, because the hippies have shaken their shoulders.

The Democratic Convention is closing its doors.

A few random thoughts, as usual:

America is a heavy island, too heavy: it would be good, for America, and for the world, for it to be demolished, for it to be reduced to powder.

The danger for America is not Mao's *Thoughts*: it is the

proliferation of cameras.

So far as I know, there were no scientists among the demonstrators: is intelligence stupid, or science too easy?

The policemen are made of rubber: their muscles are of hard rubber: the convention itself was pure rubber: Chicago is made of rubber that chews chewing gum, the policemen's thoughts are made out of soft rubber. Mayor Daley of wet rubber. . . .

As we are leaving the Democratic Convention, a young policeman looks at me. Our gazes are already a settling of scores: he has understood that I am the enemy, but not one of the policemen is aware of the natural but invisible road, like that of drugs, which has led me, underground or via the route of heaven into the United States, although the State Department refused me a visa to enter the country.

Too many star-spangled flags: here, as in Switzerland, a flag in front of every house. America is Switzerland flattened out by a steamroller. Lots of young blacks: will the delegates' hot dogs or the revolver bullet murder the democrats before it is too late?

Fabulous happening. Hippies! Glorious hippies, I address my final appeal to you: children, flower children in every country, in order to fuck all the old bastards who are giving you a hard time, unite, go underground if necessary in order to join the burned children of Vietnam.

Translated by Richard Seaver.

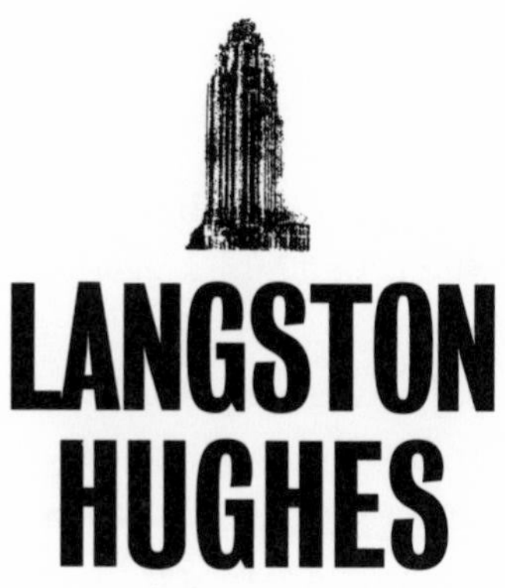

LANGSTON HUGHES

In the Dark

"WHAT YOU KNOW, daddy-o?" hailed Simple.

"Where have you been so long lately?" I demanded.

"Chicago on my last two War Bonds," answered Simple, "to see my Cousin Art's new baby to which I am godfather—against the wife's will, because she is holy and sanctified."

"What is the trend of affairs in Chicago?" I inquired.

"Balling and brawling," said Simple. "And me with 'em."

"Did you take in the DeLisa?"

"No, I did not take in the DeLisa," said Simple, but I

Langston Hughes is widely known for his jazz- and blues-influenced poetry. While poet-in-residence at the University of Chicago, he used his considerable talent to voice the woes, desires, and rhythms of the people he felt were his family—the singers, roustabouts, and common laborers he met in the South Side.

went to the Brass Rail, also Square's, also that club on 63rd and South Park which jumps out loud. Also the Blue Dahlia."

"You got around, then."

"Sure did! I went to a couple of them new cocktail lounges, too, what don't have no light in 'em at all hardly. Chicago has the darkest bars in the world. So dark it is just like walking into a movie. Man, you have to stop and pause till you can see the bar. The booths are like Lovers' Lane, man. I thought my eyesight was failing the first time I went in one. Everything's the same color under them lightless lights. Ain't no telling whiskey from gin with the natural eye."

"You were probably intoxicated," I said.

"I was expecting to get high," said Simple, "but I did not succeed. The glass was thick that night and the whiskey thin. But I met a old chick who looked *fine* setting there in the dark, although I couldn't of seen her had she not had on a white hat. I asked her what her name was and she told me Bea.

"'But don't get me wrong, King Kong, because I told you my name,' she said, 'I am a lady! My mamma calls me Bea-Baby at home.'

"I said, 'What does your daddy call you?'

"She said, 'I has no daddy.'

"I said, 'You must be looking for *me* then.'

"She said, 'I *heard* you before I saw you so I could not have been *looking* for you. You abstract attention to yourself. But since you asked me, I drink Scotch.'

"So I ordered her some Teacher's. But that girl was thirsty! She drunk me up—at Sixty-Five Cents a shot! I said, 'Bea-Baby, let's get some air.'

"She said, 'Air? I growed up in air! I got plenty of air when I were a child. Sixteen miles south of Selma there weren't nothing but air.'

"'Selma is far enough South, but *sixteen miles south of*

there is too much! How long you been up North, girl?'

"'Two years,' she said, 'and if I live to be a hundred, I will be up here seventy-five more.'

"'You mean you are not going back to Selma?'

"'Period,' she said.

"'In other words, you are going to stay in Chicago?'

"'Oh, but I am,' she said.

"'Well, we are not going to stay in this bar seventy-five years,' I whispered. 'Come on, Bea-Baby, let's walk.'

"'Walk where?' she hollered, insulted.

"'Follow me and you will see,' I said.

"'I will not follow you, unless you tell me where we are going.'

'I will not tell you where we are going, unless you follow,' I said.

"But when we got out of that darker-than-a-movie bar, under the street lights on Indiana Avenue, I got a good look at her and she got a good look at me. We *both* said 'Good-by!' In that dim dark old dusky cocktail lounge, I thought she was mellow. But she were not! I thought she was a chippy, but she were at least forty-five.

"And the first thing she said when she saw my face was, 'I thought you was a *young* man—but you ain't. You old as my Uncle Herman.'

"I said, 'I done had so many unpleasant surprises in my life, baby, until my age is writ in my face. *You* is one more unpleasantness.'

"I thought she said 'Farewell,' but it could of been 'Go to hell.'

"Anyhow, she cured me of them dark Chicago bars. *Never make friends in the dark*, is what I learned in Chicago."

"I am glad you learned something," I said.

"Thank you," said Simple. "Now, come on let's have a

beer to welcome me back to Harlem. Not to change the subjects but lend me a quarter. I'm broke.

"I'm broke, too."

"Then you can't have a beer, daddy-o," regretted Simple. "What is worse, neither can I."

THEODORE DREISER

Sister Carrie

WHEN CAROLINE MEEBER boarded the afternoon train for Chicago, her total outfit consisted of a small trunk, a cheap imitation alligator-skin satchel, a small lunch in a paper box, and a yellow leather snap purse, containing her ticket, a scrap of paper with her sister's address in Van Buren Street, and four dollars in money. It was August, 1889. She was eighteen years of age, bright, timid, and full of the illusions of ignorance and youth. Whatever touch of regret at parting characterized her

---

Writer and reporter for The Chicago Globe, *Theodore Dreiser was a founding father of the Chicago group, a turn-of-the-century salon that coined the term "American Realism." Basing his first novel,* Sister Carrie, *on the life of his own sister, Emma, Dreiser endured its dismal failure upon publication. In 1900,* Sister Carrie *was too real in its depiction of a sinful woman who evades moral retribution.*

thoughts, it was certainly not for advantages now being given up. A gush of tears at her mother's farewell kiss, a touch in her throat when the cars clacked by the flour mill where her father worked by day, a pathetic sigh as the familiar green environs of the village passed in review, and the threads which bound her so lightly to girlhood and home were irretrievably broken.

To be sure there was always the next station, where one might descend and return. There was the great city, bound more closely by these very trains which came up daily. Columbia City was not so very far away, even once she was in Chicago. What, pray, is a few hours—a few hundred miles? She looked at the little slip bearing her sister's address and wondered. She gazed at the green landscape, now passing in swift review, until her swifter thoughts replaced its impression with vague conjectures of what Chicago might be.

When a girl leaves her home at eighteen, she does one of two things. Either she falls into saving hands and becomes better, or she rapidly assumes the cosmopolitan standard of virtue and becomes worse. Of an intermediate balance, under the circumstances, there is no possibility. The city has its cunning wiles, no less than the infinitely smaller and more human tempter. There are large forces which allure with all the soulfulness of expression possible in the most cultured human. The gleam of a thousand lights is often as effective as the persuasive light in a wooing and fascinating eye. Half the undoing of the unsophisticated and natural mind is accomplished by forces wholly superhuman. A blare of sound, a roar of life, a vast array of human hives, appeal to the astonished senses in equivocal terms. Without a counsellor at hand to whisper cautious interpretations, what falsehoods may not these things breathe into the unguarded ear! Unrecognized for what they are, their beauty, like music, too often relaxes, then weakens, then perverts the simpler human perceptions.

Caroline, or Sister Carrie, as she had been half affectionately termed by the family, was possessed of a mind rudimentary in its power of observation and analysis. Self-interest with her was high, but not strong. It was, nevertheless, her guiding characteristic. Warm with the fancies of youth, pretty with the insipid prettiness of the formative period, possessed of a figure promising eventual shapeliness and an eye alight with certain native intelligence, she was a fair example of the middle American class—two generations removed from the emigrant. Books were beyond her interest—knowledge a sealed book. In the intuitive graces she was still crude. She could scarcely toss her head gracefully. Her hands were almost ineffectual. The feet, though small, were set flatly. And yet she was interested in her charms, quick to understand the keener pleasures of life, ambitious to gain in material things. A half-equipped little knight she was, venturing to reconnoiter the mysterious city and dreaming wild dreams of some vague, far-off supremacy, which should make it prey and subject—the proper penitent, grovelling at a woman's slipper.

"That," said a voice in her ear, "is one of the prettiest little resorts in Wisconsin."

"Is it?" she answered nervously.

The train was just pulling out of Waukesha. For some time she had been conscious of a man behind. She felt him observing her mass of hair. He had been fidgeting, and with natural intuition she felt a certain interest growing in that quarter. Her maidenly reserve, and a certain sense of what was conventional under the circumstances, called her to forestall and deny this familiarity, but the daring and magnetism of the individual, born of past experiences and triumphs, prevailed. She answered.

He leaned forward to put his elbows upon the back of her seat and proceeded to make himself volubly agreeable.

"Yes, that is a great resort for Chicago people. The hotels are swell. You are not familiar with this part of the country, are you?"

"Oh, yes, I am," answered Carrie. "That is, I live at Columbia City. I have never been through here, though."

"And so this is your first visit to Chicago," he observed.

All the time she was conscious of certain features out of the side of her eye. Flush, colourful cheeks, a light moustache, a grey fedora hat. She now turned and looked upon him in full, the instincts of self-protection and coquetry mingling confusedly in her brain.

"I didn't say that," she said.

"Oh," he answered, in a very pleasing way and with an assumed air of mistake, "I thought you did."

Here was a type of the travelling canvasser for a manufacturing house—a class which at that time was first being dubbed by the slang of the day "drummers." He came within the meaning of a still newer term, which had sprung into general use among Americans in 1880, and which concisely expressed the thought of one whose dress or manners are calculated to elicit the admiration of susceptible young women—a "masher." His suit was of a striped and crossed pattern of brown wool, new at that time, but since become familiar as a business suit. The low crotch of the vest revealed a stiff shirt bosom of white and pink stripes. From his coat sleeves protruded a pair of linen cuffs of the same pattern, fastened with large, gold plate buttons, set with the common yellow agates known as "cat's-eyes." His fingers bore several rings—one, the ever-enduring heavy seal—and from his vest dangled a neat gold watch chain, from which was suspended the secret insignia of the Order of Elks. The whole suit was rather tight-fitting, and was finished off with heavy-soled tan shoes, highly polished, and the grey fedora hat. He was, for the order of intellect represented, attractive, and whatever he had to recommend him, you may be sure was not lost upon Carrie, in this, her first glance.

Lest this order of individual should permanently pass, let me put down some of the most striking characteristics of his most successful manner and method. Good clothes, of course, were the first essential, the things without which he was nothing. A strong physical nature, actuated by a keen desire for the feminine, was the next. A mind free of any consideration of the problems or forces of the world and actuated not by greed, but by an insatiable love of variable pleasure. His method was always simple. Its principal element was daring, backed, of course, by an intense desire and admiration for the sex. Let him meet with a young woman twice and he would straighten her necktie for her and perhaps address her by her first name. In the great department stores he was at his ease. If he caught the attention of some young woman while waiting for the cash boy to come back with his change, he would find out her name, her favourite flower, where a note would reach her, and perhaps pursue the delicate task of friendship until it proved unpromising, when it would be relinquished. He would do very well with more pretentious women, though the burden of expense was a slight deterrent. Upon entering a parlour car, for instance, he would select a chair next to the most promising bit of femininity and soon inquire if she cared to have the shade lowered. Before the train cleared the yards he would have the porter bring her a footstool. At the next lull in his conversational progress he would find her something to read, and from then on, by dint of compliment gently insinuated, personal narrative, exaggeration and service, he would win her tolerance, and, mayhap, regard.

A woman should some day write the complete philosophy of clothes. No matter how young, it is one of the things she wholly comprehends. There is an indescribably faint line in the matter of man's apparel which somehow divides for her those who are worth glancing at and those who are not. Once an individual has passed this faint line on the way downward he will get no glance from her. There is another line at which the dress of a man will cause her to study her own. This line the individual at her elbow now marked for Carrie. She became conscious of an inequality. Her own plain blue dress, with its black cotton tape trimmings, now seemed to her shabby. She felt the worn state of her shoes.

"Let's see," he went on, "I know quite a number of people in your town. Morgenroth the clothier and Gibson the dry goods man."

"Oh, do you?" she interrupted, aroused by memories of longings their show windows had cost her.

At last he had a clue to her interest, and followed it deftly. In a few minutes he had come about into her seat. He talked of sales of clothing, his travels, Chicago, and the amusements of that city.

"If you are going there, you will enjoy it immensely. Have you relatives?"

"I am going to visit my sister," she explained.

"You want to see Lincoln Park," he said, "and Michigan Boulevard. They are putting up great buildings there. It's a second New York—great. So much to see—theatres, crowds, fine houses—oh, you'll like that."

There was a little ache in her fancy of all he described. Her insignificance in the presence of so much magnificence faintly affected her. She realized that hers was not to be a round of pleasure, and yet there was something promising in all the material prospect he set forth. There was something satisfactory in the attention of this individual with his good clothes. She could not help smiling as he told her of some popular actress of whom she reminded him. She was not silly, and yet attention of this sort had its weight.

"You will be in Chicago some little time, won't you?" he observed at one turn of the now easy conversation.

"I don't know," said Carrie vaguely—a flash vision of the possibility of her not securing employment rising in her mind.

"Several weeks, anyhow," he said looking steadily into her eyes.

There was much more passing now than the mere words indicated. He recognized the indescribable thing that made up for fascination and beauty in her. She realized that she was of interest to him from the one standpoint which a woman both delights in and fears. Her manner was simple, though for the very reason that she had not yet learned the many little affectations with which women conceal their true feelings. Some thing she did appeared bold. A clever companion—had she ever had one—would have warned her never to look a man in the eyes so steadily.

"Why do you ask?" she said.

"Well, I'm going to be there several weeks. I'm going to study stock at our place and get new samples. I might show you 'round."

"I don't know whether you can or not. I mean I don't know whether I can. I shall be living with my sister, and—"

"Well, if she minds, we'll fix that." He took out his pencil and a little pocket note-book as if it were all settled. "What is your address there?"

She fumbled her purse which contained the address slip.

He reached down in his hip pocket and took out a fat purse. It was filled with slips of paper, some mileage books, a roll of greenbacks. It impressed her deeply. Such a purse had never been carried by any one attentive to her. Indeed, an experienced traveler, a brisk man of the world, had never come within such close range before. The purse, the shiny tan shoes, the smart new suit, and the *air* with which he did things, built up for her a dim world of fortune, of which he was the center. It disposed her pleasantly toward all he might do.

He took out a neat business card, on which was engraved Bartlett, Caryoe & Company, and down in the left-hand corner, Chas. H. Drouet.

"That's me," he said, putting the card in her hand and touching his name. "It's pronounced Drew-eh. Our family was French, on my father's side."

She looked at it while he put up his purse. Then he got out a letter from a bunch in his coat pocket. "This is the house I travel for," he went on, pointing to a picture on it, "corner of State and Lake." There was pride in his voice. He felt that it was something to be connected with such a place, and he made her feel that way.

"What is your address?" he began again, fixing his pencil to write.

She looked at his hand.

"Carrie Meeber," she said slowly. "Three hundred and fifty four West Van Buren Street, care S. C. Hanson."

He wrote it carefully down and got out the purse again. "You'll be at home if I come around Monday night?" he said.

"I think so," she answered.

How true it is that words are but the vague shadows of the volumes we mean. Little audible links, they are, chaining together great inaudible feelings and purposes. Here were these two, bandying little phrases, drawing purses, looking at cards, and both unconscious of how inarticulate all their real feelings were. Neither was wise enough to be sure of the working of the mind of the other. He could not tell how his luring succeeded. She could not realize that she was drifting, until he secured her address. Now she felt that she had yielded something—he, that he had gained a victory. Already they felt that they were somehow associated. Already he took control in directing the conversation. His words were easy. Her manner was relaxed.

They were nearing Chicago. Signs were everywhere numerous. Trains flashed by them. Across wide stretches of flat, open prairie they could see lines of telegraph poles stalking across the fields toward the great city. Far away were indications of suburban towns, some big smoke-stacks towering high in the air.

Frequently there were two-story frame houses standing out in the open fields, without fence or trees, lone outposts of the approaching army of homes.

To the child, the genius with imagination, or the wholly untravelled, the approach to a great city for the first time is a wonderful thing. Particularly if it be evening—that mystic period between the glare and gloom of the world when life is changing from one sphere or condition to another. Ah, the promise of the night. What does it not hold for the weary! What old illusion of hope is not here forever repeated! Says the soul of the toiler to itself, "I shall soon be free. I shall be in the ways and the hosts of the merry. The streets, the lamps, the lighted chamber set for dining, are for me. The theatre, the halls, the parties, the ways of rest and the paths of song—these are mine in the night." Though all humanity be still enclosed in the shops, the thrill runs abroad. It is in the air. The dullest feeling something which they may not always express or describe. It is the lifting of the burden of toil.

Sister Carrie gazed out of the window. Her companion, affected by her wonder, so contagious are all things, felt anew some interest in the city and pointed out its marvels.

"This is Northwest Chicago," said Drouet. "This is the Chicago River," and he pointed to a little muddy creek, crowded with the huge masted wanderers from far-off waters nosing the black-posted banks. With a puff, a clang, and a clatter of rails it was gone. "Chicago is getting to be a great town," he went on. "It's a wonder. You'll find lots to see here."

She did not hear this very well. Her heart was troubled by a kind of terror. The fact that she was alone, away from home, rushing into a great sea of life and endeavour, began to tell. She could not help but feel a little choked for breath—a little sick as her heart beat so fast. She half closed her eyes and tried to think it was nothing, that Columbia City was only a little way off.

"Chicago! Chicago!" called the brakeman, slamming open the door. They were rushing into a more crowded yard, alive with the clatter and clang of life. She began to gather up her poor little grip and closed her hand firmly upon her purse. Drouet arose, kicked his legs to straighten his trousers, and seized his clean yellow grip.

"I suppose your people will be here to meet you?" he said. "Let me carry your grip."

"Oh, no," she said. "I'd rather you wouldn't. I'd rather you wouldn't be with me when I meet my sister."

"All right," he said in all kindness. "I'll be near, though, in case she isn't here, and take you out there safely."

"You're so kind," said Carrie, feeling the goodness of such attention in her strange situation.

"Chicago!" called the brakeman, drawing the word out long. They were under a great shadowy train shed, where the lamps were already beginning to shine out, with passenger cars all about and the train moving at a snail's pace. The people in the car were all up and crowding about the door.

"Well, here we are," said Drouet, leading the way to the door. "Good-bye, till I see you Monday."

"Good-bye," she answered, taking his proffered hand.

"Remember, I'll be looking till you find your sister."

She smiled into his eyes.

They filed out, and he affected to take no notice of her. A lean-faced, rather commonplace woman recognized Carrie on the platform and hurried forward.

"Why, Sister Carrie!" she began, and there was a perfunctory embrace of welcome.

Carrie realized the change of affectional atmosphere at once. Amid all the maze, uproar, and novelty she felt cold reality taking her by the hand. No world of light and merriment. No round of amusement. Her sister carried with her most of the grimness of shift and toil.

"Why, how are all the folks at home?" she began, "how is father, and mother?"

Carrie answered, but was looking away. Down the aisle, toward the gate leading into the waiting-room and the street, stood Drouet. He was looking back. When he saw that she saw him and was safe with her sister he turned to go, sending back the shadow of a smile. Only Carrie saw it. She felt something lost to her when he moved away. When he disappeared she felt his absence thoroughly. With her sister she was much alone, a lone figure in a tossing, thoughtless sea.

MAYA ANGELOU

The Reunion

Nobody could have told me that she'd be out with a black man; out, like going out. But there she was, in 1958, sitting up in the Blue Palm Café, when I played the Sunday matinee with Cal Callen's band.

Here's how it was. After we got on the stage, the place was packed, first Cal led us into "D. B. Blues." Of course I know just like everybody else that Cal's got a thing for Lester Young. Maybe because Cal plays the tenor sax, or maybe because he's about as red as Lester Young, or maybe just

---

A gifted singer, playwright, dancer, and writer, Maya Angelou has spent her life documenting the African-American experience with her poetry and now-classic autobiographies, I Know Why the Caged Bird Sings, Gather Together in My Name, *and* Singin' and Swingin' and Gettin' Merry Like Christmas. *She graced Chicago briefly as a reporter for* The Chicago Tribune.

because Lester is the Prez. Anybody that's played with Cal knows that the kickoff tune is gotta be "D. B. Blues." So I was ready. We romped.

I'd played with some of those guys, but never all together, but we took off on that tune like we were headed for Birdland in New York City. The audience liked it. Applauded as much as black audiences ever applaud. Black folks act like they are sure that with a little bit of study they could do whatever you're doing on the stage as well as you do it. If not better. So they clap for your luck. Lucky for you that they're not up there to show you where it's really at.

Anyway, after the applause, Cal started to introduce the band. That's his style. Everybody knows that too. After he's through introducing everybody, he's not going to say anything else till the next set, it doesn't matter how many times we play. So he's got a little comedy worked into the introduction patter. He started with Olly, the trumpet man. . . . "And here we have a real Chicagoan . . . by way of Atlanta, Georgia . . . bringing soul to Soulville . . . Mr. Olly Martin."

He went on. I looked out into the audience. People sitting, not listening, or better, listening with one side of their ears and talking with both sides of their mouths. Some couples were making a little love . . . and some whites were trying hard to act natural . . . like they come to the South Side of Chicago every day or maybe like they live there . . . then I saw her. Saw Miss Beth Ann Baker, sitting up with her blond self with a big black man . . . pretty black man. What? White girls, when they look alike, can look so much alike, I thought maybe it wasn't Beth. I looked again. It was her. I remember too well the turn of her cheek. The sliding way her jaw goes up to her hair. That was her. I might have missed a few notes, I might have in fact missed the whole interlude music.

What was she doing in Chicago? On the South Side.

And with a black man? Beth Ann Baker of the Baker Cotton Gin. Miss Cotton Queen Baker of Georgia . . . .

Then I heard Cal get round to me. He saved me for the last. Mainly cause I'm female and he can get a little rise out of the audience if he says, as he did say, "And our piano man is a lady. And what a lady. A cooker and a looker. Ladies and Gentlemen, I'd like to introduce to you Miss Philomena Jenkins. Folks call her Meanie." I noticed some applause, but mainly I was watching Beth. She heard my name and she looked right into my eyes. Her blue ones got as big as my black ones. She recognized me, in fact in a second we tipped eyelids at each other. Not winking. Just squinting, to see better. There was something that I couldn't recognize. Something I'd never seen in all those years in Baker, Georgia. Not panic, and it wasn't fear. Whatever was in that face seemed familiar, but before I could really read it, Cal announced our next number. "Round 'bout Midnight."

That used to be my song, for so many reasons. In Baker, the only time I could practice jazz, in the church, was round 'bout midnight. When the best chord changes came to me it was generally round 'bout midnight. When my first lover held me in his arms, it was round 'bout midnight. Usually when it's time to play that tune I dig right in it. But this time, I was too busy thinking about Beth and her family . . . and what she was doing in Chicago, on the South Side, escorted by the grooviest looking cat I'd seen in a long time. I was really trying to figure it out, then Cal's saxophone pushed it's way into my figurings. Forced me to remember "Round 'bout Midnight." Reminded me of the years of loneliness, the doing-without days, the C.M.E. church, and the old ladies with hands like men and the round 'bout midnight dreams of crossing over Jordan. Then I took thirty-two bars. My fingers found the places between the keys where the blues and the truth lay hiding. I dug out the story of a woman without a man, and a man without hope. I tried to wedge myself in and lay down in the groove between B-flat and B-natural. I must of gotten close to it, because the audience brought me out with their clapping. Even Cal said, "Yeah baby, that's it." I nodded to him then to the audience and looked around for Beth.

How did she like them apples? What did she think of little Philomena that used to shake the farts out of her sheets, wash her dirty drawers, pick up after her slovenly mama? What did she think now? Did she know that I was still aching from the hurt Georgia put on me? But Beth was gone. So was her boyfriend.

I had lived with my parents until I was thirteen, in the servants' quarters. A house behind the Baker main house. Daddy was the butler, my mother was the cook, and I went to a segregated school on the other side of town where the other kids called me the Baker Nigger. Momma's nimble fingers were never able to sew away the truth of Beth's hand-me-down and thrown away clothing. I had a lot to say to Beth, and she was gone.

That was a bring-down. I guess what I wanted was to rub her face in "See now, you thought all I would ever be was you and your mama's flunky." And "See now, how folks, even you, pay to listen to me" and "See now, I'm saying something nobody else can say. Not the way I say it, anyway." But her table was empty.

We did the rest of the set. Some of my favorite tunes, "Sophisticated Lady," "Misty," and "Cool Blues." I admit that I never got back into the groove until we did "When Your Lover Has Gone."

After the closing tune, "Lester Leaps In," which Cal set at a tempo like he was trying to catch the last train to Mobile, was over, the audience gave us their usual thank-you, and we were off for a twenty-minute intermission.

Some of the guys went out to turn on and a couple went

to tables where they had ladies waiting for them. But I went to the back of the dark smoky bar where even the occasional sunlight from the front door made no difference. My blood was still fluttering in my fingertips, throbbing. If she was listed in the phone directory I would call her. Hello Miss Beth . . . this is Philomena . . . who was your maid, whose whole family worked for you. Or could I say, Hello Beth. Is this Beth? Well, this is Miss Jenkins. I saw you yesterday at the Blue Palm Café. I used to know your parents. In fact your mother said my mother was a gem, and my father was a treasure. I used to laugh 'cause your mother drank so much whiskey, but my Momma said, "Judge not, that ye be not judged." Then I found out that your father had three children down in our part of town and they all looked just like you, only prettier. Oh Beth, now . . . now . . . shouldn't have a chip . . . mustn't be bitter. . . . She of course would hang up.

Just imagining what I would have said to her cheered me up. I ordered a drink from the bartender and settled back into my reverie. . . . Hello Beth . . . this is a friend from Baker. What were you doing with that black man Sunday? . . .

"Philomena? Remember me?" She stood before me absorbing the light. The drawl was still there. The soft accent rich white girls practice in Georgia to show that they had breeding. I couldn't think of anything to say. Did I remember her? There was no way I could answer the question.

"I asked Willard to wait for me in the car. I wanted to talk to you."

I sipped my drink and looked in the mirror over the bar and wondered what she really wanted. Her reflection wasn't threatening at all.

"I told him that we grew up . . . in the same town."

I was relieved that she hadn't said we grew up together. By the time I was ten, I knew growing up meant going to work. She smiled and I held my drink.

"I'm engaged to Willard and very happy."

I'm proud of my face. It didn't jump up and walk the bar.

She gave a practiced nod to the bartender and ordered a drink. "He teaches high school here on the South Side." Her drink came and she lifted the glass and our eyes met in the mirror. "I met him two years ago in Canada. We are very happy."

Why the hell was she telling me her fairy story? We weren't kin. So she had a black man. Did she think like most whites in mixed marriages that she had done the whole race a favor?

"My parents . . ." her voice became small, whispery. "My parents don't understand. They think I'm with Willard just to spite them. They . . . When's the last time you went home, Mena?" She didn't wait for my answer.

"They hate him. So much, they say they will disown me." Disbelief made her voice strong again. "They said I could never set foot in Baker again." She tried to catch my eyes in the mirror but I looked down at my drink. "I know there's a lot wrong with Baker, but it's my home." The drawl was turning into a whine. "Mother said, now mind you, she has never laid eyes on Willard, she said, if she had dreamed when I was a baby that I would grow up to marry a nig . . . a black man, she'd have choked me to death on her breast. That's a cruel thing for a mother to say. I told her so."

She bent forward and I shifted to see her expression, but her profile was hidden by the blond hair. "He doesn't understand, and me either. He didn't grow up in the South." I thought, no matter where he grew up, he wasn't white and rich and spoiled. "I just wanted to talk to somebody who knew me. Knew Baker. You know, a person can get lonely. . . . I don't see any of my friends, anymore. Do you understand, Mena? My parents gave me everything."

Well, they owned everything.

"Willard is the first thing I ever got for myself. And I'm not going to give him up."

We faced each other for the first time. She sounded like her mother and looked like a ten-year-old just before a tantrum.

"He's mine. He belongs to me."

The musicians were tuning up on the bandstand. I drained my glass and stood.

"Mena, I really enjoyed seeing you again, and talking about old times. I live in New York, but I come to Chicago every other weekend. Say, will you come to our wedding? We haven't set the date yet. Please come. It's going to be here . . . in a black church . . . somewhere."

"Good-bye Beth. Tell your parents I said go to hell and take you with them, just for company."

I sat down at the piano. She still had everything. Her mother would understand the stubbornness and send her off to Paris or the Moon. Her father couldn't deny that black skin was beautiful. She had money and a wonderful-looking man to play with. If she stopped wanting him she could always walk away. She'd still be white.

The band was halfway into the "D. B. Blues" release before I thought, she had the money, but I had the music. She and her parents had had the power to hurt me when I was young, but look, the stuff in me lifted me up high above them. No matter how bad times became, I would always be the song struggling to be heard.

The piano keys were slippery with tears. I know, I sure as hell wasn't crying for myself.

NELSON ALGREN

Chicago: City on the Make

It used to be a writer's town and it's always been a fighter's town. For writers and fighters and furtive torpedoes, cat-bandits, baggage thieves, hallway head-lockers on the prowl, baby photographers and stylish coneroos, this is the spot that is always most convenient, being so centrally located, for settling ancestral grudges. Whether the power is in a .38, a typewriter ribbon or a pair of six-ouncers, the place has grown great on bone-deep grudges: of writers and fighters and furtive torpedoes.

Nelson Algren the self-proclaimed "tin whistle of American letters," wrote about the seamier side of life in Chicago for over forty years. The prose poem City on the Make *contributed to his reputation as the poet of the Chicago slums. P.E.N. and* The Chicago Tribune *have established fiction contests in his name.*

"City of the big shoulders" was how the white-haired poet put it. Maybe meaning that the shoulders had to get that wide because they had so many bone-deep grudges to settle. The big dark grudge cast by the four standing in white muslin robes, hands cuffed behind, at the gallows' head. For the hope of the eight-hour day.

The grudge between Grover Cleveland and John Peter Altgeld. The long deep grudges still borne for McCormick the Reaper, for Pullman and Pullman's Gary. Grudges like heavy hangovers from men and women whose fathers were not yet born when the bomb was thrown, the court was rigged, and the deed was done.

And maybe it's a poet's town for the same reason it's a working stiff's town, both poet and working stiff being boys out to get even for funny cards dealt by an overpaid houseman weary long years ago.

And maybe it's a working stiff's and a poet's town because it's also an American Legionnaire's town, real Chamber of Commerce territory, the big banker-and-broker's burg, where a softclothes dick with a paunch and no brain at all, simply no brain at all, decides what movies and plays we ought to see and what we mustn't. An arrangement sufficient to make a sensitive burglar as well as a sensitive poet look around for the tools closest to hand.

Town of the hard and bitter strikes and the trigger-happy cops, where any good burglar with a sheet a foot long can buy a pass at a C-note per sheet: half a sheet, half a bill. Two sheets, two bills. Yes, and where the aces will tell the boy behind the bars, "Come on out of there, punk. You ain't doin' us no good in there. Out on the street 'n get it up—everythin' over a C you get to keep for yourself 'n be in court with it at nine tomorrow or we'll pick you up without it 'n fit you for a jacket."

Where undried blood on the pavement and undried

blood on the field yet remembers Haymarket and Memorial Day.

Most radical of all American cities: Gene Debs' town, Big Bill Haywood's town, the One-Big-Union town. Where woodworkers once came out on the First of May wearing pine shavings in their caps, brewers followed still wearing their aprons, and behind them the bakers, the barbers, the cornice-makers, tin-roofers and lumber-shovers, trailed by clerks and salesmen. As well as the town where the race riots of 1919 broke and the place where the professional anti-Semites still set up shop confident of a strong play from the North Shore.

Town of the flagpole sitters, iron city, where everything looks so old yet the people look so young. And the girl who breaks the world's record for being frozen into blocks of ice between sprints at the Coliseum Walkathon breaks the self-same record every night. And of that adolescent who paused in his gum-chewing, upon hearing the sentence of death by electrocution passed upon him, to remember ever so softly: "Knew I'd never get to be twenny-one anyhow."

Town of the small, cheerful apartments, the beer in the icebox, the pipes in the rack, the children well behaved and the TV well tuned, the armchairs fatly upholstered and the record albums filed: 33 rpm, 45 rpm, 78 rpm. Where the 33 rpm husband and proud father eats all his vitamin-stuffed dinner cautiously and then streaks to the bar across the street to drink himself senseless among strangers, at 78 rpm, all alone.

Town of the great international clowns, where the transcontinental Barnum-and-Bailey buffoons stand on their heads for a picture on the sports page, a round of applause, a wardful of votes, a dividend or a friendly smile: Big Bill Thompson, King Levinsky, Yellow Kid Weil, Gorgeous George, Sewell Avery, Elizabeth Dilling, Joe Beauharnais, Sam Insull, Botsy Connors, Shipwreck Kelly, The Great I Am, and

Oliver J. Dragon. And, of course, the Only-One-on-Earth, the inventor of modern warfare, our very own dime-store Napoleon, Colonel McGooseneck.

Town of the classic boners and the All-Time All-American bums, where they score ten runs after two are gone in the last of the ninth when the left-fielder drops an easy popup that should have been the third out. Final score: 10–8. Where somebody is always forgetting to touch second. And the local invincible, the boy most likely to be champion, faints open-eyed on the ropes in the very first round without being struck a blow because the champion is coming right toward him.

"I'll do any damned thing you boys want me to do," Mayor Kelly told his boys gratefully, and he kept his word.

Town of the great Lincolnian liberals, the ones who stuck out their stubborn necks in the ceaseless battle between the rights of Owners and the rights of Man, the stiff-necked wonders who could be broken but couldn't be bent: Dreiser, Altgeld, Debs.

The only town for certain where a Philadelphia first-baseman can answer an attractive brunette's invitation to step into her room: "I have a surprise for you"—and meet a shotgun blast under the heart. "The urge kept nagging at me and the tension built up. I thought killing someone would relieve it." For the sad heart's long remembrance.

Town of the blind and crippled newsies and the pinboys whose eyes you never see at all. Of the Montgomery-Ward sleepwalkers and all the careworn hopers from home with Expressman Death in their eyes reading all about it on the Garfield Park Local.

Town of the topless department stores, floor upon floor upon floor, where a sea-green light from the thousand-globed chandeliers drifts down the scented air, across oriental rugs and along long gleaming glass: where wait the fresh-cut sirloin tips, the great bloody T-bones and the choice center-cut pork chops, all with a freezing disdain for the ground hamburger.

A Jekyll-and-Hyde sort of burg, where one university's faculty members can protest sincerely against restrictive covenants on the blighted streets bordering their campus—not knowing that the local payroll draws on real estate covered by covenants like a tent. Let's get back to them saints, Professor. It's awful cold out there.

As the carillons of twelve A.M. divide the campus from the slum.

"THE SLUMS TAKE their revenge," the white-haired poet warned us thirty-two American League seasons and Lord-Knows-How-Many-Swindles-Ago. "Always somehow or other their retribution can be figured in any community."

The slums take their revenge. And you can take your pick of the avengers among the fast international set at any district-station lockup on any Saturday night. The lockups are always open and there are always new faces. Always someone you never met before, and where they all come from nobody knows and where they'll go from here nobody cares

The giants cannot come again; all the bright faces of tomorrow are careworn hustlers' faces.

And the place always gets this look of some careworn hustler's tomorrow by night, as the arch of spring is mounted and May turns into June. It is then that the women come out of the summer hotels to sit one stone step above the pavement, surveying the men curb-sitting one step below it. Between them pass the nobodies from nowhere, the nobodies nobody knows, with faces cut from the same cloth as their caps, and the women whose eyes reflect nothing but the pavement.

The nameless, useless nobodies who sleep behind the taverns, who sleep beneath the El. Who sleep in burnt-out busses with the windows freshly curtained; in winterized chicken coops or patched-up truck bodies. The useless, helpless nobodies nobody knows: that go as the snow goes, where the wind blows, there and there and there, down any old cat-and-ashcan alley at all. There, unloved and lost forever, lost and unloved for keeps and a day, there far below the ceaseless flow of TV waves and FM waves, way way down there where no one has yet heard of phonevision nor considered the wonders of technicolor video—there, there below the miles and miles of high-tension wires servicing the miles and miles of low-pressure cookers, there, there where they sleep on someone else's pool table, in someone else's hall or someone else's jail, there where they chop kindling for heat, cook over coal stoves, still burn kerosene for light, there where they sleep the all-night movies through and wait for rain or peace or snow: there, there beats Chicago's heart.

There, unheard by the millions who ride the waves above and sleep, and sleep and dream, night after night after night, loving and well beloved, guarding and well guarded, beats the great city's troubled heart.

And all the stately halls of science, the newest Broadway hit, the endowed museums, the endowed opera, the endowed art galleries, are not for their cold pavement-colored eyes. For the masses who do the city's labor also keep the city's heart. And they think there's something fishy about someone giving them a museum for nothing and free admission on Saturday afternoons.

They sense somebody got a bargain, and they are so right. The city's arts are built upon the uneasy consciences that milked the city of millions on the grain exchange, in traction and utilities and sausage-stuffing and then bought conscience-ease with a minute fraction of the profits. A museum for a traction system, an opera building for a utilities empire. Therefore the arts themselves here, like the acres of Lorado Taft's deadly handiwork, are largely statuary. Mere monuments to the luckier brokers of the past. So the people shy away from their gifts, they're never sure quite why.

The place remains a broker's portage. And an old-time way station for pimps as well. Both professions requiring the same essential hope of something for nothing and a soft-as-goosefeathers way to go. A portage too for the fabulous engines: the Harvester, the sleeping car and the Bessemer Process.

Yet never a harvest in sight hereabouts for humanity's spirit, uprooted over half the world and well deceived here at home.

No room, no time, no breath for the Bessemer processes of the heart.

JANE ADDAMS

Twenty Years at Hull House

FROM OUR VERY first months at Hull House we found it much easier to deal with the first generation of crowded city life than with the second or third, because it is more natural and cast in a simpler mold. The Italian and Bohemian peasants who live in Chicago, still put on their bright holiday clothes on a Sunday and go to visit their cousins. They tramp along with at least a suggestion of having once walked over plowed fields and breathed country air. The second generation of city poor too often have no holiday clothes and consider their relations a "bad lot." I have heard a drunken man in a maudlin stage, babble of

---

Jane Addams was founder of Hull House, considered to be the prototype settlement house in American, and a leader in social work and pacifism. She wrote two autobiographical books: Twenty Years at Hull House *and* The Second Twenty Years at Hull House.

his good country mother and imagine he was driving the cows home, and I knew that his little son who laughed loud at him, would be drunk earlier in life and would have no such pastoral interlude to his ravings. Hospitality still survives among foreigners, although it is buried under false pride among the poorest Americans. One thing seemed clear in regard to entertaining immigrants; to preserve and keep whatever of value their past life contained and to bring them in contact with a better type of Americans. For several years, every Saturday evening the entire families of our Italian neighbors were our guests. These evenings were very popular during our first winters at Hull House. Many educated Italians helped us, and the house became known as a place where Italians were welcome and where national holidays were observed. They come to us with their petty lawsuits, sad relics of the *vendetta*, with their aspirations for American clothes, and with their needs for an interpreter.

An editor of an Italian paper made a genuine connection between us and the Italian colony, not only with the Neapolitans and the Sicilians of the immediate neighborhood, but with the educated *connazionali* throughout the city, until he went south to start an agricultural colony in Alabama, in the establishment of which Hull House heartily cooperated.

Possibly the South Italians more than any other immigrants represent the pathetic stupidity of agricultural people crowded into city tenements, and we were much gratified when thirty peasant families were induced to move upon the land which they knew so well how to cultivate. The starting of this colony, however, was a very expensive affair in spite of the fact that the colonists purchased the land at two dollars an acre; they needed much more than raw land, and although it was possible to collect the small sums necessary to sustain them during the hard time of the first two years, we were fully convinced that undertakings of this sort could be conducted properly only by colonization societies such as England has established, or, better still, by enlarging the functions of the Federal Department of Immigration.

An evening similar in purpose to the one devoted to the Italians was organized for the Germans, in our first year. Owing to the superior education of our Teutonic guests and the clever leading of a cultivated German woman, these evenings reflected something of that cozy social intercourse which is found in its perfection in the fatherland. Our guests sang a great deal in the tender minor of the German folksong or in the rousing spirit of the Rhine, and they slowly but persistently pursued a course in German history and literature, recovering something of that poetry and romance which they had long since resigned with other good things. We found strong family affection between them and their English-speaking children, but their pleasures were not in common, and they seldom went out together. Perhaps the greatest value of the Settlement to them was in placing large and pleasant rooms with musical facilities at their disposal, and in reviving their almost forgotten enthusiasms. I have seen sons and daughters stand in complete surprise as their mother's knitting needles softly beat time to the song she was singing, or her worn face turned rosy under the hand-clapping as she made an old-fashioned curtsey at the end of a German poem. It was easy to fancy a growing touch of respect in her children's manner to her, and a rising enthusiasm for German literature and reminiscence on the part of all the family, an effort to bring together the old life and the new, a respect for the older cultivation, and not quite so much assurance that the new was the best.

This tendency upon the part of the older immigrants to lose the amenities of European life without sharing those of America, has often been deplored by keen observers from the home countries. When Professor Masurek of Prague gave a course of lectures in the University of Chicago, he was much distressed over the materialism into which the Bohemians of Chicago had fallen. The early immigrants had been so stirred by the opportunity to own real estate, an appeal perhaps to the Slavic land hunger, and their energies had become so completely absorbed in money-making that all other interests had apparently dropped away. And yet I recall a very touching incident in connection with a lecture Professor Masurek gave at Hull House, in which he had appealed to his countrymen to arouse themselves from this tendency to fall below their home civilization and to forget the great enthusiasm which had united them into the Pan-Slavic Movement. A Bohemian widow who supported herself and her two children by scrubbing, hastily sent her youngest child to purchase, with the twenty-five cents which was to have supplied them with food the next day, a bunch of red roses which she presented to the lecturer in appreciation of his testimony to the reality of the things of the spirit.

An overmastering desire to reveal the humbler immigrant parents to their own children lay at the base of what has come to be called the Hull House Labor Museum. This was first suggested to my mind one early spring day when I saw an old Italian woman, her distaff against her homesick face, patiently spinning a thread by the simple stick spindle so reminiscent of all southern Europe. I was walking down Polk Street, perturbed in spirit, because it seemed so difficult to come into genuine relations with the Italian women and because they themselves so often lost their hold upon their Americanized children. It seemed to me that Hull House ought to be able to devise some educational enterprise, which should build a bridge between European and American experiences in such wise as to give them both more meaning and a sense of relation. I meditated that perhaps the power to see life as a whole, is more needed in the immigrant quarter of a large city than anywhere else, and that the lack of this power is the most fruitful source of misunderstanding between European immigrants and their children, as it is between them and their American neighbors; and why should that chasm between fathers and sons, yawning at the feet of each generation, be made so unnecessarily cruel and impassable to these bewildered immigrants? Suddenly I looked up and saw the old woman with her distaff, sitting in the sun on the steps of a tenement house. She might have served as a model for one of Michaelangelo's Fates, but her face brightened as I passed and, holding up her spindle for me to see, she called out that when she had spun a little more yarn, she would knit a pair of stockings for her goddaughter. The occupation of the old woman gave me the clue that was needed. Could we not interest the young people working in the neighboring factories, in these older forms of industry, so that, through their own parents and grandparents, they would find a dramatic representation of the inherited resources of their daily occupation. If these young people could actually see that the complicated machinery of the factory had been evolved from simple tools, they might at least make a beginning towards that education which Dr. Dewey defines as "a continuing reconstruction of experience." They might also lay a foundation for reverence of the past which Goethe declares to be the basis of all sound progress.

My exciting walk on Polk Street was followed by many talks with Dr. Dewey and with one of the teachers in his school who was a resident at Hull House. Within a month a room was fitted up to which we might invite those of our neighbors who were possessed of old crafts and who were eager to use them.

We found in the immediate neighborhood, at least four varieties of these most primitive methods of spinning and three distinct variations of the same spindle in connection with wheels. It was possible to put these seven into historic sequence and order and to connect the whole with the present method of factory spinning. The same thing was done for weaving, and on every Saturday evening a little exhibit was made of these various forms of labor in the textile industry. Within one room a Syrian woman, a Greek, an Italian, a Russian, and an Irish-woman enabled even the most casual observer to see that there is no break in orderly evolution if we look at history from the industrial standpoint; that industry develops similarly and peacefully year by year among the workers of each nation, heedless of differences in language, religion, and political experiences.

And then we grew ambitious and arranged lectures upon industrial history. I remember that after an interesting lecture upon the industrial revolution in England and a portrayal of the appalling conditions throughout the weaving districts of the north, which resulted from the hasty gathering of the weavers into the new towns, a Russian tailor in the audience was moved to make a speech. He suggested that whereas time had done much to alleviate the first difficulties in the transition of weaving from hand work to steam power, that in the application of steam to sewing we are still in the first stages, illustrated by the isolated woman who tries to support herself by hand needlework at home until driven out by starvation, as many of the hand weavers had been.

The historical analogy seemed to bring a certain comfort to the tailor as did a chart upon the wall, showing the infinitesimal amount of time that steam had been applied to manufacturing processes compared to the centuries of hand labor. Human progress is slow and perhaps never more cruel than in the advance of industry, but is not the worker comforted by knowing that other historical periods have existed similar to the one in which he finds himself, and that the readjustment may be shortened and alleviated by judicious action; and is he not entitled to the solace which an artistic portrayal of the situation might give him? I remember the evening of the tailor's speech that I felt reproached because no poet or artist has endeared the sweaters' victim to us as George Eliot has made us love the belated weaver, Silas Marner. The textile museum is connected directly with the basket weaving, sewing, millinery, embroidery, and dressmaking constantly being taught at Hull House, and so far as possible with the other educational departments; we have also been able to make a collection of products, of early implements, and of photographs which are full of suggestion., Yet far beyond its direct educational value, we prize it because it so often puts the immigrants into the position of teachers, and we imagine that it affords them a pleasant change from the tutelage in which all Americans, including their own children, are so apt to hold them. I recall a number of Russian women working in a sewing-room near Hull House, who heard one Christmas week that the House was going to give a party to which they might come. They arrived one afternoon when, unfortunately, there was no party on hand and, although the residents did their best to entertain them with impromptu music and refreshments, it was quite evident that they were greatly disappointed. Finally it was suggested that they be shown the Labor Museum—where gradually the thirty sodden, tired women were transformed. They knew how to use the spindles and were delighted to find the Russian spinning frame. Many of them had never seen the spinning wheel, which has not penetrated to certain parts of Russia, and they regarded it as a new and wonderful invention. They turned up their dresses to show their homespun petticoats; they tried the looms; they explained the difficulty of the old patterns; in short, from having been stupidly entertained, they themselves did the entertaining. Because of a direct appeal to former experiences, the immigrant visitors were able for the moment to instruct their American hostesses in an old and honored craft, as was indeed becoming to their age and experience.

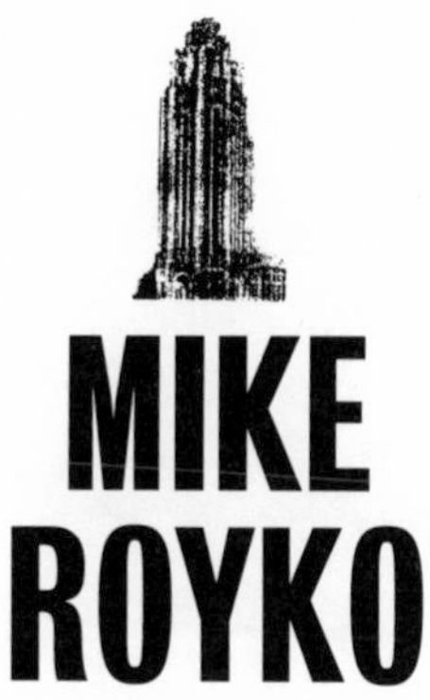

MIKE ROYKO

Boss

Kunstler: Mayor Daley, do you know a federal judge by the name of Judge Lynch?
Witness: Do I know him?
Kunstler: Yes.
Witness: . . . We have been boyhood friends all our lives.

HE GREW UP a small-town boy, which used to be possible even in the big city. Not anymore, because of the car, the shifting society, and the suburban sprawl. But Chicago, until as late as the 1950s, was a place where people stayed put for a while, cre-

---

Renowned Chicago journalist Mike Royko wrote a daily column for the Chicago Tribune. *His recounting of Chicago's backroom wheeling and dealing culminated in his most famous and controversial work,* Boss: Richard J. Daley of Chicago.

ating tightly knit neighborhoods, as small-townish as any village in the wheat fields.

The neighborhood-towns were part of larger ethnic states. To the north of the Loop was Germany. To the northwest was Poland. To the west were Italy and Israel. To the southwest were Bohemia and Lithuania. And to the south was Ireland.

It wasn't perfectly defined because the borders shifted as newcomers moved in on the older settlers, sending them fleeing in terror and disgust. Here and there were outlying colonies, with Poles also on the South Side, and Irish up north.

But you could always tell, even with your eyes closed, which state you were in by the odors of the food stores and the open kitchen windows, the sound of the foreign or familiar language, and by whether a stranger hit you in the head with a rock.

In every neighborhood could be found all the ingredients of the small town: the local tavern, the funeral parlor, the bakery, the vegetable store, the butcher shop, the drugstore, the neighborhood drunk, the neighborhood trollop, the neighborhood idiot, the neighborhood war hero, the neighborhood police station, the neighborhood team, the neighborhood sports star, the ball field, the barber shop, the pool hall, the clubs, and the main street.

Every neighborhood had a main street for shopping and public transportation. The city is laid out with a main street every half mile, residential streets between. But even better than in a small town, a neighborhood person didn't have to go over to the main street to get essentials, such as food and drink. On the side streets were taverns and little grocery stores. To buy new underwear, though, you had to go to Main Street.

With everything right there, why go anywhere else? If you went somewhere else, you couldn't get credit, you'd have to waste a nickel on the streetcar, and when you finally got there, they might not speak the language.

Some people had to leave the neighborhood to work,

but many didn't, because the houses were interlaced with industry.

On Sunday, people might ride a streetcar to visit a relative, but they usually remained within the ethnic state, unless there had been an unfortunate marriage in the family.

The borders of neighborhoods were the main streets, railroad tracks, branches of the Chicago River, branches of the branches, strips of industry, parks, and anything else that could be glared across.

The ethnic states got along just about as pleasantly as did the nations of Europe. With their tote bags, the immigrants brought along all their old prejudices, and immediately picked up some new ones. An Irishman who came here hating only the Englishmen and Irish Protestants soon hated Poles, Italians, and blacks. A Pole who was free arrived hating only Jews and Russians, but soon learned to hate the Irish, the Italians, and the blacks.

That was another good reason to stay close to home and in your own neighborhood-town and ethnic state. Go that way, past the viaduct, and the wops will jump you, or chase you into Jew town. Go the other way, beyond the park, and the Polacks would stomp on you. Cross those streetcar tracks, and the Micks will shower you with Irish confetti from the brickyards. And who can tell what the niggers might do?

But in the neighborhood, you were safe. At least if you did not cross beyond, say, to the other side of the school. While it might be part of your ethnic state, it was still the edge of another neighborhood, and their gang was just as mean as your gang.

So, for a variety of reasons, ranging from convenience to fear to economics, people stayed in their own neighborhood, loving it, enjoying the closeness, the friendliness, the familiarity, and trying to save enough money to move out.

INTO SUCH A self-contained neighborhood was born Richard J. Daley. For his time, and his destiny, he could not have chosen a better place.

His was the great and powerful Irish South Side, bordered on the east by blacks and on the west by a variety of slavs.

The Irish settled in Chicago around 1840 to dig a canal, live in shanties, and work in the industries that followed their strong backs. The area became known as Back of the Yards, because of its greatest wonder—the stockyards. Then the nation's busiest slaughterhouse, it gave meat to the nation, jobs to the South Side, and a stink to the air that was unforgettable.

Daley's neighborhood was Bridgeport, located at the north end of the ethnic state. The people lived in small homes and flats, there were ten Catholic churches, about the same number of smaller Protestant churches, countless saloons, and a natural body of water, known a Bubbly Creek, into which the stockyards dumped wastes and local thugs dumped victims.

In Bridgeport's early days, the people grew cabbage on vacant land in their yards, and it was known for a time as the Cabbage Patch. But by the time Daley was born, most people had stopped raising cabbage and had taken to raising politicians. Daley was to become the third consecutive mayor produced by Bridgeport. It would also produce an extraordinary number of lesser office-holders, appointed officials, and, legend says, even more votes than it had voters.

It was a community that drank out of the beer pail and ate out of the lunch bucket. The men worked hard in the stockyards, nearby factories, breweries, and construction sites. It was a union neighborhood. They bought small frame homes or rented flats. It had as many Catholic schools as public schools, and the enrollment at the parochial schools was bigger.

Daley was born on May 15, 1902, in a flat at 3602 South Lowe, less than a block from where he later lived as mayor.

His father, Michael, was a short, wiry, quiet man, a sheet-metal worker. His parents had come from County Waterford. His mother, Lillian Dunne Daley, had been born in Bridgeport of parents from Limerick.

When Daley was born, his father was twenty-two and his mother was thirty. He was their only child.

Daley has said little about his childhood, other than that it was happy and typical. His mother baked bread and his father worked hard. His earliest memory, was of being taken into the Church of the Nativity, where his mother was an energetic volunteer church worker. His political memories begin with his mother's taking him along when she joined in women's suffrage marches.

His old friends, such as Judge William Lynch, say he was always shy, even as a little boy, and that he always dressed well, better than most of the children in the neighborhood. "I think the reason he's always had trouble talking," an old Bridgeport resident said, "was that there weren't any other children in his home, and his parents were quiet people. His father never said much and his mother pretty well ran things. His mother kept an eye on him. He always had nice clothes, she saw to that. With only one child, they could afford it."

Daley was enrolled in the elementary school at the Nativity Church, under the strict discipline of the nuns. The Nativity Church was the center of the community, towering over the small homes. The church and the local political office provided most of the social welfare benefits of the day. Families that were down on their luck could get a small loan, food, a job referral.

Throughout boyhood, Daley always had a part-time or a weekend job. He sold papers at the streetcar stops on Halsted Street and sometimes boarded the cars to sell papers in the aisles. He picked up pocket money by working on a horse-drawn vegetable wagon, running up the back steps with orders.

Bridgeport families, with their low incomes, could not make plans for college educations for their children. If it happened, fine; but it was more realistic to prepare them for a job.

So when Daley finished elementary school, his parents enrolled him at De La Salle Institute, a three-year commercial high school, operated by the Christian Brothers.

The school taught typing, shorthand, bookkeeping and other office skills. Those were the days when men worked as secretaries. While some general academic courses were provided, the diploma was accepted only by Catholic colleges.

The school gave Daley his first glimpse of institutional segregation. Drab and already old looking, it was located in the Negro area east of Bridgeport. The 350 students were white, about ninety percent of them Irish.

The Christian Brothers provided him with another ample dose of discipline and order. "They were good teachers," one of Daley's classmates remembers, "but if you got out of line, they wouldn't hesitate to punch you in the head." One of the teaching brothers, after slamming a student's head into the blackboard, let the brow-sized dent remain in the board for years as a stimulant to learning.

Most of the students did not have to be punched. They came from hard-working families, to whom the fifty dollars a year tuition, ten dollars typewriter rental, and the daily streetcar fare were a substantial investment. To a laborer, it represented three or four pay envelopes. Students brought home weekly report slips to be signed by their parents printed on different colored slips, pink meaning failure, as a hedge against an illiterate parent's being deceived.

The school had little to offer besides a ticket to a job. The sports program was intramural softball in a little courtyard. The lunchroom sold a plate of beans for a nickel. Anybody caught smoking was fined one dollar. Daley never took it up. The students didn't hang around after school because the neighborhood was black, and there were racial fights. Daley arrived and left each day with a group from Bridgeport. Most of the student cliques were along neighborhood lines.

Between the discipline and the course of studies, it was not an easy place for anyone to become a big man on campus. If anybody filled that role, it wasn't Daley.

They remember him as having been "a hard worker . . . maybe a little above average . . . just an average kid . . . short, stocky, even then . . . built like a brick outhouse . . . affable . . . always a heavyweight, not belligerent, but he could handle himself and he had a deep voice."

Only one of his classmates, who later spent many years holding down a desk in City Hall, saw him in a completely different light: "He was a brilliant person, even then. I could see the greatness in him. Everybody could. He got along with everybody. People sought him out. He was a brilliant student. He did everything well. He was an outstanding softball player."

Daley's class graduated in June 1919, and the school accomplished its objective: almost all of the graduates got office work. The school found jobs for some. It had a working relationship with private firms and City Hall, and one youth found himself clerking in a downtown court that specialized in prostitution cases. Few went to college, but some did well in business. And at their reunions many years later, they were unanimous in their satisfaction with their strict, functional education, in their contempt for modern youth and dissent, and in their distrust of blacks.

If June 1919 was a memorable month for Daley's class, the next month was even more memorable for them, and the rest of the South Side.

On July 27, a black youth, swimming off the Twenty-seventh Street beach, made the mistake of drifting south until he was off the Twenty-ninth Street beach. In doing so, he had crossed an invisible line that separated the white and black beaches.

When he tried to come ashore, the whites stoned him, and he swam back out. Black bathers ran to his aide, fights broke out, more stones were thrown, and the black youth drowned.

It wasn't the first such incident on the South Side. Besides the threat they posed in housing and job competition, the blacks had antagonized the heavily Democratic white neighborhoods by voting Republican. They were given credit for Republican Mayor William Thompson's slim victory that spring.

But nothing had ever happened on the scale of the rioting that broke out that oppressively hot day after word of the youth's death swept the black area, and rumors of a black uprising mobilized the whites.

The biggest race war in Chicago's history erupted. It raged for four days and left 15 whites and 23 blacks dead, 178 whites and 342 blacks injured. About one thousand homes were burned.

Daley has never discussed his memories of the riot, but he surely has some, because his neighborhood was part of the battleground. The heaviest rioting took place on the South Side, and most of the deaths and serious injuries were in the Back of the Yards and the adjoining black area.

The Illinois Commission of Human Relations, which conducted a three year study of the riot, said "Forty-one percent of the clashes occurred in the white neighborhood near the Stockyards, between the South branch of the Chicago River and 55th St."

Dozens of white mobs prowled the streets. Blacks going home were dragged from streetcars, beaten, and killed. Raiding parties drove into black areas and lobbed bombs into homes.

The blacks retaliated by killing white delivery men and greeting white raiders with gunfire.

Fighting broke out in the Loop and spilled into the West Side Italian area, which a Negro workman entered on a bike, but left in a box.

THE QUESTION HAS been raised by newspapers from time to time: Was young Daley a participant in the violence? Blacks passing through his neighborhood were beaten within screaming distance of his home. Daley has never answered, or even acknowledged, the question. The 1919 riot itself is something he has never talked about. But if he wasn't part of it, if he sat out his neighborhood's bloody battle, it is certain that some of his friends participated, because Daley belonged to a close-knit neighborhood club known as the Hamburg Social and Athletic Club. And this is what the riot study had to say of the club:

"Responsibility for many attacks was definitely placed by many witnesses upon the 'athletic clubs' including Ragen's Colts, the Hamburgers, Aylwards, Our Flag, Standard . . . and several others. The mobs were made up for the most part of boys between 15 and 22.

"Gangs, particularly of white youths, formed definite nuclei for crowd and mob formations. Athletic clubs supplied the leaders of many gangs."

In later years, Daley described the Hamburgs as something of a cross between the Boy Scouts of America and the YMCA, saying:

"Its purpose was social and athletic and some of the finest athletes, priests, and citizens of Chicago have been members."

And Judge Lynch said: "It was a great debating place We talked about the issues of the day, national affairs, local politics, and, of course, sports."

But others, looking in from the outside, or from the

sidewalk up, saw it in a different way.

A policeman, talking to the riot commission interviewers, said of the Back of the Yards "athletic clubs":

"There is the Canaryville bunch in there and the Hamburg bunch. It is a pretty tough hole."

John Waner, a Republican city politician who was defeated by Daley for mayor in 1967, grew up in the Slavic area west of Bridgeport, and he recalls that in the 1920s, "Gee, you'd never think of just walking into their neighborhood, or you'd get the hell knocked out of you by the Hamburgs."

Social and athletic club, made up of men who would be priests and leaders, or a tough, street fighting mob of brawlers?

It was probably both, just as Daley's neighborhood, almost fifty years later, was composed of hard-working church-going citizens, who nevertheless poured into his street and became a mob when a black college student moved into a flat.

When the 1919 riots occurred, the Hamburgs had already won neighborhood fame for their street battles with the rival Ragen's Colts from the Canaryville neighborhood to the north. They never had the Colts' reputation for criminality, but were handy with a brick.

The Hamburgs, by then, were a political force in Bridgeport, and the rest of what was then the Thirteenth Ward.

In 1914 the president of the Hamburg Club, Tommy Doyle, twenty-eight, decided to challenge an alderman who had been in office for twenty years.

Doyle won. And according to news accounts of the day, he won because 350 young men from the club went out in teams of ten every night and "campaigned" for him.

Four years later, the Hamburgs helped send Doyle to the state legislature, and another Hamburg hero, Big Joe McDonough was elected to the City Council.

Doyle went on to become a congressman, one of the few

to carry a gun in a belt holster, and McDonough in a few years was the leader of the ward and one of the most powerful Democrats in the city.

By 1924, Daley was elected the club's president, and he remained in office for about fifteen years. As mayor, he would appoint old-time Hamburg members and their sons to some of the city's top administrative posts. The Hamburgs, still with headquarters in a store on Halsted Street, have more power than some of the city's most prestigious private businessmen's clubs. If it never made *Who's Who in America*, it is part of what's what in Chicago.

After graduation, Daley had his last experience with private enterprise. And therein lies a Daley legend.

He is portrayed by his publicists as having been a young "cowboy" in the stockyard, herding cattle on horseback, a Bridgeport John Wayne. For years, the legend goes, he herded cattle during the day and dragged himself to law school at night, weary but unfaltering in his determination to improve himself. Even Abe Lincoln couldn't have worked harder.

"That is just so much bull," says Benjamin Adamowski, once a friend, and later Daley's most bitter political enemy. "He got on a public payroll almost as soon as he was able to vote, and he's been there since."

It does appear that Adamowski's version of Daley's cowboy years is closer to the truth than the legends.

Daley did go to work in the stockyards after graduation, but his secretarial skills soon had him working at a desk. If he rode horses, it was not a long trail drive.

At twenty-one, he was a precinct captain in McDonough's ward organization and a member of the Hamburgs. Then, as now, being a precinct captain in a solid ward organization usually meant some kind of public payroll job. Add to that the Hamburg status, and you do not have somebody who needed to stomp around in cow dung.

Daley's memory gets foggy when asked about this period. The closest he has ever come to being specific about his period of stockyard employment is "about three or four years."

That would bring him to about twenty or twenty-one years of age, which is when he found a place on McDonough's lap and became his personal ward secretary and a protégé. It was also the time when William Dever, a Democrat, was elected a reform mayor. Since Chicago reforms begin with the firing of city workers from the other parties, the Democrats were grabbing all the patronage jobs. This, then, is when Daley apparently got his first City Hall job, as a clerk in the City Council. He would be on public payrolls for the next forty-eight years, at least.

If the regular pay was important to him, the opportunity to learn was of even greater long-range significance.

As McDonough's personal secretary in the ward organization, he could observe political science, as applied at the local level: the doling out of patronage jobs to the deserving and the firing of the undeserving; the helping of friends through the fix and the punishing of enemies through pressure from city inspectors; the adjustment of a case at the police station; the adding up of votes so they come out the right way; and all the other skills a ward leader must have and not get caught at.

Then down to the clerical job in City Hall for more learning. The first lesson is always the same: never repeat what you see or hear, or somebody might get indicted.

The City Council, where Daley was put to work shuffling papers and fetching coffee, was where many of the party powerhouses were. He was able to observe how driveway permits were sold to property owners, how and why rate increases were granted to utilities and public transportation lines, how rezoning could send a piece of property spiraling in value with the stroke of a pen, and where the bottles were kept in the cloak room.

It had to be a jaw-dropping experience for a shy, churchgoing youth from a proper family, all those cigar-chomping bandits sitting among their spittoons and dividing up the town.

The city had just come off eight years of rule by raucous Big Bill Thompson, who had put up buildings and bridges, widened streets, and made countless contractors happy. They, in turn, made countless politicians happy.

He also made the gangsters happy by giving them the run of the town, and they made the Police Department happy by giving them a piece of the profit. Everybody was happy except the people being shot and the citizens who thought things were getting a bit outlandish, even for Chicago.

Reform was demanded by the civic leaders in 1923, and Thompson didn't run for a third term. And that brought in Mayor Dever, a judge, and by Chicago standards, a decent man. He set out to reform City Hall, but there was only so much he could do, since most of the members of his party considered reform to be the redirecting of graft from Republicans to themselves.

Dever did manage to get Al Capone out of Chicago, after Thompson had almost given him the key to the city. Capone moved his headquarters to Cicero, a nearby suburb. He promptly went into Cicero politics, running his own slate of candidates. On election day, three people were killed, several were kidnapped, many were beaten, and Capone's candidates won. The Syndicate took over Cicero and never completely let go. It still has its strip of bars where gambling and whoring are unnoticed. The only thing they won't tolerate in Cicero are Negroes.

From Cicero, Capone had no difficulty running his bootleg empire, which brought in millions of dollars a week, and the killing went on, although Dever managed to close down hundreds of speakeasies.

As much as Chicagoans wanted reform, they wanted their bootleg gin more, so after four years of Dever, they returned Thompson to power. Capone came back downtown and had things his own way until the federal government imprisoned him for tax evasion. He came out wasting away with syphilis, but Capone, with Thompson's tacit consent, had built the model American municipal crime syndicate. His successors never again ran the town, as he did, but they always had a piece of the action.

These were Chicago's "Roaring Twenties." And through those fast-paced years plodded young Richard Daley.

During the day he worked in City Hall. After work, he went to DePaul University's School of Law, four nights a week, 6 P.M. to 8 P.M. The rest of his time was taken up with ward politics and the Hamburg Club athletics. He managed the club's softball team.

Another boyhood friend, Steven Bailey, who became head of the Plumbers' Union, said, "I used to go out dancing at night, but Dick would go home and hit the books."

One of Daley's fellow students was Louis Wexler, a Russian-born immigrant, who got off the boat and zipped through elementary and high school in four years.

"Daley was a nice fellow, very quiet, a hard worker, and always neatly dressed. He never missed a class and always got there on time. But there was nothing about him that would make him stand out, as far as becoming something special in life. Even then, he misused the language so that you noticed it. He had trouble expressing himself and his grammar wasn't good." But thirty years later, Daley's grammar was good enough to say "yes" when Wexler appealed to their old night school ties, and Wexler became a judge.

If the pace was plodding, the future, at least, held promise. In Alderman McDonough, the ward leader, Daley had a political godfather with upward mobility and long coattails.

McDonough had wisely allied himself in the City Council with Anton (Tony) Cermak, a one-time coal miner who had become the political leader of the Bohemian community. Uneducated, tough, crude, but politically brilliant, Cermak had the gall to challenge the traditional South Side Irish domination of the Democratic party. More than gall, he had the sense to count up all the Irish votes, then he counted all the Italian, Jews, Germans, Poles, and Bohemians. The minority Irish domination didn't make sense to him. He organized a city-wide saloon keepers' league, dedicated to fighting closing laws and prohibition. With the saloon keepers behind him, he couldn't be stopped. He became president of the Cook County Board, took over the party machinery, and ran for mayor in 1931.

Most of the South Side Irish leaders thought of Cermak as the worst thing since the potato famine. They didn't realize that he was doing them a favor while cuffing them about. He didn't realize it either.

By creating the ethnically balanced ticket, something new, he put together the most powerful political machine in Chicago history. It is the direct ancestor of the organization Daley inherited.

Soon after Cermak was elected mayor, he was on a speaking platform in Miami when a mad assassin took a shot at President Roosevelt and got him instead.

The Chicago Machine gave him a hero's funeral, the biggest in city history, changed the name of Twenty-second Street to Cermak Road, wiped away its tears, and then the South Side put Ed Kelly in as mayor and let Pat Nash run the party. The famine was over.

Two years earlier, however, Cermak had slated his friend McDonough as the candidate for county treasurer. If McDonough won, Daley knew it would be his ticket out of the

City Council, to a job in the treasurer's office.

He worked hard, as did the rest of Bridgeport, to bring in the vote for McDonough, throwing back his head and leading rallies in McDonough's personal campaign song:

Whataya gonna do for McDonough?
Whataya gonna do for YOU?
Are ya gonna carry your precinct?
Are you gonna be true blue?
Whenever ya wanted a favor,
McDonough was ready to do.
Whataya gonna do for McDonough,
After what he done for you?

McDonough and the rest of the Democratic ticket won easily, and Daley got his desk in the treasurer's office as an administrative assistant. It paid better and it was another chance to learn. The council had taught him what it had to offer, and now he could immerse himself in the complexities of tax collection, banking of county funds, and the management of a large patronage office.

Somebody had to do the work, because McDonough didn't want to. To McDonough, a stubby 280-pounder, the charm of elective office was not mucking about with papers and figures. The office meant more jobs, more power. The management was left to trusted and skilled assistants. McDonough had other interests that took his time. He loved the horses, and never missed a Kentucky Derby.

When his long absences from the County Building became noticeable to the press, McDonough offered a novel excuse: because he was known to be a generous and soft-hearted man, people were constantly coming to him for loans, jobs, and other favors; therefore, he said, the only way he could get any work done was to stay away from his office.

Daley eagerly took over much of the responsibility of the county treasurer, although the voters didn't know it. And he may have acquired an added incentive for wanting to make a good showing. The summer before the election, he had met a young lady.

By all accounts, Daley was not a lady's man. Shy and reserved around men, he was a paralytic near women. The glib tongue of the Irish had been swallowed somewhere in his ancestry.

His idea of a big time was a Hamburg softball game and a few beers and some poker at The Pump on Halsted Street or Babe Connelly's Bar on Thirty-seventh Street.

It was at a softball game that a casual acquaintance named Lloyd Guilfoyle introduced Daley, then twenty-eight, to his sister, Eleanor Guilfoyle, nineteen, a paint company secretary.

The Guilfoyles were a large family from neighboring Canaryville, and Miss Guilfoyle had an upbringing and education as Catholic as Daley's.

Shyness aside, Daley was a handsome man in his youth, with strong clean features, thick black hair, and an erect posture. He was stocky, but not fat.

The couple began keeping company in 1930, and six years after they met, they were married. Daley's pace was consistent in all matters.

In 1934, Daley got his long sought law degree, but he didn't go into private practice. During the Depression, LaSalle Street was full of good lawyers who didn't have the price of lunch, but Daley had a regular paycheck. The legal knowledge was useful, and the degree and license another step forward, but practicing law was not his ambition. He has never practiced it, although he and Lynch had a firm between 1946 and 1955. Of Daley as a lawyer, Tom Keane, his council leader, and a rich lawyer himself says:

"Daley wouldn't know what the inside of a courtroom

looks like. He never practiced law. Lynch handled all the firm's work. All Daley ever cared about was politics, and he spent his time running for office."

In his pursuit of elective office it looked like a long wait in 1934. Despite the Democrats' control of state, county, and city offices, there wasn't much open at Daley's level. Tom Doyle, the hard-drinking congressman, had returned from Washington to replace McDonough as alderman. And Doyle was only forty-eight. McDonough was a mere forty-five. Ahead of Daley in ward organization influence was Babe Connelly, a saloon keeper, bookie, and former speakeasy operator who was only forty-three. It could be years before something opened up. How long can a man be happy as president of the Hamburg Club?

It all changed quickly. In 1934, McDonough was stricken with pneumonia and died. His funeral was the biggest since Cermak's. Thousands filled the streets outside the Church of the Nativity and watched every big shot, from the governor down, mourn him. One thousand cars went to the cemetery. The biggest names in politics were his honorary pallbearers. But Daley and Babe Connelly carried the casket.

A year later, Alderman Doyle got pneumonia and he died as quickly as had McDonough. Connelly replaced Doyle in the City Council. The turnover in ward leadership was complete. Babe Connelly was now the boss, and Daley and a few other ambitious young men were right behind him.

Meanwhile, Daley was working for three more county treasurers, and an interesting trio they were.

When McDonough died, the party asked Thomas Nash, a first cousin of Party Chairman Pat Nash, to complete the unexpired term. Tom Nash was a ward leader and a prosperous criminal lawyer who defended Capone and other gangsters. And if the client died of an overdose of bullets, he was not too proud to go to their funerals. It wasn't uncommon for Chicago politicians to join in the mourning at the funerals of gangsters, with aldermen weeping and judges praying. There was good reason for them to weep and pray, as they had to deal with somebody new. Tom Nash's law firm produced more Chicago and state judges than any other.

Then there was Robert M. Sweitzer, a veteran office-holder, who became county treasurer in December 1934. Within a year he was found to have lost $453,000 in county funds in an unsuccessful private business venture—he had tried to manufacture synthetic coal briquettes. He was ousted, tried, pleaded good intentions, and was acquitted.

This brought in Joe Gill, another ward boss, who is believed to have gone on his first public payroll before the turn of the century; he lived long enough to spend his twilight years as a park commissioner and, in 1968, to tell the strange Yippie creatures that they could not camp in the parks during the Democratic Convention.

In 1936, Daley's big break finally came. Again somebody died. This time it was an elderly state legislator, David Shanahan, who had been Speaker of the Illinois House. He died only fifteen days before the November 3 elections, with his name already on the ballots. It seemed like a terrible waste to elect a dead man to office, especially in the legislative districts that included Bridgeport, where there were so many live ones.

It was too late to reprint the ballots, so the Machine organized a write-in campaign for Daley. The precinct captains did their jobs, getting eighty-six hundred people to write in his name, and on November 4, 1936, Daley had won his first elective office.

The only thing that kept the victory from being perfect was the fact that Shanahan had been a Republican, running unopposed. So Daley's name had to be written in on the

Republican side of the ballot. Richard Daley was elected to his first public office as, of all things, a Republican.

In fact, when he got to the legislature, he had to spend his first morning on the Republican side of the aisle. Ironically, the Democratic minority leader was Adamowski, his future enemy, and Adamowski offered the resolution to let Daley come sit among the Democrats.

The Republicans, still angered by the Bridgeport opportunism that cheated them of a seat, made Daley suffer for it. Their leader pointed a long finger at Daley and said: "I don't care about the resolution. I want to know where Representative Daley wants to sit. Where do you want to sit, Representative Daley?"

Daley pointed at the Democrats and, in a soft voice, said, "There."

"Then go on over there," the Republican leader barked, "because we don't want you over here."

He did, gratefully. And two years later somebody else in his neighborhood dropped dead and Daley took his place in the state Senate, going in by the front door, finally, as a Democrat.

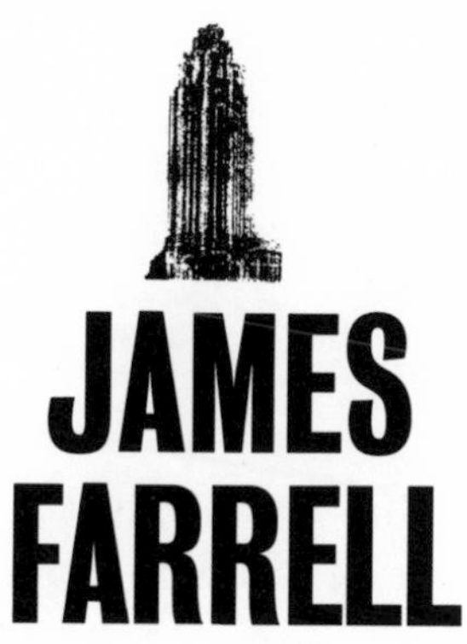

JAMES FARRELL

Studs Lonigan

STUDS LONIGAN, looking tough, sat on the fireplug before the drug store on the northeast corner of Fifty-eighth and Prairie. Since cleaning up Red Kelly, he, along with Tommy Doyle, had become a leading member of the Fifty-eighth Street bunch. Studs and Tommy were figured a good draw. Studs sat. His jaw was swollen with tobacco. The tobacco tasted bitter, and he didn't like it, but he sat, squirting juice from the corner

---

The patriarch of contemporary Chicago writing, James Farrell, was raised in the South Side. He created the definitive Chicago hero in his most famous and respected work, the trilogy Studs Lonigan. *Patron of the underdog, Farrell believed that a man's mind was the product of his environment; he spent much of his career examining the consequences of life on the Chicago streets.*

of his mouth, rolling the chewed wad from jaw to jaw. His cap was pulled over his right eye in hard-boiled fashion. He had a piece of cardboard in the back of his cap to make it square, just like all the tough Irish from Wentworth Avenue, and he had a bushy Regan haircut. He sat. He had a competition with himself in tobacco juice spitting to determine whether he could do better plopping it from the right or the left side of his mouth. The right hand side was Studs; the left hand side was a series of rivals, challenging him for the championship. The contests were important ones, like heavyweight championship fights, and they put Studs Lonigan in the public eye, like Jess Willard and Freddy Welsh. Seriously, cautiously, concernedly, he let the brown juice fly, first from the left, then from the right side of his mouth. Now and then the juice slobbered down his chin, and that made Studs feel as goofy as if he was a young punk with falling socks.

People paraded to and fro along Fifty-eighth, and many turned on and off of Prairie Avenue. It was a typically warm summer day. Studs vaguely saw the people pass, and he was, in a distant way, aware of them as his audience. They saw him, looked at him, envied and admired him, noticed him, and thought that he must be a pretty tough young guy. The ugliest guy in the world passed. He was all out of joint. His face was colorless, and the jaws were sunken. He had the most Jewish nose in the world, and his lips were like a baboon's. He was round-shouldered, bow-legged and knock-kneed. His hands were too long, and as he walked he looked like a parabola from the side, and from the front like an approaching series of cubistic planes. And he wore colored glasses. Studs looked at him, laughed, even half-admired a guy who could be so twisted, and wondered who old plug-ugly was, and what he did. Then Leon ta-taed along, pausing to ask Studs about taking music lessons. He put his hands on Studs' shoulders, and Studs felt uncomfortable, as if maybe Leon had horse apples in his hands. Leon wanted Studs to take a walk, but Studs said he couldn't because he was waiting for some guys to come along. Leon shook himself along, and Studs felt as if he needed a bath. Old Fox-in-the-Bush, the priest or minister or whatever he was of the Greek Catholic Church across from St. Patrick's, walked by, carrying a cane. Studs told himself the guy was funny all right; he was Gilly's bosom friend. Studs laughed, because it must be funny, even to Gilly, listening to a guy talk through whiskers like that. Mrs. O'Brien came down the street, loaded with groceries, and Studs snapped his head around, like he was dodging something, and became interested in the sky, so that she wouldn't see him, not only because he was chewing, but also because if he saw her, he'd have to ask her if he could carry her groceries home for her. Hell, he was no errand boy, or a do-a-good-deed-a-day boy scout. And there was old Abraham Isidorivitch, or whatever his name was, the batty old half-blind Jew who was eighty, or ninety or maybe one hundred and thirty years old, and who was always talking loud on the corners. Abraham, or whatever his name was, did repair work for Davey Cohen's old man sometimes, and the two of them must be a circus when they're together. Mothers passed with their babies, some of them brats that squawled all over the place. Helen Borax, with her nose in the air, like she was trying to avoid an ugly smell. Mrs. Dennis P. Gorman, with a young kid carrying a package of her groceries that was too heavy for him. Studs got the gob of tobacco out just in the nick of time. She stopped and asked him how his dear mother was. She said he should be sure and tell her and his father to telephone them sometimes, and to come over for tea. And she asked him how he was enjoying the summer. Dorothy was just doing fine. She was very busy with her music, and she was going to summer school at Englewood, because she wanted to do the four years high school in three. And she said that Mr.

Robinson, head master of the troop of boy scouts in the neighborhood, had been over to her house the other evening, and he talked about getting more boys in his organization, because that kept them out of mischief. The boy scouts, she explained, were an excellent organization which made gentlemen out of boys, gave them opportunities for clean, organized fun and sport, and they taught boys to do all sorts of kind deeds like helping blind ladies across the street. The little boy helping her with groceries was a boy scout, and his good deed every day was to carry her groceries home; and he wouldn't take a penny for it. And her husband said that the boy scouts gave boys preliminary military training and discipline so that it would be easier for them later on in the army, if they were called to defend their country, as they might have to do with that old Kaiser trying to conquer the world. She expected to see Studs and all the other boys on Indiana Avenue join the boy scouts. She started to move on, and said in parting:

"Now, do tell your dear mother and your father to come and see us, and now don't you forget to, like little boys often do."

The boy scout struggled after her with the bundle that was too heavy for him. Studs watched them, and thought unprintable things about old lady Gorman.

He stacked some more tobacco in his mug. He sat there. He put on a show to please himself, and imagined that everybody noticed him. He tired of his tobacco juice spitting contest, and quit. He watched snot-nosed Phil Rolfe, the twelve-year-old little pest, tear after a motor truck heading north. The runt got his hitch, even though Studs yelled after him to confuse him, and wished that he'd break his kike neck. Old Man Cohen, dirty, bearded, paused and accusingly asked Studs if he had seen Davey. Studs said no. Studs felt sorry for Davey, with an old man like that. He sat there.

Nate shuffled by, and, seeing Studs, came over. Nate was a toothless, graying little man, with an insane stare in his smallish black eyes. He wore a faded and unpressed green suit that had cobwebs on it and a thick, winter cap of the kind that teamsters wore.

"What's on your mind, Nate?" Studs asked, using the same tone and manner that the older guys around Bathceller's pool room used with him.

Nate said he was getting some new French post cards, and told Studs that he'd sell them for a dime apiece. They were *some* pictures. Oh, boy! They showed everything. Studs said that he'd take a dozen or two when Nate brought them around. Nate tried to collect in advance, but Studs was no soap for that. Nate started to shuffle away and Studs asked him where the fire was.

"Work, my boy! I was jus' tellin' myself about the chicken I made lay eggs today. I was deliverin' some groceries over on South Park Avenoo, and this chicken was the maid. See! Well! Well, I delivers my groceries, and she says the missus ain't in, and she looks at me, you know the way a chicken looks at a guy!"

Nate winked, leered and poked Studs in the ribs expressively. He continued:

She says I should leave the groceries, and you know that ain't good business, so I calls ole man Hirschfield, but he says its o.k. So I leave the groceries. She tanks me, and she says she has jus' made a cup of tea, an' I should siddown and have one wid her. She was a looker, so I takes the tea wid her, and we gets to barbering about one ting an' anoder, about one ting and anoder . . ."

Nate paused to wipe the slobber off his whiskery chin.

"We gasses about on ting an' anoder, and soon she ups and walks by me to go to the sink, so I pinches her, and it was de nicest I ever pinched, an', my boy, I pinched many in my day, because I'm old enough to be yer grandaddy. Well, first ting you know . . ."

Nate leered.

"The first ting you know . . . why . . . I schlipt her a little luck."

"Yeh?"

Nate poked Studs confidentially, leered. and said: "Yeh, I schlipt her a little luck."

"Yeh?"

"Yeh!"

Nate turned to gape at a passing chicken, and Studs goosed him. Nate jumped.

He shuffled away, furious, telling himself about the damn brats who got too wise before their diapers were changed.

Studs laughed.

He took out another chew, and resumed his competition. The right hand side of his mouth won easily. He thought of Lucy who was probably still sore at him. The old feeling for Lucy flowed through him, warm. She seemed to him like a . . . like a saint or a beautiful queen, or a goddess. But the tough outside part of Studs told the tender inside part of him that nobody really knew, that he had better forget all that bull. He tried to, and it wasn't very easy. He let fly a juicy gob that landed square on a line, three cracks from him. Perfect! He saw Lucy, and acted very busy with his tobacco juice squirting. He let fly another gob that was a perfect hit. She laughed aloud at him, and said:

"Think you're funny, Mr. Smarty!"

Studs let fly another gob. She laughed again, and walked on. Studs sat, not looking nor feeling so much like a tough guy. He didn't turn and see Lucy twist around to glance at him. He threw his wad away. He sat, heedless of the noisy street. A dago peddler parked his fruit wagon in back of Studs, and he was there calling his wares for some time before Studs laughed, like he laughed at all batty foreigners. He thought of Lucy. Lucy . . .

she could go plum to . . . LUCY! He shoved another thumb of tobacco in his puss, but didn't chew it with the same concentration. He almost swallowed the damn stuff. Mr. Dennis P. Gorman passed, after his trying day at the police court. Studs coughed from the bad taste in his mouth.

Kenny Killarney appeared, and Studs smiled to see him. Kenny was thin, taller than Studs, Irish, blue-eyed, dizzyfaced, untidy, darkish, quick, and he had a nervous, original walk.

"Hi!" said Studs.

"Hi!" said Kenny, raising his palms, hands outward.

"Hi!" said Studs.

"Hi!" said Kenny; he salaamed in oriental fashion.

"Hi!" laughed Studs.

"Hi!" said Kenny.

"Hi!" said Studs. "Jesus Christ!" said Studs.

"Hi, Low, Jack, and the Game," said goofy Kenny.

They laughed and stuffed chews in their faces. Studs marveled at Kenny's skill in chewing. Juice rolled down his own chin, and he had to spit the tobacco out again.

Kenny gave a rambling talk. Studs didn't listen, and only heard the end, when Kenny said:

"And I said I'm from Tirty-turd and de tracks, see, an' I lives on de top floor ob de las' house on de left-hand side of de street, and deres a skull an' crossbones on de chimney, and blood on de door, and my back yard's de graveyard for my dead."

Studs laughed, because you had to laugh when Kenny pulled his gags. Kenny was a funny guy. He ought to be in vaudeville, even if he was still young.

"Well, Lonigan, you old so-and-so, what's happening?"

"It's dead as a doornail, you old sonofabitch," Studs said.

Kenny looked at Studs; he told him not to say that; he cried:

"Take that back!"

"What's eatin' you?"

"Nothing'. But I don't care if you're kiddin' or not. I love my mother, and she's the only friend I got, and if I was hung tomorrow, she'd still be my mother, and be at my side forgivin' me, and I can't stand and let anybody call her names, even if it's kiddin'; and I don't care if you are Studs Lonigan and can fight, you can't say anything about my mother," Kenny said. He drew back a step, wiped the tears from his face with his shirt sleeve, and picked up a wooden slab that lay on the sidewalk.

Studs looked questioningly at Kenny, who stood there nervously clenching and unclenching his free fist, determined, his face ready to break into tears at any moment.

"Hell, Kenny! I was only kiddin'. I take it all back," said Studs.

They faced each other, and in a minute or two the incident was forgotten. Kenny became his old self.

"It's too hot, or we could go raidin' ice boxes. But I don't feel like much effort today," Kenny said.

"Let's go swimmin'," suggested Studs.

"O.K.," said Kenny.

"All right. I'll get my suit and meet you here in twenty minutes," said Studs.

"But I'll have to get a suit. I ain't got none," said Kenny.

"Whose will you borrow?" asked Studs.

Kenny winked.

"What beach'll we go to?" asked Studs.

"Fifty-first Street," said Kenny.

"Ain't there a lot of Jews there?" asked Studs.

"Where ain't there kikes? They're all over. You watch. First it's the hebes, and then it's the niggers that's gonna overrun the south side," Kenny said.

"And then where ull a white man go to?" asked Studs.

"He'll have to go to Africa or . . . Jew-rusalem," said Kenny.

Kenny sang Solomon Levi with all the sheeny motions, and it was funny, because Kenny was funny, all right, and could always make a guy laugh.

Afterward Studs said:

"If we go to Jackson Park, it might be better."

"There's Polacks there," said Killarney.

"Well, how about Seventy-fifth Street beach?" asked Studs.

"It's O.K. But listen, sometimes Iris is at Fifty-first."

"That's a different story. I got to meet this here Iris," said Studs.

"Yeh," said Kenny.

"I hope she's there."

"She's sweet. Boy, she's just UMMMMMMMMMMM-MMMMMM," said Kenny.

"Is she really good?" asked Studs.

"Best I ever had," said Kenny like he was an older guy with much experience.

"Well, I'm going to be a disappointed guy if she ain't," said Studs.

"But listen! Don't work so fast. Suppose she don't give you a tumble. Sometimes she gets temperment, and then she's no soap until some guy she gets a grudge against beats it . . . She's like a primadonna," said Kenny.

"I thought she was like a sweetheart of the navy," Studs said.

"Well, sometimes she is and sometimes she isn't."

"Yeah. But anyway, you just lead me to her," boasted Studs.

"Well, at that, you're talkin' horse sense," said Kenny.

"Horsey sense," said Studs.

"Well, anyway, I got to get my suit," said Kenny.

Kenny told Studs to walk down Fifty-eighth toward Indiana.

"And when I come tearin' along, you run, too, and cut through the lot on Indiana, and down the alley, and through that trick gangway to Michigan," he added.

Studs did. In a moment, Kenny came running along, and they carried out their plan of escaping though no one was chasing them. On Michigan, Kenny pulled out the two-piece bathing suit he had copped; the trunks were blue, the top white.

"If it only fits now," he said.

They laughed together, and Studs said that Kenny had real style. Kenny laughed, and said it was nothing to cop things from drug stores. Studs told himself that Killarney was a guy, all right.

They put their suits on under their clothes at Studs'. The suit fitted Kenny. They went over to South Park and bummed rides to Fifty-first, and did the same thing along Fifty-first and Hyde Park Boulevard. They had fun on Hyde Park Boulevard. It was a ritzy neighborhood where everybody had the kale and all the men wore knickers and played tennis and golf, and all the guys were sissies. Kenny had chalked his K.K. initials all over the Fifty-eighth Street neighborhood, so he started putting mysterious K.K. signs on the Boulevard. And he kept walking on the grass, making fun of the footmen and wriggling his ears at the well-dressed women. They saw one hot dame, in clothes that must have cost a million bucks, and Kenny commented on the large breastworks she had. He spoke too loud, and she heard him. She went up in the air like a kite, and talked very indignantly about ragamuffins from the slums. When they got out of her hearing, they laughed.

The lake was very calm, and way out it was as blue as the sky on a swell summer evening. And the sun came down over it like a blessing. And they were tanned, so they didn't have to worry about getting sunburned and blistered. They ran out from the lockers with feelings of animal glee. The first touch of the water was cold, and they experienced sharp sensations. But they dove under water, and then it was warm. The lake was just right. They went out, splashing, diving under water, trying to duck each other, laughing and shouting. The diving board was crowded but they climbed up and took some dives. Kenny did all kinds of dippy dives, back flaps and rolls. The people about the diving board watched them and thought Kenny was pretty good. He started a stump-the-leader game on the board but he was too good for them, so they all lost interest.

Kenny and Studs swam out where it was cold and deep, and there was no one around them. They dove, splashed, floated, splashed, swam, snorted. They were like happy seals. Studs got off by himself and wheeled and turned over in the water like a rolling barrel. He called over to Kenny that it was the nuts. Kenny yelled back that boy it was jake. They swam breast-stroke, and it was nice and easy; then they did the crawl. They went out further. Only the lake was ahead of them, vast and blue-gray and nice with the sun on it; and it gave them feelings they couldn't describe. Studs floated, and looked up at the round sky, his head resting easy on the water line, himself just drifting, the sun firing away at his legs. It was too nice for anything. He just floated and didn't have anything to think about. He looked up at the drifting clouds. He felt just like a cloud that didn't have any bothers and just sailed across the sky. He told himself: Gee, it was a big sky. He asked himself: I wonder why God made the sky? He floated. He floated, and suddenly he liked himself a lot. Sometimes he was ashamed of his body, like when the old man came in to use the bathroom when he was taking a bath and didn't have anything on, or like on the night he graduated, when he was in bed and had a time trying to sleep. Now he liked his body, and wasn't at all ashamed of it. It moved through the water like a slow ship that just went along and didn't have any place particular to go and just sailed. About ten yards away he heard Kenny wahooing and singing about Captain Decker who sailed on the bounding main, and lost his . . . and Kenny seemed almost as far away as if he was on the other side of the lake. He splashed with his hands. Then he held his toes up and tried to wiggle them, but he got a mouthful. He turned and swam a little way, taking in a mouthful of water and holding it. He turned over and floated, spouting the water, pretending he was the most powerful whale in all the seas and oceans, floating along, minding its business, because all the sharks were leery of attacking it. He had a sudden fear that he might get cramps and drown, and he was afraid of drowning and dying, so he turned over and swam. But he wasn't afraid for long. Then he and Kenny tried to see who could stay under water the longest, and they waved in to attract attention, so people on the diving board might think they were drowning and get all excited. He dove down, imagining he was a submarine, and the water kept getting cooler, and he kept his eyes open but could only see the water, clear, all around him. He felt far away from all the world now, and he didn't care. He came up, choking for air, and it was like coming to out of a goofy dream where you are falling or dying or something. Kenny was up before him, and Studs, after he had gotten a good breath, told Kenny he wasn't so good.

"Drowning ain't my specialty. That's not my trick!" Kenny yelled back.

They swam slowly in.

When they got on the beach, they gazed about and ran all around, looking for Iris and eyeing all the women to get some good squints. Kenny said it would be swell, like heaven, if all women wore the same kinds of swimming suits that Annette Kellerman did. Studs said it would be better if they didn't wear anything. Kenny said women sometimes did go swimming without anything on. Studs said he'd give his ear to see them.

Finally, they sprawled face downward in the sand, the sun fine and warm on their backs, evaporating all the wet. They didn't talk. They just sprawled there. It was too good to talk. Studs forgot everything, and felt almost as good as when he had been by himself way out in the deep water. He just lay there and pretended that he wasn't Studs or anybody at all and he let his thoughts take care of themselves. He was far away from himself, and the slap of the waves on the shore, the splash of people in the water, all the noise and shouts of the beach were not in the same world with him. They were like echoes in the night coming from a long way off. He was snapped out of it by Kenny cursing the goddamn flies and the kids who ran scuffing sand all over everybody. Studs looked up. Then he looked out over the lake where the water and sky seemed to meet and become just nothing. He thought of swimming far, far out, farther than he and Kenny had, swimming out into the nothingness, and just floating, floating with nothing there, and no noises, no fights, no old men, no girls, no thinking of Lucy, no nothing but floating, floating. Kenny broke off his thoughts. He talked about swimming across the lake, arguing that a good life guard could swim all the way to Michigan City or Benton Harbor. Studs said that Kenny was nuts, but then he couldn't talk as fast as Killarney, so he lost the argument. Kenny just talked anyway, and it didn't matter what he talked about or make him less funny.

At six they went home, and moving along Hyde Park Boulevard, trying to bum rides and cursing everybody who passed them by, Kenny said:

"It was swell today."

"Yeh! it was swell," Studs said.

"Only I wish Iris had been there," said Kenny.

"Yeh," said Studs.

"I'm so hungry, I could eat a horse," said Kenny.

"Wouldn't it have been nice to have had her there and have her let us lay our heads in her lap, and have a feel-day, or go out with her way out, or swim around to the breakwater, where nobody was, and out there get our ashes hauled," said Studs.

"Almost as nice as eating a steak would be this very minute," said Kenny.

"Sure," said Studs.

They walked on. When Studs had been lying in the sand, he had been at peace, almost like some happy guy in a story, and he hadn't thought that way about girls, and it hadn't bothered him like it did other times, or made him do things he was ashamed of way deep down inside himself. Now his peace was all gone like a scrap of burned-up paper. He was nervous again, and girls kept coming into his mind, bothering all hell out of him. And that made him feel queer, and he got ashamed of the thoughts he had . . . because of Lucy. And he couldn't think of anything else.

At home they had steak, and Studs, like a healthy boy, forgot everything but the steak put before him.

THE JULY NIGHT leaked heat all over Fifty-eighth Street, and the fitful death of the sun shed softening colors that spread gauze-like and glamorous over the street, stilling those harshnesses and commercial uglinesses that were emphasized by the brighter revelations of day. About the street there seemed to be a supervening beauty of reflected life. The dust, the scraps of paper, the piled-up store windows, the first electric lights sizzling into brightness. Sammie Schmaltz, the paper man, yelling his final box-score editions, a boy's broken hoop left forgotten against the elevated girder, the people hurrying out of the elevated station and others walking lazily about, all bespoke the life of a community, the tang and sorrow and joy of a people that lived, worked, suffered, procreated, aspired, filled out their little days, and died.

And the flower of this community, its young men, were grouped about the pool room, choking the few squares of sidewalk outside it. The pool room was two doors east of the elevated station, which was midway between Calumet and Prairie Avenues. It had barber poles in front, and its windows bore the scratched legend, Bathcellar's Billiard Parlor and Barber Shop. The entrance was a narrow slit, filled with the forms of young men, while from inside came the click of billiard balls and the talk of other young men.

Old toothless Nate shuffled along home from his day's work.

"Hello, Nate!" said Swan, the slicker who wore a tout's gray checked suit with narrow-cuffed trousers, a pink silk shirt with soft collar, and a loud purplish tie; his bright-banded straw hat was rakishly angled on his blond head.

"Hello, Moneybags!" said Jew Percentage, a middle-aged, vaguely corpulent, brown-suited, purple-shirted guy with a cigar stuck in his tan, prosperous-looking mug.

"Hello, Nate! How's the answer to a K.M's prayer on this fine evenin'?" asked Pat Coady, a young guy dressed like a race-track follower.

"How're the house maids?" asked young Studs Lonigan, who stood with the big guys, proud of knowing them, ashamed of his size, age and short breeches.

The older guys all laughed at Young Lonigan's wise-crack. Slew Weber, the blond guy with the size-eleven shoes, looked up from his newspaper and asked Nate if he was still on the trail of the house maids.

Nate had been holding a dialogue with himself. He interrupted it to tell them that he was getting his.

Slew Weber went back to his newspaper. He said:

"Say, I see there's six suicides in the paper tonight."

"Jesus, I knew it," said Swan.

"This guy Weber is a guy, all right. All he needs to do is smell a paper, and he can tell you how many birds has croaked themselves. He's got an eagle eye fur suicides," said Pat Coady.

Nate started to talk; he said:

"Say, goddamnit, I'm tired. I'm tired, I'm gonna quit this goddamn wurk. Jesus Christ! the things people wancha tuh do. Now, today I was hikin' an order, and some old bitch without a stitch on . . ."

"Naughty! Naughty! Naughty Nate!" interrupted Percentage, crossing his fingers in a child's gesture of shame.

"She was without a stitch on, and she wants me to go an get her a pack of cigaretts, and I looks at her, and I said, I said . . . but Jesus, it was funny, because I coulda killed her with the look I gave her; but I said, I said, Lady I'm workin' since seven this mornin', and I still gotta store full of orders to deliver. Now Lady how do you expect me ever to get finished, and Lady if I go runnin' for Turkish Trophies for every one that wants 'em . . . Well, sir! Ha! Ha! She shuts up like a clam. And then I always gotta deal with these nigger maids dat keep yellin' for you tuh wipe yer feet. I said, give uh nigger an inch, and dey wants a hull mile. And my rheumatism is botherin' me again. But say you oughta see the chicken I got today . . ."

Saliva and brown tobacco juice trickled down Nate's chin.

"Well Nate, the first hundred years is the hardest," said Percentage.

"Yeh, Nate, it's a tough life it you don't weaken," said Swan.

"Say, Nate, did you ever buy a tin lizzie?" said Studs, trying to be funny like the older guys.

"Think yuh'll ever amount to much, Nate?" asked Pat Coady.

"Say, listen, when you guys is as old as me you'll be in the ground," said Nate.

"Say, I'll bet Nate's got the first dollar he ever earned," said Slew.

"And a lot more," said Pat.

Nate told them never to mind; then he started to talk of

the Swedish maid he had on the string. He poked Slew confidentially, and said that every Thursday afternoon, you know. Then he said he was getting in a new stock of French picture cards, and tried to collect in advance, but they told him to bring them around first.

A girl passed, and they told Nate there was something for him. Nate turned and gaped at her with a moron's excited eyes.

Percentage told Nate he had a swell new tobacco which he was going to let him try. Nate asked the name and price. Percentage said it was a secret he couldn't reveal, because it was not on the market yet, but he was going to give him a pipeful. He asked Nate for his pipe, and Nate handed him the corncob. Percentage held the pipe and started to thumb through his pockets. He winked to Swan, who poked the other guys. They crowded around Nate so he couldn't see, and got him interested in telling about all the chickens he made while he delivered groceries. Percentage slipped the pipe to Studs, and pointed to the street. Studs caught on, and quickly filled the pipe with dry manure. Percentage made a long funny spiel, and gave the pipe to Nate. The guys had a hell of a time not laughing, and nearly all of them pulled out handkerchiefs. Studs felt good, because he'd been let in on a practical joke they played on someone else; it sort of stamped him as an equal. Nate fumbled about, wasting six matches trying to light the pipe. He cursed. Percentage said it was swell tobacco, but a little difficult to light, and again their faces went a-chewing into their handkerchiefs. Nate said they must all have colds. Nate said that whenever he had a cold he took lemon and honey. Percentage said that once you got this tobacco going, it was a swell smoke, and all the colds got suddenly worse.

Nate shuffled on, trying to light his pipe and talking to himself.

Percentage took Studs through the barber shop and back

into the pool room to wash his hands. Studs said hello, casually, to Frank who always cut his hair; Frank was cutting the hair of some new guy in the neighborhood, who was reading the *Police Gazette* while Frank worked. The pool room was long and narrow; it was like a furnace, and its air was weighted with smoke. Three of the six tables were in use, and in the rear a group of lads sat around a card table, playing poker. The scene thrilled Studs, and he thought of the time he could come in and play pool and call Charley Bathcellar by his first name. He was elated as he washed his hands in the filthy lavatory.

He came out and saw that Barney was around. Barney was a bubble-bellied, dark-haired, middle-aged guy. He looked like a politician, or something similarly important.

"Say, Barney, you think you'll ever amount to much?" asked Barlowe.

"Sure, he's something already," said Swan.

"What?"

"He's a hoisting engineer," said Swan, who accompanied his statement with the appropriate drinking gesture.

"Yeh, he's a first-class hoistin' engineer," said Emmet Kelly, one of Red's brothers.

"He hoists down a barrel of beer a week, don't you, Barney?" said Mickey O'Callaghan.

They laughed. Studs told himself that, goddamn it, they were funny all right.

"You two-bit wiseacres can mind your own business," said Barney.

They all laughed.

"But, Barney, no foolin' . . . I want to ask you a question in all sincerity," said Percentage.

"Save the effort and don't get a brainstorm, hebe," said Barney.

"Why don't you go to work?" asked Percentage.

"Times are hard, jobs are scarce and good men is plentiful," said Barney.

They all laughed.

"Well, anyway, Barney, did you get yer beers last Sunday?" asked Weber.

"Listen, brother! Them Sunday blue laws don't mean nothin' to me," said Barney.

"Nope, I guess you'd get your beer even if the Suffragettes put Prohibition down our necks," said Pat Coady.

"Why, hell! I seen him over in Duffy's saloon last Sunday, soppin' up the beers like there was no law against buyin' drinks on Sunday. He was drinkin' so much, I thought he was gonna get his false teeth drowned in beer," Barlowe said, and they all laughed.

Studs noticed the people passing. Some of them were fat guys and they had the same sleepy look his old man always had when he went for a walk. . . . Those old dopey-looking guys must envy the gang here, young and free like they were. Old Izzy Hersch, the consumptive, went by. He looked yellow and almost like a ghost; he ran the delicatessen-bakery down next to Morty Ascher's tailor shop near the corner of Calumet, but nobody bought anything from him because he had the con, and anyway you were liable to get cockroaches or mice in anything you bought. Izzy looked like he was going to have a funeral in his honor any one of these days. Studs felt that Izzy must envy these guys. They were young and strong, and they were the real stuff; and it wouldn't be long before he'd be one of them and then he'd be the real stuff.

Suddenly he thought of death. He didn't know why. Death just came into his thoughts, dripping black night-gloom. Death put you in a black coffin, like it was going to put Izzy Hersch. It gave you to the grave-diggers, and they dumped you in the ground. They shoveled dirt on you, and it thudded, plunked, plump-plumped over you. It would be swell if people didn't have to die; if he, anyway, didn't have to; if he could grow up and be big and strong and tough and the real stuff, like Barlowe was there, and never change. Well, anyway, he had a long time to go.

People kept dribbling by and the guys stood there, barbering in that funny way of theirs.

Lee came along, and the guys asked him why he was getting around so late.

"Oh, my wife invited me to stay home for supper, just for a change, and I thought I'd surprise her and accept the invitation," Lee said.

"Hey, you guys! did you get that? Did you? Lee here said his old woman asked him to come to supper, just to vary the monotony a little, and he did. He actually . . . dined with his old woman," Percentage said.

"Next think you know he'll be going to work and supportin' her," said Pat Coady.

"Jesus, that's a good one. Hey, Lee, tell me some more . . . I got lots of Irish . . . credulity," said Barney.

They laughed.

"That's a better on," said Lee, pointing to a girl whom everybody marveled at because they said she was built like a brick out-house.

"She has legs, boy," said Studs, trying to horn back into the conversation.

They didn't pay any attention to him.

"Well, I object!" said Percentage.

"Why?"

"I OBJECT!"

"Why?"

"Goddamnit, it ain't right! I tell you it ain't right that stuff like that moll be wasted, with such good men and true around here . . . I say that it is damn wanton extravagance," said Percentage.

"Hey, Percentage, you shoulda been a Philadelphia lawyer, with them there words you use," said Barlowe.

The guys laughed, and Percentage said he was the objection saw sustained.

Swan, Percentage and Coady had a kidding match about who was the best man. It was interrupted by Barney. An ugly-looking, old-maidish female passed, and Barney said to the three kidders:

"That's your speed!"

They trained their guns on Barney, and told him how dried up he was.

Another dame ambled by, and Percentage repeated his objection, and they kidded each other.

A third dame went by, and Percentage again objected.

"Them's my sentiments," said Fitz, the corner pest.

A good-looking Negress passed.

"Barney, how'd you like that?" Studs asked.

"Never mind, punk! . . . And listen, the niggers ain't as bad as the Irish," said Barney.

"Where's there a difference?" asked Percentage.

"Well, if you ask me, Barney is a combination of eight ball, mick, and shonicker," said McArdle, one of the corner topers.

"And the Irish part is pig-Irish," said Studs.

"The kid's got your number," said Percentage as they all gave Barney some more merry ha-ha's.

Studs felt grown up, all right.

Barney called Studs a goofy young punk. But they all laughed at him. Studs laughed weakly, and hated bloated-belly Barney. He told himself he'd been a damn fool for not having put on his long pants before he came out.

They hung around and talked about the heat and the

passing gals. It grew dark, and more lights flashed on. Andy Le Gare came along. He spoke to Studs, but Studs didn't answer him; Studs turned to Barlowe, and said the punk had wheels in his head. Barlowe said yeh; he remembered him in his diaper days down around Forty-seventh; but his brother George was a nice guy, and a scrapper. Studs again felt good, because Barlowe had talked to him like one equal to another. Andy stopped before Hirschfield's grocery store, and started erasing the chalked announcement. He rubbed out the lower part of the B on the brick butter announcement, and stood off to laugh in that idiotic way of his. The guys encouraged the punk. They talked about baseball. Swan spilled some gab about the races. Then he told of what he had seen at the Johnson-Willard and Willard-Moran fights. He said that Willard was a ham, and that Fred Fulton would mow him down if they ever got yellow Willard in the same ring with the Minnesotan. Studs said the Irishman Jim Coffey was pretty good. Swan said he was a cheese. He said the best of them all, better than Fulton even, was Gunboat Smith, who had the frog, Carpentier, licked that time in London or Paris or wherever they fought. They wondered what they would do, and talked about the heat. Barney suggested seeing the girlies, and they said o.k. Barlowe said he couldn't go. They asked why.

"I still got my dose," he said.

They told him it was tough, and he wanted to take care of it. Coady asked him if it was bad.

"It's started again," he said casually.

"Well, be careful," Coady said.

The other lads piled into a hack, and were off. Studs watched them go, wide-eyed with admiration and envy, and yet quite disappointed. He watched Barlowe limp down the street, a big husky guy. Then he thought of the time when he'd be able to pile into a hack and go with the lads. He thought of Barlowe. He was afraid of things like that, and yet he wished he could stand on the corner and say he had it. Well, it wouldn't be long now before he'd be the big-time stuff.

Davey Cohen, Tommy Doyle, Haggerty, Red Kelly and Killarney happened along. Killarney had a pepper cellar, and they went over to the park to look for Jews and throw pepper in their eyes. Over in the park, Studs saw a pretty nurse, and he started objecting that molls like that should walk around and not have guys taking care of them; it was a lot of good stuff gone to waste, he repeated, and the kids all laughed, because it was a good wisecrack.

STUDS AND PAULIE walked south along Prairie Avenue, eating the last of the candy. The candy came from the famous raid on Schreiber's ice cream parlor. Schreiber's place was between Prairie and Indiana on Fifty-eighth. Schreiber was a good guy, but you know he liked his nooky, and he was always mixed up with some woman or other. They caught up with him. One day when Studs was walking down Fifty-eighth Street, he saw two dicks taking the guy away. The bunch found out, through Red Kelly, whose old man was a police sergeant, that Schreiber was in on a white slavery rap. Three-Star Hennessey discovered that the back door of the candy store wasn't locked, and all the kids in the neighborhood raided the place. For five days they were filling up on sodas, having fights with ice cream and whipped cream, carting away candy. They stole wagons from little kids, and bikes, and carted the stuff to George Kahler's basement. It was a swell feed they had. Most of them couldn't eat supper for a week. But with so many hogging it, the loot didn't last as long as it should have. Anyway, it was a time to remember for your grandchildren. They talked about it, and laughed.

"Well, it's August already," Paulie said.

"Yeh, Goddamn it!"

"I wonder what school I'll go to next year?" Paulie said.

"Can't you go back to St. Patrick's?" asked Studs.

"Jesus, I don't think so. And if I did get back, they probably wouldn't pass me anyway. . . . Say, why in hell is school?" asked Paulie.

Studs shrugged his shoulders and cursed school.

"Say, why don't you bring your old lady up to see Bernadette," said Studs.

"Maybe I will. Hell, St. Patrick's gets more holidays and is out sooner in June than the public schools. Only I got bounced out of there three times already," said Paulie.

"Well, maybe you can break the record," said Studs.

"That's something," said Paulie.

They walked along. Paulie sniped a butt and lit it.

"Doesn't Iris live here?" asked Studs, pointing at a red brick, three-story building.

"Yeh, and I'd like to bump into her," Paulie said.

"Me, too," said Studs.

Studs suddenly resented Paulie. Paulie couldn't fight as well as he but got more girls, and knew what it was all about.

Iris, fourteen, bobbed-haired, blue-eyed, innocent with a sunny smile, walked out of the building. She had a body too old for her years; the legs were nice and her breasts were already well-formed.

Iris was glad to see them. Paulie asked her how was tricks. She said what tricks. Paulie said just tricks. She said he was naughty-naughty. She flung lascivious looks at them, and Studs was thrilled as he had never been thrilled by Lucy. He shifted his weight from foot to foot, and studied the sky. Then he became absorbed in his shoes. They were high ones, scuffed and dirty, very much like army shoes. Paulie asked how about it. She said her mother was home. Paulie said they could go over to the park. She said no, because she had to help her old woman clean house. She cursed her mother, glibly. Hearing a girl call her mother names was different from hearing a guy, and it shocked Studs. Paulie asked how about it. She said some other afternoon. She told Studs she especially wanted him to come and see her some time, because she had never met him before and everybody said nice things about him. She looked at him in that way of hers, and said she'd be nice to him. Then she tripped toward Fifty-fifth Street, and they watched her wriggle along. They had a discussion about the way girls wriggled along. Studs said the one who had them all beat at wriggling was Helen Borax. Paulie said Iris was no slouch though. Studs wondered if girls wriggled on purpose, and how about decent ones. He told this to Paulie, and added that he hadn't ever noticed if his sister did or not. Paulie said all girls had to wriggle when they walked, and he guessed there was nothing wrong with it. He said that anything a girl did was o.k. with him, as long as she was good-looking.

They met Weary at Fifty-eighth Street. Weary had his long jeans on. He looked at Studs; Studs sort of glowered back. Paulie suggested that it was foolish not to shake hands and settle old scores. They shook.

Studs tried to be a little friendly. He asked:

"What you been doing?"

"Workin' in an office downtown," said Weary.

"Off today?" asked Paulie.

"I took the day off, and my old lady got sore and yelled at me. I had a big scrap with the family. The gaffer was home and he tried to pitch in, too, and my sister Fran, she got wise. They noticed that my hip pocket was bulgin' a little. And when I leaned down to pick somethin' up, they saw my twenty-two. They shot their gabs off till I got sick of listenin' to them, and I got sore and cursed them out. I told them just what they could do without mincing my words, and they all gaped at me like I was a circus. The ole lady jerked on the tears, and started blessing herself, and Fran got snotty, like she never heard the words before, and she bawled, and the old man said he'd bust my snoot, but he knew better than try it. So I tells them they could all take a fast and furious, flyin', leapin' jump at Sandy Claus, and I walks out, and I'll be damned if I go home. Maybe I might try stickin' somebody up," he said.

They were shocked, but they admired Weary tremendously. They acted casual and gave him some advice. He showed them his rusty twenty-two, and said he needed bullets. Paulie said it might be a little dangerous carrying a loaded gat around, but Weary didn't care. Studs wished that he could walk dramatically out of the house like Weary did; he told himself that he might some day. Paulie asked Weary what he'd been doing, and Weary said he had been hangin' out at White City; he'd picked up a couple of nice janes there. One of them was eighteen and didn't live at home, and wanted him to live with her. They looked at Weary. Weary was a real adventurous kid, after all was said and done, even if he was something of a bastard. Suddenly Weary left, walking toward Fifty-seventh. They watched him. He met a girl . . . it was Iris . . . and the two of them disappeared in her entrance way.

"Well, I say she's no good," Studs said.

"Well, I'll be damned," said Paulie, scratching his head.

They looked at each other, knowingly, expressing with their faces what even the lousiest words they could think of to call Iris couldn't express.

"Some day I'm gonna up and bust that jane right in her snoot," said Paulie.

"And a guy I licked . . . I ought to hang a couple more on him," Studs said.

"Yeh," said Paulie.

Studs wished to hell there were more swear words in the list so he could use them to curse the world.

CARL SANDBURG

Chicago

HOG BUTCHER for the World,
Tool Maker, Stacker of Wheat,
Player with Railroads and the Nation's Freight
Handler;
Stormy, husky, brawling,
City of the Big Shoulders:

They tell me you are wicked and I believe them, for I have seen
your painted women under the gas lamps luring the

"Chicago," the intensely patriotic excerpt from Carl Sandburg's Chicago Poems, *reveals the passion with which the poet regarded his city. A self-styled hobo, Sandburg strived to capture the roaming, untamed spirit of America on paper. He is noted for saying that he would be found on his deathbed trying to compose a poem about his nation.*

farm boys.
And they tell me you are crooked and I answer: Yes, it is true I
have seen the gunman kill and go free and kill again.
And they tell me you are brutal and my reply: On the faces of
women and children I have seen the marks of wanton hunger.
And having answered so I turn once more to those who sneer at this
my city, and I give them back the sneer and say to them:
Come and show me another city with lifted head singing so proud
to be alive and coarse and strong and cunning.
Flinging magnetic curses amid the toil of piling job on job, here
is a tall bold slugger set vivid against the little soft cities;
Fierce as a dog with tongue lapping for action, cunning as a savage
pitted against the wilderness,

Bareheaded,
Shoveling,
Wrecking,
Planning,
Building, breaking, rebuilding,

Under the smoke, dust all over his mouth, laughing with white teeth,
Under the terrible burden of destiny laughing as a young man laughs,
Laughing even as an ignorant fighter laughs who has never lost a battle,
Bragging and laughing that under his wrist is the pulse, and under his
ribs the heart of the people,
Laughing!
Laughing the stormy, husky, brawling laughter of Youth, half-naked,
sweating, proud to be Hog Butcher, Tool Maker, Stacker of Wheat,
Player with Railroads and Freight Handler to the Nation.

CLARENCE DARROW

The Loeb-Leopold Tragedy

IN THE SUMMER of 1924 I was called into the defense of the Loeb-Leopold case in Chicago. Few cases, if any, ever attracted such wide discussion and publicity; not only in America, but anywhere in the world. Two boys, named Richard Loeb, who was seventeen years old, and Nathan Leopold, eighteen years old, were indicted for murder. Both were sons of wealthy families, well known and highly respected in Chicago and elsewhere.

A young boy, named Robert Franks, fourteen years old, had disappeared on his way home from school. He did not return that night, and the parents were greatly alarmed over his absence. The next day the father received a letter saying that his

---

As the legendary defense attorney for the Scopes trial, Clarence Darrow protected the right to teach a secular, Darwinian view of creation. This excerpt, from his autobiography, The Story of My Life, *recounts his involvement with another famous trial: the Loeb-Leopold murder.*

son was safe and would be returned on the payment of a ransom of ten thousand dollars. The letter contained explicit directions as to how the money should be delivered. Mr Franks was to put it in a package, stand on the rear platform of a certain train leaving Chicago about four o'clock that afternoon, and throw the money off at a lonely spot near a grain-elevator south of Englewood. Mr. Franks went to the bank for the money and was preparing to go to the train when the afternoon papers printed a story about the discovery of a dead boy lying naked in a culvert under a railroad crossing some twenty miles south of the city. Everything led to the belief that it was Robert Franks. The information was telephoned to the Franks home, and the father felt satisfied that the poor boy was his son, and he really was.

Before going to the place on the prairie where the money was to be delivered, both Loeb and Leopold saw the story in the papers, so, of course, they did not go after the money. The authorities immediately began an investigation. A number of suspects were brought in within a few days and put through strict grillings, as is usual in cases of murder. Two or three of these were seriously injured in their standing, and suffered notoriety and loss of positions from which they have never recovered, although wholly innocent of the charge.

In the inspection of the place and surroundings where the dead boy was discovered, a pair of eyeglasses was found. The oculist who sold them was traced, and he stated that he never sold but two pairs just like that—one of these purchasers was now in Europe, so obviously he could not have been in any way connected with the crime; the other customer was a young man named Nathan Leopold. The Leopold home was near the Franks residence. These two families and the Loeb family had been neighbors and friends for years. Young Leopold was a graduate of the University of Chicago and was then in his second year of the law course in that university. He was to leave for Europe in a few days. This trip had been planned for some time. His father had given him the money for this summer vacation, and the tickets were purchased.

The eyeglasses having been sold to Nathan Leopold, the State's attorney sent for him and questioned him as to his whereabouts that night. Leopold answered everything that was asked, saying that on that night he and Loeb were automobiling in the parks and the country around Chicago, driving Leopold's car. No one in the State's attorney's office or anywhere else had the slightest idea that Leopold could possibly be involved in the case, but out of prudence it was thought best to hold him a short time for further investigation. The boy, after advising with his father and Mr. Benjamin Bachrach, consented to this, the two older men having not the faintest suspicion that young Leopold had anything whatever to do with the affair.

The next day the officers sent for Richard Loeb and asked him about that evening; he said he did not remember where he was, but thought that he and Leopold went driving, but could not tell where they went. It seemed to have been agreed that if anything happened and they were arrested within a week they should tell their pre-arranged story, as afterwards told by Leopold; but if arrested after that they were to say that they did not remember where they drove. As fate would have it, Nathan was arrested before the week was over, and Loeb after its expiration. Still, the officers did not lay any stress on the variance in their statements. Both boys were of wealthy families and always had plenty of money; no one could think of any possible motive for committing such a deed. It occurred to one of the officers, however, to send for Leopold's chauffeur and question him. The chauffeur said that Leopold's car was not used that night; that it was in the garage for repairs. This story was easily verified, and the boys were questioned further. In a day or two they broke down and confessed and told their story with all its ghastly details. The clothes were taken off the Franks boy so that identity might not be disclosed; some of them were placed in the lagoon in Jackson Park; some of them were buried; and some were burned. The boys were taken to all the places covered by their route, including the place where the clothes were buried, and their story was fully corroborated by what was found.

It seemed that Loeb had gotten it into his head that he could commit a perfect crime, which should involve kidnapping, murder, and ransom. He had unfolded his scheme to Leopold because he needed some one to help him plan and carry it out. For this plot Leopold had no liking whatever, but he had an exalted opinion of Loeb. Leopold was rather undersized; he could not excel in sports and games. Loeb was strong and athletic. He was good at baseball and football, and a general favorite with all who knew him. Both of them always had money. Loeb had two thousand dollars in cash, a number of Liberty Bonds whose coupons had not been cashed, and a standing order to draw money whenever he wanted it by asking the cashier at his father's office.

Several times there was trouble between the boys about going on with their plan. At one time their correspondence, offered in evidence, and published by the press, revealed that they nearly reached the point of open breach, and extreme violence.

When their plans were actually completed they arranged to get a car from a renting office, and Leopold, under another name, was to refer to Loeb, also under another name, as reference for the expense and safe return of the car. Loeb's assumed name was given as that of a resident of the Hotel Morrison, where he had rented a room and deposited a valise in which there happened to be a book drawn by him from the University of Chicago Library.

Before this they had written the ransom letter. This was addressed "Dear Sir," as they had no idea whose boy would be taken and to whom the letter would be mailed.

Around four o'clock one afternoon they got into the car, drove within a few squares of Loeb's home, along one of the best residence districts of Chicago, over to a private school that Loeb had formerly attended, arriving there just as the afternoon session was over and the boys were coming out. One after another was surveyed by the boys in the car until poor Robert Franks came along. He was invited into the car for a ride; he got into the front seat with Leopold, who was driving; and within ten minutes he was hit on the head by a chisel in the hands of Loeb, was stunned by the blow, and soon bled to death. All this happened in a thickly populated section of Chicago and close to the homes of all three of the boys.

The car was then driven slowly for twenty miles through the main streets and parts of the south side of the city, solidly built up and congested with automobiles going in all directions. It was summertime; the afternoons were long and evenings late. Leopold was a botanist and a lover of birds. He had often been in that far section gathering flowers and catching birds; he had a rare collection and was creating a museum for himself; he had mounted the birds with great skill, and many of them were very valuable. During these excursions he had become thoroughly familiar with that out-of-the-way locality and remembered the culvert under the railroad tracks, which could be reached only by an unfrequented road. When they got into that vicinity the sun had not yet disappeared, so they drove for an hour or two waiting for the twilight to fade into deeper darkness. Then they placed the boy in the culvert and drove away.

When they got back to town they took out the ransom letter and addressed it to Mr. Jacob Franks, the father of the boy that they had left out in the country. They then went to a restaurant, ate a hearty meal, and drove to Leopold's home. This residence was in a well-settled block next door to a large apartment building. The boy was killed in the rented car and it was soaked with blood, not only inside but also on the outside. They left the car standing in the street in front of the house while they went up to Leopold's room and discussed the events of the day until a late hour, when Loeb went home.

In the morning after the killing Loeb came back to Leopold's home. They took the car into the garage and washed it as best they could, but did not remove all the stains, as the evidence brought out. When the car was dry, Leopold took it back to the agency where he had hired it.

Loeb is a good-natured, friendly boy. I realize that most people will not be able to understand this, and perhaps will not believe it. Some may remember Daniel Webster's address to a jury in a murder case. He pictured the accused: his low brow, his murderous eye, his every feature loudly proclaimed him a fiend incarnate. One would suppose from Daniel Webster's foolish argument that the defendant would be recognized as a murderer wherever he went. A part of this tirade was published in the old school-reader, and we used to "speak" it on the last day of the term. We youngsters wondered why the Lord needed to put a mark on Cain's brow, for after reading Daniel Webster's recipe we could go out on the street and pick out killers everywhere, for all seemed to be marked. But Daniel Webster was not a psychologist; he was a politician and an orator, and that was enough for one man.

"Dicky" Loeb was not only a kindly *looking* boy but he *was* and *is* a kindly boy. He was never too busy to personally do a favor for any one that he chanced to know. There was no reason why he should be put into prison for life excepting for the strange and unfortunate circumstances that might not occur again in a thousand years.

Leopold had not the slightest instinct toward what we are pleased to call crime. He had, and has, the most brilliant intellect that I ever met in a boy. At eighteen he had acquired nine or ten languages; he was an advanced botanist; he was an authority on birds; he enjoyed good books. He was often invited to lecture before clubs and other assemblages; he was genial, kindly, and likeable. His father was wealthy, and this son was his great pride. Every one prophesied an uncommon career for this gifted lad. He is now in prison for life for the most foolish, most motiveless, act that was ever conceived in a diseased brain by his boon companion.

Leopold had scarcely seen Robert Franks before the fatal day. Loeb had played tennis with him and they were good friends. Why, then, did these two boys commit this rash and horrible deed? I presume they know less about the reason than others who have studied the case and the boys well. There are many things that human beings cannot understand, and of all the fathomless questions that confront and confuse men, the most baffling is the human mind. No one can tell what will be the outcome of any life. To quote Oscar Wilde:

> "For none can tell to what Red Hell
> His sightless soul may stray."

The terrible deed had been committed. The two boys were in the shadow of the gallows; their confession had been made; their families were in the depths of despair, and they came to me to assist the lawyers already employed. My feelings were much upset; I wanted to lend a hand, and I wanted to stay out of the case. The act was a shocking and bizarre performance; the public and press were almost solidly against them.

In a terrible crisis there is only one element more helpless than the poor, and that is the rich. I knew then, and I know now, that except for the wealth of the families a plea of guilty and a life sentence would have been accepted without a contest. I knew this, and I dreaded the fight.

No client of mine had ever been put to death, and I felt that it would almost, if not quite, kill me if it should ever happen. I have never been able to read a story of an execution. I always left town if possible on the day of a hanging. I am strongly—call it morbidly, who will—against killing. I felt that I would get a fair fee if I went into the case, but money never influenced my stand one way or the other. I knew of no good reason for refusing, but I was sixty-eight years old, and very weary. I had grown tired of standing in the lean and lonely front lines facing the greatest enemy that ever confronted man—public opinion.

But, I went in, to do what I could for sanity and humanity against the wave of hatred and malice that, as ever, was masquerading under its usual nom de plume: "Justice."

DAVID MAMET

The Museum of Science and Industry Story

A helicopter shot of the Museum of Science and Industry.

MUSEUM GUIDE (*voice over*): . . . between the South Side community of Hyde Park, and Lake Michigan; a Recreation, an Educational experience, a Monument to Humankind's struggle to Rise from the Muck and Goo, and get the upperhand over its environment . . .

(*A shot of the foyer of the museum, by the main doors. The* MUSEUM GUIDE *is seen ushering out a group of Japanese businessmen, to whom he has been giving his lecture.* [*Their translator can be heard mumbling softly behind the lecture.*] ALBERT LITKO, *a good-looking fellow in his twenties, is seen on the upper level of*

Director, playwright, screenwriter, and Chicago native David Mamet uses the slang and banter of blue-collar Chicago neighborhoods to give his works (such as the award-winning plays American Buffalo *and* Glengarry Glen Ross*) their distinct atmosphere.*

the foyer, staring at the main doors.)

. . . Chicago's famed Museum of Science and Industry . . .

(*The* MUSEUM GUIDE *continues to usher his charges out the main doors, along with other groups and individuals, who file out toward the parking lot. It is obviously closing time. An* OLD WOMAN *leaving the museum steps on* ALBERT'S *foot.)*

OLD WOMAN: I stepped on your foot.

ALBERT: Mmmmm.

(*The* OLD WOMAN *continues on her way.)*

GUIDE: . . . home of the famous Two-Speed Clock; The Living Cantaloupe; . . . The U-505 Submarine (the First Foreign Man of War captured on the High Seas in a Coon's Age) . . .

(*The* GUIDE *continues as voice over,* ALBERT *is seen to leave his vantage point and move to the public telephones.)*

. . . Planes, Trains, all sorts of Weird Objects, various Exhibits, a Huge model Railroad, and stuff too numerous to mention; open most of the time to one and all, and now bidding you, each and every one, from the citizens of Chicago, to the denizens of famed Nippon, a fond "Sayonara."

(ALBERT *is now seated at a phone, has dialed, and listens to ringing.)*

ALBERT: Hello?

Where *are* you?

Albert.

Albert *Litko.*

(*As* ALBERT *talks we see the lights, section by section, being extinguished in the museum.)*

At the Museum.

Waiting for *you.*

Well, we *did.*

We certainly *did.*

Well, *I* thought we did.

I'm sorry, too.

At the Museum, I told you.

It's okay. What are you doing *tonight?*

Oh. (*Long pause.*)

(*The camera tracks through the upper level of the museum, shooting down at the main floor, revealing total absence of humanity, and darkness.*)

What are you doing *tomorrow* night?

Oh.

No. I'm not. I'm not.

No. Don't be silly.

No. Okay.

I . . . uh . . . look, good-bye, okay?

(*The camera returns to* ALBERT *seated at the telephone.*)

I swear I'm not hurt. On my mother's deathbed. I swear.

Okay. I will.

Okay.

Okay, good-bye.

(*The phone is obviously hung up on the other end. We hear a disconnect signal coming from the phone, which* ALBERT *still holds in his hand. A pause, then* ALBERT *utters an inchoate cry and whacks the telephone with the handset. We hear a slight "ding."* ALBERT *checks the coin return and finds out that it's his dime.*)

Ha ha ha ha ha.

(*He hangs up the phone. He gets up and starts to walk, in a controlled and dignified manner, to the doors. The camera follows behind him. He arrives at the closed doors, tries the handle. It is locked. He tries another door, he tries the last door. He finds that he is, in fact, locked in. He screams and starts pounding on the door.*)

Vixen! Siren! I give my *heart* to you, I give my *soul* to you, I get locked *in*, it's *dark* (Oh, God, I'm *such* a sucker for a kind word) . . . I'm *scared*, it *does not pay to get involved.* I don't *care*, I'm going on *record*, I've said it, and I'm glad.

(*He stops pounding and composes himself. He adjusts his clothing and starts trying to find a way out of the museum. The camera follows him walking through the main hall. As he walks he mumbles.*)

. . . safety precautions . . .

. . . inadequate *crowd* control . . .

. . . social consciousness . . .

. . . *savoir faire* . . .

. . . 'preciate me someday when I'm dead . . .

(*Over his mumbling we hear a voice singing "K. C. Moan."* ALBERT *stops and tries to identify the direction from whence the voice comes. Having identified it, he proceeds toward it. The camera follows him into the hall containing the Santa Fe model railroad. The song has now changed to "The Atcheson Topeka, and the Santa Fe."* ALBERT *follows the song around to the east end of the exhibit, and finds an old black man seated at the controls, singing. This is* RUDY. *He is dressed in traditional railroad work attire which is incredibly worn and old. He is working the controls.* RUDY *stops singing and begins shouting at the trains.*)

RUDY: 'Kay, less gettem rollin', ain't got all night. Lettem go, three cars. Three cars.

ALBERT: 'Scuse me.

RUDY: Yup?

ALBERT: I'm locked in.

RUDY: Gest you was. (*To exhibit:*) Come on, *hump* those cars.

ALBERT: Uh . . . uh, what are you doing?

RUDY: *Look* like I'm doin'? (*To exhibit:*) *Now* you talkin'. You talkin' now. Keep rollin'. (*To* ALBERT:) I'm switchin'.

ALBERT: Oh.

RUDY (*to exhibit*): Two more, two more, lettem go. (*To* ALBERT:) Stan' back there, willya, son?

ALBERT: I'm locked in here.

RUDY: I see that. (*Hands him plug tobacco.*) Have a chaw, feel better.

ALBERT: No thank you, I don't chew.

RUDY: Bes' thing in the worl', you *loss*, sit down, have a chaw, think things over.

ALBERT: I'm not lost. I'm locked in.

RUDY: 'Mounts to the same thing. You jes' here for the night, then.

ALBERT: What do you mean?

RUDY: All I mean, you jes' here for the *night*. (*To exhibit:*) Whoa! *Slow* it down, there. Ho up. Ho up. Take a break. (*To* ALBERT:) We goan take a little break here. Chaw?

ALBERT: Uh, no thank you.

RUDY: Yes *sir. Hell* of a good deal workin' indoors. Course, the *trains* are smaller . . .

ALBERT: Uh huh . . .

RUDY: But that's jes' common *sense*. You gonna work indoors, you got reglar size rollin' stock, you got to get y'self a buildin' size of I don't know *what*. Huh?

(ALBERT *nods his head.*)

Ain't so bad in here. No. You only stayin' the night, huh?

ALBERT: I got locked in.

RUDY: I been here mos' eleven years. Nigh on twelve years. Yup.

(RUDY *leaves the control board and wanders to the real locomotive located about twenty feet from same. He seats himself at the controls,* ALBERT *follows him.*)

Close on twelve years. (*Pause.*) Pensioned off in Sixty, Ruth died Sixty . . . uh . . Sixty-Two. . . wandered in here one day . . .

Nineteen and Sixty-Three. I think I'm going to sing here.

(Rudy *sings "Rudy's Song." A song of his fascination with trains since boyhood . . . of his wish to be an engineer . . . of his youth working in Pullman cars . . . of his working as a fireman . . . of his wife, their marriage, their children . . . of his compulsory retirement, the death of his wife, and his old age. He finishes the song.*)

Yup.

Albert: And so now you work for the Museum now? You work for the Museum Railroad?

Rudy: I'm not an idiot, son. I'm *old*, but I got my senses intack. The Museum don't got a *railroad*, what the Museum got, the Museum got a *model* railroad.

Albert: Yes.

Rudy: Well, it's apparent. An' I doan work *for* them . . .

Albert: No?

Rudy: No, I jes' kind of . . . *work* here. I mean, what for they goan pay someone good cash come in here switch all the *rollin'* stock at night? It's a useless expenditure their part. Huh?

Albert: I suppose so.

Rudy: No supposin' in it. It's outright featherbedding. (An' I have been a Union Man all my life, y'unnerstand, but some things I do not hold with.)

Albert: Uh-huh.

Rudy: What I mean, a man has got to have his *pride* (This is common knowledge). You stick him on a job he doan *do* nothin' . . . I mean, you stick him on a job he doan *do* nothin' all day long, all day long he got nothin' to *do*. (You see what I'm sayin'?)

Albert: Yes.

Rudy: An' in the same spirit, you take a man, prime of his life, not a goddamned thing in the *worl'* the matter with him, an' you tell him to punch out, go home, doan come back . . . well, I doan got to *tell* you what *this* is. (*Pause.*) So, in answer to your question, no, I do not work for the Museum, as any fool can plainly see.

ALBERT: Oh.

(*Pause.*)

RUDY: I free-lance.

ALBERT: Can you help me get outta here?

RUDY: What?

ALBERT: I want to go home.

RUDY: Doan you *go* home, then?

ALBERT: The Museum is locked.

RUDY: Doan you *relax*, then? (See what I'm sayin'?) Come on, I'm goan take a break anyway. See if we can't get you out of here.

(*They leave the Santa Fe exhibit, and walk toward the Harvester Farm.*)

You ever live in the country?

ALBERT: No. We lived in the *suburbs* a little.

RUDY: Ain't the same thing.

(*A huge war cry is heard, and a boomerang narrowly misses* RUDY'*s head.*)

(*Loudly*): Sonsabitches.

PIERRE (*voice over*): Get you next time.

RUDY: Hell you say. (*He picks up boomerang. To* ALBERT:) Sonofabitch can't even get the goddam thing come *back*.

(*They walk on.*)

Born an' *raised* in the country. Yup. Doan tell *me* 'bout country life. Uh-*uh. Hate* it in the country. Got out firs' chance I got.

(*They approach the farm.*)

Smoke, noise, *action*, some kine *movement* . . . you see what I'm gettin' at?

ALBERT: Yes.

RUDY: You hungry?

ALBERT: I . . . uh . . . a little. I'm a bit confused.

RUDY: You wan' a chaw?

ALBERT: No thank you.

(*They come upon a pastoral scene at the farm [appropriately enough]. Six or eight aged hippies dressed in denim overalls and grown a bit paunchy [perhaps led by Bruce Vilanch] are seated at a table covered with dishes full of candy bars, Twinkies, etc., and pitchers of Pepsi.* JOHN, *the leader of the farmers, approaches* RUDY *and* ALBERT.)

JOHN: Rudy.

RUDY: Evenin', John.

JOHN: Who's your friend?

RUDY: *Frien'* of mine.

ALBERT: Albert Litko, I got locked in.

JOHN: Glad to meet you.

ALBERT: Likewise.

JOHN: Sit down, sit down.

(ALBERT *sits down.*)

Make yourself at home, any friend of Rudy's is always welcome.

RUDY: Glad to hear you say that, John.

JOHN: Wouldn't say it if I didn't mean it.

RUDY: That so?

JOHN: Yes. (*To* ALBERT:) Dig in, dig in. Bet you aren't used to country food, eh?

ALBERT: No.

JOHN: No two ways about it. No substitute for it. Eh, Rudy?

RUDY: *Hate* the country.

JOHN: Cloris! Cloris, bring these boys some milk. (*To* ALBERT:)

Never too old for milk.

(CLORIS, *an attractive woman in her early thirties, decked out in hippie farm fashion, appears with a pitcher full of Pepsi.* CLORIS *pours a glass of Pepsi for* ALBERT.)

ALBERT: This is not milk.

JOHN: I know that.

ALBERT: This is Pepsi.

JOHN: Of course it's Pepsi. If you only use the common sense God gave you you will see that yonder cows are about as fradulent as they could ever *be*. They're made of *wood*. They cannot *give* milk. We *know* this.

RUDY: Can't *get* milk from a cow like that.

ALBERT: I see that.

RUDY: Only thing you get is disappointed.

ALBERT: I can see that.

JOHN (*To* ALBERT): Would you please pass the milk pitcher. (ALBERT *does so; to assembled* FARMERS:) Friends, I think it would not be inappropriate at this point to offer a small display of gratitude for this meal which we enjoy.

(*The* FARMERS *stop and sing "The Farmers Song." The song of how good it is to get back to the land and discover one's roots and embrace nature. When they finish their song,* ALBERT *pulls* RUDY *aside and interrogates him.*)

ALBERT: Who are these people?

RUDY: Farmers. Live in the Farm.

ALBERT: Uh, where do they come from?

RUDY: Mostly they folk wander over from the University Chicago, side to stay.

ALBERT: What are they *doing* here?

RUDY: They farmin'. That one he puts bunches of knots in string, and they got a girl signed to make up poems 'bout the reaper.

They real into handicraft.

(JOHN *rises and sings "The Song of the Arid Intellectual Life." The following dialogue takes place in back of his first chorus:*)

ALBERT: But they can't live off *farming.*

RUDY: They live off th' vending machines downstairs.

ALBERT: Oh.

RUDY: See, you got John a little mad, talkin' bout the milk. Milk machine's buss, so they got to drink Pepsi.

ALBERT: Oh.

(JOHN *finishes "The Song of the Arid Intellectual Life," and sits down to the approbation of his comrades.*)

RUDY: Real well sung, John.

JOHN: I'm glad you think so. (*To* ALBERT:) So, what do *you* think?

ALBERT: I'm locked in.

JOHN (*as to some novelty*): Oh!

ALBERT: Could you help me get out?

JOHN: It would be my pleasure to.

RUDY: Please pass the Twinkies.

ALBERT: Thank you.

JOHN: Not at all. Cloris!

(CLORIS *appears.*)

CLORIS: John?

JOHN: This is . . .

ALBERT: Albert Litko.

(CLORIS *nods.*)

JOHN: Albert has been locked in . . .

CLORIS: Uh huh . . .

JOHN: And would like to be shown the way out.

CLORIS: Glad to do it.

JOHN (*rising*): You're in good hands.

ALBERT: I'm sure. I, uh, well . . . (*He rises and moves to* CLORIS. *To* RUDY:) Well, it's been a pleasure meeting you.

RUDY (*rising from his plate*): Likewise.

(CLORIS *begins to lead* ALBERT *out of the museum. As they move away from the table and into the darkened museum we hear the eating noises of the* FARMERS *in the background:* "Anybody want a Snickers?" *etc.*)

ALBERT: Someone threw a boomerang at us earlier.

CLORIS: Goddamn Potawatamies.

ALBERT: Oh. Does, uh, does anybody know you people are in here?

CLORIS: Well, of course.

ALBERT: Oh.

CLORIS: We are not loafers, we are not moochers. We are not here at the whim of some demented officialdom. We perform a useful agrarian function.

ALBERT: Yes?

CLORIS: Yes. Many things. We, uh . . . we polish the *cows* . . . *Many* things . . .

(*As they walk past the entrance to the coal mine they hear singing. They see a group of old men [some in wheelchairs] clustered around the entrance, and before them, on a soapbox, is* TIMMY, *a seventy-year-old man dressed in the style of the thirties. He has on baggy pants, suspenders, a shirt with the collar detached, and a battered felt hat on the back of his head. He is trying to lead the men before him in a rendition of* "*Miner's Life.*")

ALBERT: What's that?

CLORIS: Miners' meeting.

ALBERT: Could we watch for a minute?

CLORIS: You're the guest.

(*They stop and listen. The song is finished, and* TIMMY *starts to speak.*)

TIMMY: World's full of freeloaders, friends: "Lemme see what the Union's going to do for me." Full of fellas kind enough bet on a sure thing came in yesterday. Well, friends, this does not work. This ain't going to make you *happy*, and it ain't going to make you *strong*, and it ain't going to build a *Union*, and there's no way in the *world* it will. No sir. You don't get strong unless you do the work yourself . . . it's the same if you're down at the *face*, and it's the same if you're on a picket line. Brothers, here's how you get strong: (*Espies* CLORIS.) Evening, Cloris.

CLORIS: Evening, Timmy.

(*The* MINERS, *severally, say hello to* CLORIS, *she acknowledges them.*)

TIMMY (*to* CLORIS): Where was I?

CLORIS: Right before "You get strong if you *are* strong."

TIMMY: Thank you. (*To* MINERS:) Friends, you get strong if you *are* strong . . . (*To* CLORIS:) Who's your friend?

ALBERT: Albert Litko, I got locked in.

CLORIS: I'm getting him out.

TIMMY (*confidentially, to* CLORIS:) Nice lookin' fella.

CLORIS: Not bad.

TIMMY (*To* ALBERT): Timmy O'Shea.

ALBERT: Pleased to meet you.

(*They shake hands.*)

TIMMY: Rest of the group: Lars Svenson, Bo Lund, Stosh Zabisco . . . feller in the funny hat's named Harry.

HARRY: Hiya, Pal.

ALBERT: Hi.

TIMMY (*to* ALBERT): Why don't you sit *down* a minute. Holdin' a meeting.

ALBERT: Well, thanks, but we're kind of . . . uh, what Union do you work for?

TIMMY: Don't work for any union. *Used* to work for the U.M.W. of A. Now, I'm on a pension, same's these fellas here. Siddown. (*To* MINERS:) Friends:

ALBERT: Do you guys actually mine coal in here?

TIMMY: Nope. All show. Miners're real, though.

STOSH: Goddam right.

TIMMY: Known Stosh all my life. Grew up together.

ALBERT: And he never joined the Union?

STOSH: Joined the Union 1928. Mass Meeting. John L. on the Dais. Never forget it. Fought all m'life. Dug, fought . . .

ALBERT: You're a Union member?

BO: Ve vas *all* Union.

ALBERT: But, then, what's the lecture for?

TIMMY: Pass the time . . . old times . . . bringing back old times. Just passing the time . . .

BO: Ve vas *all* in de Union.

ALBERT: And, uh, what do you do in the Museum now?

TIMMY: Reminisce.

ALBERT: Ah.

TIMMY: Yup.

HARRY: We're doin' a little rem*inis*cin'. Ain't been inside a mine, 1952. 'Tober fourth, 1952. Worked 21 years in the mines.

(TIMMY *starts to sing "The Song of the Thirties." The song of the Depression, the little steel strike, and violent labor troubles, Ethiopia, Spain, the Lincoln Brigade.*)

Yup. Had things happen to me you wouldn't believe. Seen things *I* didn't believe. West Virginia . . . Pennsylvania . . . spent sixty-two hours once in a four-foot seam . . .

(*The* MINERS *join* TIMMY *in song.*)

LARS: Feller must share de action and excitement of his time, on pain of having been judged not to have lived. Oliver Vendell Holmes, a great American.

TIMMY (*to* ALBERT): What do *you* do?

ALBERT: Well, I'm out of work right now.

HARRY: No shame in that.

ALBERT: No.

HARRY: Might as well be, though, huh?

ALBERT: Yes.

TIMMY: You know anything about organizing? I like the way you look.

ALBERT: Well, no, I uh . . . I'm *flattered* but . . . I really should be getting . . . home.

TIMMY: Wide-open *field* . . .

ALBERT: Uh, no, I uh . . . I mean, my father was a Republican.

HARRY: He outta work?

TIMMY: Well, if you ever change your *mind* . . .

ALBERT: Yes. Thank you. Thank you very much.

(*A tableau. Both groups, obviously taken with each other, are loathe to part.*)

Well I guess we really should be getting on.

(ALBERT *and* CLORIS *start to walk away.*)

HARRY: You take it easy now, Brother.

ALBERT: You, too, it's a pleasure to have met you.

(*As they walk away the voice of* TIMMY *haranguing the* MINERS *can be heard.* TIMMY *shouts after* CLORIS.)

TIMMY: Cloris, where was I?

CLORIS: "The way to get strong is to be strong."

TIMMY: Right. (*To* MINERS:) The way to get strong is to *be* strong.

Country wasn't founded by a bunch of sissies: "What's in this for *me*" . . . founded by a bunch of men and women not afraid to take a chance . . . (*His voice fades out.*)

ALBERT: What nice guys.

CLORIS: You said it.

ALBERT: And you support them, huh?

CLORIS: They support us.

(*Their stroll takes them through the turn-of-the-century street.*)

'Member you got a boomerang thrown at you?

ALBERT: Yes. I do.

CLORIS: Potawatamies. Neo-Potawatamies. Bunch of nowhere creeps. Trying to knock off Rudy.

ALBERT: Why?

CLORIS: For his pension check. Everybody in here lives off the pension checks of the old folks.

ALBERT: Oh.

CLORIS: So prices go up and Pierre and his Neo-Potawatamies come up with the bright idea that if we whack out the old folks and take their checks, there's more food for the lot of us.

ALBERT: That's terrible.

CLORIS: The terrible thing is that Pierre has been talking with John and the Farmers, trying to get their help getting rid of the old folks . . .

ALBERT: (Senior citizens.)

CLORIS: (We just call 'em old folks) . . . and John is starting to come around.

ALBERT: No.

CLORIS: Yes. Pierre comes in there with all this garbage about Survival of the Fittest, Natural Selection, The Law of Life, and so on, and the Farmers listen. (You can convince an intellectual of anything, ever notice that?) (*Pause.*) It's terrible. I mean, growing old is no joke . . .

ALBERT: No . . .

CLORIS: But it's not a *crime*, huh? How you going to beat Entropy? It's a surefire losing proposition. (*Pause.*) Had a guy used to live here, used to be the office boy for Robert Todd Lincoln. Used to tell us stories Robert Todd told him, his father told him. I mean, we're talking about the transmission of infor*ma*tion, here.

ALBERT: Yes.

CLORIS: I mean, we're talking about *real* history here. (You don't get close with the old people, who's going to tell you about life, Nevins and Commager?) What are you going to do when *you* get up there, jump off a building? It's very adolescent.

ALBERT: Uh huh.

CLORIS: Best goddamn organizer in the Country. John L. treated him like a son. *I'm* glad to have him here. (Sonofagun knows a lot of *songs*.) Goddamn Potawatamies should be ashamed of themselves. What kind of a society is frightened of its history? (*Pause.*)

ALBERT: I like the way you talk.

(CLORIS *shrugs.*)

I like it a lot. You impress me. Would you like to come home with me?

CLORIS: I live *here*. And besides I hardly know you.

ALBERT: Oh. (*Pause.*) It's been a very rough day.

CLORIS: That doesn't necessarily mean that I should go to bed with you.

ALBERT: No, you're right. I got stood up.

CLORIS: I'm sorry.

ALBERT: I like the way you look.

CLORIS: I'm glad. (*Pause.*)

(ALBERT *sings the sad song of "The Myth of Free Love and the Myth and Reality of Promiscuity."* CLORIS *joins him. At the end of the song there is a long pause. The two look at each other.* DIETER, *a wizened man in a somewhat military-looking fatigue costume approaches. He is in his sixties.*)

DIETER: *Guten abend.*

CLORIS: *N'abend.*

ALBERT: *N'abend.*

(*Pause.*)

DIETER: Someone srew a boomerang at me.

CLORIS: They're starting.

DIETER: Zis is terrible. Terrible.

CLORIS: I know it.

DIETER: Somesing must be done.

CLORIS: The question is but what. (*To* ALBERT:) This is Dieter Gross.

ALBERT: Albert Litko.

DIETER: Enchanted.

CLORIS: He got locked inside.

DIETER: He didn't.

ALBERT: Yes, I did.

DIETER: That is too bad.

CLORIS: Dieter used to work on the U-505 submarine.

ALBERT: Yes? What, as a janitor?

DIETER: No, I vas radioman and forvard damage control. (*Pause.*)

ALBERT: When did you work on it?

DIETER: Sirty-nine srough forty-sree.

ALBERT: Oh.

DIETER: I vent home on leave, I get sick, I am separated from ze ship.

ALBERT: Oh.

DIETER: I rejoin ze ship in 1959 as Janitor at her present moorings in Chicago. In 1964 I am retired, and now I just hang out.

(ALBERT *nods.*)

CLORIS: Show him your medal, Dieter.

DIETER: Nooo.

CLORIS: Go on.

(DIETER *grudgingly and ceremoniously takes a felt pouch from his clothing, and removes a medal from it, which he shows to* ALBERT.)

ALBERT: What . . . what is it for?

DIETER: Oh, nosing special. Ze North-Atlantic. Forty-one. Nosing Special.

CLORIS: It's the Iron Cross.

DIETER: I von it on dat ship. (*Points toward submarine. Pause.*)

ALBERT: And now you just hang out here?

DIETER: Ya. I like it here. You like it here?

ALBERT: Well, uh, yes.

DIETER: I like it here. It has some assmosphere, ya?

ALBERT: Yes.

DIETER: It has some ...*weight.* Zis building is a Monument to Science.

ALBERT: Yes.

DIETER: Zis building is a Monument to Orderly Understanding, and a Stark Affront to all ze ravages of Time.

CLORIS: You think so, Dieter?

DIETER: Ya, I sink so, else I vould not live here. (I live here out of choice) . . .

ALBERT: . . . uh-huh . . .

DIETER: . . . to be close to ze ship I love . . . of course . . . and out of respect for ze larger principles on which ziz building stands.

(DIETER *sings the song of his attempts to find "A Reasonable Life." He sings of his youth in Germany, of the Depression, of the Nazis, of his life in the navy, of the end of the war. At the end of his song he turns to* ALBERT.)
So you are locked in here, eh?

ALBERT: Yes, I . . . I'm on my way out.

DIETER: Hmmm. You know Szoreau? Szoreau is in jail, Emerson comes to visit him. Emerson says "Szoreau, vat are you doing in a Museum?," Szoreau says, "Ralph, what are you doing *not* in a Museum." Ziz is how I feel.

ALBERT: But I have to get home.

(DIETER *nods. The air is rent by the screams of the* POTAWATAMIES. *The camera peeks over the second level balcony to reveal the* POTAWATAMIES, *paunchy types in Glaneagles raincoats, herding the* MINERS *with spears.*)

CLORIS (*shouting*): Pierre, you sonofabitch, you leave those men alone.

TIMMY (*shouting up*): We're alright, Honey.

(TIMMY *gets whacked on the head with a spear.*)

CLORIS (*sotto voce*): FUCKING CREEPS. (*To* ALBERT:) Come on, we gotta do something.

DIETER: I go for help to ze *landsmenschen.*

CLORIS: Good luck.

(DIETER *goes for help.*)

CLORIS (*shouting*): Dammit, Pierre, you leave those guys alone.

(CLORIS, *with* ALBERT *in tow, runs down the stairs and after the* POTAWATAMIES. *A chase throughout the museum. A reprise of "The Song of the Thirties" [as it would be sung by the Soviet Army Men's Chorus] is in the background. The chase takes them through a large part of the museum and culminates in a remote part of the first floor, where* CLORIS *and* ALBERT *encounter* PIERRE *and his* POTAWATAMIES *about to do harm to the* MINERS.)

CLORIS: Okay, Pierre, give it up.

PIERRE: This is just *dialectic*, Cloris, this is the Law of life.

CLORIS: I'll *give* you the Law of life, Pierre, pick on someone your own age, for Chrissakes.

PIERRE: It's not for nothing that we're younger than they are . . .

CLORIS: No?

PIERRE: There's a plan in this.

CLORIS: This is strongarm and robbery.

PIERRE: That's a very limited view, Cloris.

CLORIS: Well, you just let 'em alone.

PIERRE: Or you are gonna what?

(*The shouts of* DIETER *are heard.*)

CLORIS (*shouting*): Dieter! We're over here. Now you're gonna get *yours*, creep.

(DIETER *appears with the* FARMERS *behind him.*)

CLORIS (*To* JOHN): Al*right* alright alright. And about time, too. (Thank God.)

JOHN: What, uh, seems to be the trouble here?

PIERRE: Hi, John.

JOHN: Pierre.

CLORIS: They want to whack out the miners.

JOHN (*to* PIERRE): This true?

PIERRE: Yes. (*Pause.*)

JOHN: You don't, uh, really want to do that, do you, Pierre?

PIERRE: Yes.

JOHN: But, why?

PIERRE: Money.

(*A pause.* PIERRE *and the* POTAWATAMIES advance on the MINERS *brandishing blunt instruments.*)

TIMMY (*to* MINERS): Sing, boys!

(MINERS *break into "Solidarity Forever," which continues behind ensuing dialogue.*)

CLORIS: You hold it right for Chrissake there, Pierre. John. John . . . (JOHN *starts surreptitiously edging away from scene of conflict.*)

CLORIS: John, where are you going?

JOHN: Going? I'm not going anywhere.

CLORIS: Then why are you getting farther away? (*Pause.*) John? John where are you going? (*Pause.*) You can't do this, John. You come back here. You come *back* here. (CLORIS *interposes self between* POTAWATAMIES *and* MINERS. *To* FARMERS:) Douggie, Fran, Bruce, where do you think you're going with him?

JOHN: We have a social function to fulfill, Cloris, which does not encompass getting hit on the head. This is a struggle for property between two naturally opposed groups, and the intervention of our faction would be the sheerest *gaucherie*. (*Pause.*) White-collar liberalism. (*Pause.*) These people are much closer to the roots of the problem than we, Cloris. There are variables in this conflict whose *existence* we are not even aware of. (*Pause.*) The urge to acquire property is a primordial and (we may assume) in the final analysis, a *constructive* urge. (*Pause. Summoning* FARMERS:) Friends . . .

(RUDY *separates self from* FARMERS *and stands with* CLORIS.)

RUDY: That is the *lowes'* bunch of verbige I ever *did* hear. You come back here, John.

JOHN: I have a responsibility to these people (*indicating* FARMERS. *A* POTAWATAMIE *advances on a* MINER.)

POTAWATAMIE: Gimme your wallet, Gramps.

ALBERT (*to* POTAWATAMIE): Okay, okay, this has gone about far enough. Here's what we're going to do . . .

(ALBERT *gets whacked across the head with a quarterstaff. He falters.*)

CLORIS: John, I swear to God . . . you come back here.

JOHN (*reverting to a childish tone*): If they're so smart, how come they're old?

ALBERT (*to* POTAWATAMIE): Why don't you put down those things and go home?

POTAWATAMIE: We live here.

CLORIS (*to* JOHN): If *you're* so smart, how come you're living in a museum on Twinkies?

JOHN (*incensed*): What did you say?

CLORIS: You heard me.

(JOHN *screams, and runs at* CLORIS. *The* POTAWATAMIES, *sensing their bloodlust condoned, turn on the* MINERS *in force.* ALBERT *interjects self into the fray.*)

ALBERT: You leave these folks alone, you goons. (*He gets another whack in the head.*)

(*A major fight.* RUDY *is seen fighting bravely.* CLORIS *and* ALBERT *gravitate toward each other in the fray.*)

POTAWATAMIE (*eerily*): Youth is Nature's Gift to the Young!!

(*The* MINERS *continue to sing. Suddenly, the tide of battle turns so that* MINERS, RUDY, CLORIS, *and* ALBERT *find themselves in a cul-de-sac. The* POTAWATAMIES *and the* FARMERS *control the exit. All, sensing the imminence of the end, fall silent. A pause. The* POTAWATAMIES *and the* FARMERS *close in on the opposing faction.* ALBERT *unconsciously slips his arm around* CLORIS. *A pause.*)

CLORIS: John, you . . .

JOHN (*cutting her off*): Sticks and stones will break my bones, but names will never hurt me. (*Pause.*)

PIERRE (*a battlecry*): "Let's hear it for *now*!!!!"

(*All the* POTAWATAMIES *scream and run at the three friends. In their charge* ALBERT *finds himself thrust against a firedoor, which opens with his weight, and he finds himself outside the museum in an early dawn. The sounds of screaming continue within the museum.* ALBERT *pounds on the door, but his pounding is not answered.*)

ALBERT (*screaming*): Let me in. Let me in.

(*He begins to run around the museum from entrance to entrance, trying all the doors in an attempt to get in. Running around the back he trips over a pair of lovers, and says* "Sorry," *and continues running. His run finally takes him to the main* [*north*] *entrance, where we see him trying the doors. We hear someone shouting at him from the entrance drive.*)

POLICEMAN: Hey. Hey. Hey, you . . .

(ALBERT *turns and we see that he is being shouted at by a* POLICEMAN *in a patrol car.*)

The Museum doesn't open for four hours. (*To his companion officer:*) I never *seen* this.

(ALBERT *turns back to the main door and continues to pound and cry* "Let me in.")

(*His* COMPANION OFFICER, *who is sleeping with his hat over his eyes, answers him.*)

SECOND POLICEMAN: What?

POLICEMAN: I don't know . . . some kind of *culture* junkie, something . . . (*To* ALBERT:) Go home, go read a book, something.

(ALBERT *does not move.*)

Did you *hear* me? I said move on.

(*Pause.* ALBERT *reluctantly starts to walk down the stairs.*)

Okay.

(*The patrol car pulls away.* ALBERT *walks sadly down the stairs. As he walks down the stairs, a yellow schoolbus pulls up. It has about fifty Shriners in full dress regalia in it. The Shriners file out of the bus and set up on the stairs to have a formal group picture taken by a fellow with an old bellows camera and flash pan. Shooting down from the roof of the museum we see the Shriners assembled,* ALBERT *trudging toward the lone car in the parking lot* [*A 1963*

Dodge Dart]. *The flash pan goes off, the Shriners file back into the schoolbus, which pulls away, leaving* ALBERT *alone in the parking lot, trudging to his car. A helicopter shot of* ALBERT *going to his car and a voice over of a traffic report.*)

TRAFFIC REPORT: . . . smooth right up to the Junction. Eden's a little heavy between Armitage and Congress, and the Ryan, as usual, backed up from the Loop to 95th Street. And now back to Jim.

JIM THE DISC JOCKEY: Thank you. Bob, we'll have another report in fifteen, but here's one we've got a *lot* of requests for, and we're sending this out to Doug from Betty.

(*The radio plays the closing song, "The Museum of Science and Industry Story." The helicopter follows* ALBERT*'s car into South Shore Drive and traffic as he heads north. Credits super.*)

STUDS TERKEL

Lucy Jefferson, 52

When I first came from Mississippi, I was so young and ignorant. But I was freer, you know? I think I had a little bit more room to move around in than I have now. Because I think the white man wasn't so afraid then. There wasn't enough of us. There's too many of us now, I think that's what frightened him. Nobody noticed you then. You were there but nobody bothered about seeing you.

Louis Terkel was born in New York City, but soon moved to Chicago and became Studs, adopting his pseudonym from the James Farrell character. Originally trained in law, Studs became a successful actor and broadcaster with his own TV talk-show. Blacklisted and kicked off the air for sympathizing with Communism, Terkel took to the streets to tape-record the native wit of the average Joe. Division Street: America *is the first collection of these conversations.*

She lives in the low-rise Robert Brooks Housing Project on the Near West Side. Hers is described as a row house. It was neatly furnished; some pies were in the oven; there were books all over.

My supervisor once said to me, "Now Lucy, you sit out here at this desk and answer the phone. And I think you should tell me what's going on because people here say things to you that they wouldn't dare say to me. And because, after all, you're just part of the furniture." Oh boy, did I give a chuckle. Yeah. I laughed to myself and I said, now here's a chance for all the hate in the world. But you know what really happened? I felt so sorry for the poor thing. Some Negro went out to the steel mill and he shot up a lot of people, and after that—Oh, I tell ya, I'm very wicked—after that I'd take her arm and say, "Miss Pruner, I want to talk to you about somethin'." And I slammed the door and she'd freeze. I wasn't going to do anything to her, but she . . . (Prolonged laughter.) I am just telling you how wicked I am. I'm an awful louse. (Soft chuckle.)

I walk down the street, I smoke a cigarette. Well, ladies aren't supposed to do that. But I'm no lady. (Laughs.) I just have the best old time. Sometimes, it amuses, you know. When I get blue and disgusted, I go get me some beer and get cockeyed drunk, stay at home. I don't go out. I don't believe in taverns. Then you say, why the hell do you drink beer? Because I like it. There's a lot of things that I don't like.

I just don't like doles. I wouldn't accept one dime from anybody. I'm not gonna raise my children on Aid. Why should I? There's enough money in America for me to raise my children. Now one is seventeen, one is twenty-one. And I absolutely refused to accept these handouts from anybody. How am I gonna teach these children of mine what a pleasure it is in accomplishment? Do you realize what it means if I'm gonna sit here and accept this check? We can't go to the zoo because there's carfare. Everything has to be pinpointed.

We took the little money that we made, brought it home, and we said, "Okay, Melvin would count it maybe one day, Corrine would count it the next payday." And they'd say, "Okay, what are you going to do this time, mom? Does the rent have to be paid?" And I'd say, "No, not this time." "Well, then, we can go to the show?" and I'd say, "Yes, we can go to the show this time. Meet me downtown when I get off from work." I'd go to the ten-cent store when I got off from work and buy a pound of candy, mixed. I'd meet 'em at the show. We'd go in. Now this means, this is about five dollars and some cents out of this paycheck. We don't go but about every two–three months. Or maybe less. I always had a picnic basket and picnic jugs and all this junk. Because these things are essential wherein they could get around and see what is happening.

I worked at Wesley Hospital for about eleven years. As an aid in physical therapy. I worked part-time and went to school part-time, as a practical nurse. There was this woman that was very kind to me. She used to tell me, "Lucy, why don't you get on Public Aid until you can finish school. Don't let your pride stop you." Maybe I didn't realize exactly what she meant by pride. But I just—gave it up. With all the stuff attached to it, maybe that's why . . . the publicity, the degradation see?

Everybody's screaming now: Oh, these women on ADC. Why hasn't somebody told these people that they're on ADC because you gave all this money to keep from hirin' em'? Years and years ago. This didn't just start, you know. You don't keep people in a certain category for hundreds of years and expect them to come out and do all these things. For generations and generations they've been just barely making it. Now what do you expect? Plums?

Hell, we're as poor as Joseph's goat, as far as that goes.

We pinch pennies every day, but truly we don't think anything about it. When I get paid we know exactly what we're gonna eat for two weeks. I buy whatever sale is on, that's what we eat. I go to Hillman's or George's or something, whatever's on sale. Say, for instance, we're gonna make spareribs today. That's okay. We might have spareribs and sauerkraut. If the steak's cheap enough we might even have steak once in a while. But for two long weeks we know exactly what kind of meat we're gonna have. So what we do, we wrap it around, we got potatoes in the house, we got rice in the house, we got frozen vegetables in the house, so we build a meal around this thing. So far as being poor is concerned, boy I bet I got a monopoly on that. (Laughs.)

It's a very fashionable hospital, Wesley. The clientele there are usually people that's got money. To me there were fascinating. All those beautiful clothes. You know, I could dream and see myself in this role. Then naturally I continued to read, self-educated almost. This man came in one day and he suffers from a backache. He usually gets a heat and massage to the low back. He knew me and of course all the clientele called me by my first name, which I resented. But it turned out to be an asset. So he came in and said, "Lucy, what are you reading?" And I said, *The Status Seekers*. And he said, "Don't read that junk." And I said, "By the way, you're in the advertising business." I had loads of fun, loads of fun.

They call you by the first name, the students, everybody. You see, this was the policy to keep the Negro in his place. But I happened to be the kind of Negro that became controversial, because I read such things as *The American Dilemma* and I walk around with the book in my hand, see? I defied them in so many ways. I almost terrified 'em.

You know, it got so every time I got on an elevator—"What are you reading? What are you reading? What are you reading?" (Laughs.) And I'd begin to enjoy this thing, you know. I was having the best old time. I was absolutely terrifying 'em. Everybody was yelling: "Lucy, Lucy!" Maybe that's why I say, the first name, it came in very handy. Because if they hadda just said, "Jefferson," nobody probably'd ever knowed it was me. But by making this so commonplace, here's this Negro woman, every time you see her she's reading a different book. You know what I'd do? I'd go to the library and get these books, and I'd just dash back home and read these. And truly it became a game with me. I don't think I ever had more fun in my life than I had working right there.

I guess I was darn near fifty then. That's the reason why I say I was havin' a ball. I'm carrying this book by Faulkner, paperback, in my pocket you know. But this particular time I didn't realize that the heading of the book was sticking out just a little above. The students, doctors interns got on . . . "Faulkner!" (Prolonged laughter.)

What is it they're afraid of?

This is what—you are just breaking down this stereo thing that all Negroes are ignorant, they won't read, they won't do this, they won't help themselves. Once they see you're trying to do it . . . You see what? They're not really worrying so much about the Negro, they're worried about themselves. When I really want to fight them, you know what I do, I glare at 'em. They cringe. (Laughter.)

I have learned that a Negro woman can do anything she wants to do if she's got enough nerve. So can a white man. But a white woman and a Negro man are slaves until this day. I'll tell you why. The white man has set his woman up on a pedestal. He's trying to prove to her how superior he is. Truly he's not superior, he's just another little boy. She has to stay there if she wants to be anybody. But if she ever learns anything and she strays, she's an outcast. Me, you know what I can do? I can do any cotton pickin' thing I feel like doin'.

The white woman is more a slave than you?

Oh, by all standards. The black woman has to have nerve, though. She has to have experience. And she needs a little education to go along with it. You know this is such a strange thing, don't know why people like mystery. Love is so beautiful. It can be beautiful, with any group of people . . . Florence Scala and I can sit here . . .

We talk about all facets of our lives, things we wouldn't dare say to anybody else in public. And somebody else, even a Negro walks in my back door, we shut up. Because it's taboo. They might say it was Uncle Tomming, or they could make it look ugly. These things are hard to understand. Two human beings could have so much in common that they can really sit down and talk about their own lives, their own failures, their own misgivings, and truly speaking tell you about some of my absolute traits that I don't like. Two women, we're just two women. So here is this cloak of mystery. Everybody, even the neighbors, gawking. When she comes in, you know. The curtains are moving and they come boldly to the door and watch, as though, well, here is the enemy.

Florence, with Florence what I tried to teach in this particular neighborhood, here's a woman everybody says, oh well, she's Italian, she doesn't have the interest. Damn that, this is a woman that you *need* to talk to. She doesn't live on Lake Shore Drive. I tried to show them the little, simple, down-to-earth qualities about this particular woman. But, my God, this Petrillo, who ever the hell he is, what are you going to tell him? The man has no interest in white or black. If you're poor, see? He's living in another world altogether.

This is the Berlin Wall right over here. You see, we don't even have a ten-cent store. Woolworth doesn't find it profitable. We don't have a bank. After all, everybody here is on Welfare. So if you want to get your check cashed, I go downtown to the bank. I usually go to Sears or Wards or somewhere where I've got a charge account. This is where you get a check cashed, unless you want to go to the currency exchange and pay somebody to get your check cashed. Well, I don't make that kind of money to give somebody money to cash my check. We don't have any facilities here that poor folks need. On Michigan Avenue, where people can get along without it, you got your ten-cent stores. I did all my shopping in a ten-cent store when I worked at Wesley.

Here again, it's the white man's standards. You know, I laugh sometimes. Just like these books we have in our schools. Dick and Jane, here's this pretty rosy-cheeked white woman and she's got on a pretty dress and a lovely little apron and she's standing out on this lawn and here's this big huge driveway, goes to two, three acres. All this stuff, and she's waving goodbye to her son. He's off on his way to school, you know. And this is what they teach the children in projects. (Laughter.) Boy, this is really something.

I was trying to live by white man's standards myself. I didn't realize it. One day the school sent for me. I'm kind of a stickler for not laying off the job, so I sent my mother. The principal told her Melvin was a problem child. He must have been about seven then. When I got off from work at five o'clock, I chased myself home to fix supper. I couldn't see the forest from the trees. I was so busy trying to get home, trying to get dinner, trying to help with homework, trying to get him to bed, so he'd get enough sleep. Do you realize what a vicious cycle this is? I didn't realize what I was doing to my children. Because I was rushing them to death. I was rushing myself to death.

I asked for help. I realized that all the voices Melvin heard were female voices. My voice, his sister's voice, his grandmother's voice, his teacher's voice. I began to get frightened. I went down to the I.S.U. something. I talked with them. They decided I was the one needed the psychoanalyzing. They had me in a conference and there were about twelve psychiatrists, all around. Somebody was taking notes and what have you. Nobody said one word about tomorrow. I explained to the people that my child, he's wandering away and I'm afraid he needs male companionship. I'm not asking you to give him anything, just a few minutes of your time. Till this day I didn't get it.

This is what would happen at work. Instead of sending a card: Mrs. Jefferson, come to school to see about your son . . . they'd call up. When the phone would ring, honest to God, you know what? My blood pressure would rise, because now I was so afraid. "Lucy!" Whenever a call came in, I knew something was wrong. And when this truant officer would phone, one of the girls would answer.

Boy, oh boy, here I go. I didn't like this, see? I was furious, because I thought this was invading my private life. The way I raise my children was my own private business. Let's say I was ashamed. This would be a better word. I wouldn't have admitted it then, but I can admit it now. Because, you see, the stigma of all Negro children are lazy, they don't do this, they don't do that, you know. See I didn't want anybody to think my children wasn't up to par, or wasn't up to the white man's standards. Well, I blowed that long ago. (Laughs.)

I couldn't afford to go to the PTA meetings. They don't do a damn thing but drink coffee anyway. I like coffee and I like to drink it in the morning, but I have to go to work, and they had PTA meetings at one o'clock in the day. I couldn't lay off my job to go down there to chitchat with them. I think they had PTA meetings twice in the last ten years at night. They're no damn good anyway.

Melvin was doing very poorly and I was getting letters. You know, they send you all these little items. Come to see me, come to school, because your child is not working up to his capacity. I don't know why they just don't tell you the truth about it, instead of using all these vague, false phrases. I thought he was just being lazy, but the child couldn't read. He couldn't spell. He was at Crane High, out there in the ghetto. I laid off from work the next day. I got up, cocked my hat up Miss Johnny Aside . . . I wanted to let him know I was plenty mad then. Oh yeah, I visited Crane. Melvin was having three study periods in a row. Gee, this is kind of crazy, studying what? I went to see this study hall. And this is the auditorium. It has a false ceiling, and there's very few lights, and there's children everywhere, male and female, and about the only thing they can do there is make love. Most of the kids can't read anyway, but if they could, they wouldn't be able to see. So I went to the counselor and he said, "It costs $10,000 to put up this business of putting lights in and the school system doesn't have the money" and blah, blah, blah. I said, "But in the meantime, what are you going to do about all these children in there, these boys and girls, these young men and women?" I said, "Maybe they can't read but they can do other things in there, such as getting babies." He said, "Well, well . . . we don't have anywhere else to put 'em."

You're talking about teachers. I bet he never had the same teacher twice in two weeks in two years. It's a disgrace to keep on calling these places schools. I think the best thing we can say about them, these are meeting places where people get up every morning, give their children a dollar, seventy-five cents, or whatever the heck they give 'em, and these kids go off. Schools you learn in. They could take a store front on Roosevelt Road or anywhere and clean it up, put some seats in there, and put some books in. But see, you can't learn anything where there is no books. Melvin went a whole half year at Crane, didn't have a book. If I woke up in a house that didn't have a book in, I'd just burn it down, it wouldn't be any good. To me, they're my lifeblood. Types of caps, gowns, all that crap, it don't mean nothing.

Oh what am I *really* looking for? For my daughter to have her baby. This is her first. Her marriage turned out bad. I would like for her to finish her college education. She's gonna need it to help her child, to rear her child. The only thrill left for me is to see my grandchild come and see what I can do about him. Won't that be fun? You know, I'll be able to afford things that would give him incentive to paint, music, literature, all these things that would free his little soul. Other than that, no bother. Melvin? Am I going to give him a chance to be a man or not? I took that chance when I let him go to Selma. I was scared to death. And I was very proud. I was afraid he was too young, because he was only sixteen, to know what was really happening. But I couldn't afford to tell him. I wouldn't have given him a chance to be a man. This was his chance. And I didn't want to steal it.

Let's face it. What counts is knowledge. And feeling. You see, there's such a thing as a feeling tone. One is friendly and one is hostile. And if you don't have this, baby, you've had it. You're dead.

Credits

"Looking for Mr. Green," from *Mosby's Memoirs & Other Stories* by Saul Bellow, © 1951, 1979. Reprinted by permission of Viking Penguin, a division of Penguin Books USA Inc.

The Untouchables by Eliot Ness, © 1947. Reprinted with permission by the American Reprint Company.

"The Members of the Assembly" by Jean Genet first appeared in *Esquire*, November 1968. © 1968. Reprinted with permission.

"In the Dark" by Langston Hughes, reprinted by permission from *Chicago's Public Wits: A Chapter in the American Comic Spirit*, edited by Kenny J. Williams and Bernard Duffey. © 1983 by Louisiana State University Press.

"The Reunion" by Maya Angelou is reprinted by permission of the Hemen Brann Agency, © Maya Angelou.

"No More Giants" from *City on the Make* by Nelson Algren, © 1951 Nelson Algren, reprinted by permission of Donadio and Associates.

Excerpt from *Boss: Richard J. Daley of Chicago* by Mike Royko. © 1971 by Mike Royko. Used by permission of the publisher, Dutton, an imprint of New American Library, a division of Penguin Books USA Inc.

Excerpt from The *Studs Lonigan* Trilogy by James Farrell reprinted by permission of the Estate of James T. Farrell.

Carl Sandburg 'Chicago': Reprinted with permission from Harcourt, Brace and Jovanovich.

Excerpt from *The Story of My Life* by Clarence Darrow reprinted with permission of Charles Scribner's Sons, an imprint of Macmillan Publishing Company. © 1932 Charles Scribner's Sons; © renewed © 1960 Mary D. Simonson.

"The Museum of Science and Industry Story" from *5 Television Plays* by David Mamet, © 1975 by David Mamet, is used by permission of Grove Press, Inc.

"The Feeling Tone [Lucy Jefferson]." From *Division Street: America*, by Studs Terkel. © 1967 by Studs Terkel. Reprinted by permission of Pantheon Books, a division of Random House, Inc.